AVALINE SADDLEBAGS

DI DYLAN MONROE INVESTIGATES: ONE

NETTA NEWBOUND
MARCUS BROWN

Junction Publishing

Netta Newbound & Marcus Brown/Junction Publishing United Kingdom

Avaline Saddlebags - DI Dylan Monroe Investigates: One

AS DIDMIO/ Netta Newbound & Marcus Brown – 1st Ed.

To our long suffering other halves (which is a laugh seeing as we're the long suffering ones, lol...)

PROLOGUE

Gina stumbled down the dark alleyway. "Fucking heels," she moaned, almost losing her footing on the cobblestones.

She regretted taking the shortcut home from the club. Her mum would go ballistic if she found out, especially after that poor woman was murdered the other week, but she was exhausted and more than ready for her bed. And besides, what were the chances of it happening twice in the same area?

A loud scraping noise from behind caused her pulse to quicken. Spinning around, she squinted, scanning the alleyway. She couldn't see a thing, but goosebumps covered her entire body. "Hello?" she called. "Is anybody there?"

A cat jumped down from the wall beside her and ran screeching past and back into the shadows.

With a guttural roar, Gina staggered backwards in fright— hyperventilating. She knew she was freaking herself out but was unable to calm her raging heartbeat.

As she took several more tentative steps, another loud bang echoed along the alleyway.

"Hey! This isn't funny now." Her anxiety levels soared, and

she quickened her pace in the stupidly high heels she vowed never to wear again.

"Gina," a mocking male voice came out of the darkness.

She stopped running, rooted to the spot.

"Who's there?" Her voice was almost a shriek. "Whoever it is, it's not funny now. You're scaring me."

"Gina," the voice called again.

Run, you stupid bitch, her inner voice yelled, and she did. Kicking off her shoes, she wasted no time and, seconds later, found herself at the bottom of the alleyway gasping for breath. Glancing back, she still couldn't see anybody, but she knew he was there.

Still five minutes from home, she chose not to take her usual route in case he followed her.

Darting across the road, she ran towards Chapel Lane, her big feet slapping on the concrete.

"Gina." The voice seemed closer this time and she turned around as a tall dark shadow approached her.

"Leave me alone." she yelled. "Or I'll call the police."

"You'll be long dead before they can get to you."

Whimpering uncontrollably, she turned to run, stubbing her toe on the uneven cobbles. She stumbled forwards, crashing to the ground.

White hot pain exploded in her knee. She cried out in agony trying to get back up. Seconds later, a kick to her side sent her crashing back to the ground. Winded, she couldn't move. "I'll do anything you want, just don't hurt me," she begged.

"I'm not going to hurt you, Gina. I'm going to kill you." He dealt her another boot to the ribs then grabbed a fistful of her hair and dragged her back up the dark alley.

She could taste the sickly sweet stench of the industrial bins and began to retch.

The man shoved her to the ground once again.

As she fell, her head splashed into a muddy puddle and her long blonde hair, her pride and joy, was caked in dirt and dog-piss.

He straddled her, leaning in and pinning her arms above her head.

"Take my bag," she begged. "I have cash in there."

He picked up the bag with his gloved hand and threw it across the alley. "You're nothing but a freak, a clown," he spat. "Walking the streets, tricking decent hard-working men into believing you're a real woman." He spoke with the hint of an accent Gina couldn't place.

"I *am* a real woman," she protested.

He leaned forward and whispered in her ear. "But you weren't born a woman, were you, Gina? Or should I call you George?"

She flinched. It had been nearly seven years since anybody had used that name.

"I don't know what you're talking about," she cried.

His hand gripped her throat and squeezed hard.

"Please, you're hurting me," she choked. "If you let me go, I won't say a word to anyone."

He was strong and used one hand to pin both of hers behind her head before punching her in the face.

Gina cried out in agony as blood poured from her left nostril. He leaned in closely and she tried to get a good look at him, but it was still too dark.

"You're a screwed up, perverted faggot just like the last one," he growled into her face.

"And you're a twisted fucker who probably can't get it up," she replied, defiantly.

"Freak." He kneed her between the legs.

She screamed and her body was once more racked with white-hot pain.

He punched her face again.

Gina's head bounced off the cobblestones and she cried out once more. "I'm sorry, please, just let me go. I told my daughter I wouldn't be late. Just do what you want and let me go."

"Daughter? Who are you trying to kid? Do you tell people you carried her to term? Men can't give birth, Georgie. Surely, even you're not that deluded?"

The moon suddenly made an appearance giving Gina her first proper look at him. Dressed entirely in black, a cap's visor shielded his eyes and a black pollution mask covered his nose and the lower portion of his face. Something was amiss, but she couldn't place what it was, however, judging by how he was dressed, she knew this wasn't a random act—he meant business. If she had any chance of escaping, she would have to fight. A staunch pacifist, she abhorred violence of any kind, but her life was at stake and she hadn't spent the best part of ten years transitioning to meet her maker at the hands of this lunatic.

"You wanna fuck me, don't you," she said bravely, trying a change of tactic. "Isn't that what this is all about? You like cock, but you're too scared to try it. Well, sorry to disappoint you, but my cock was tucked away a long time ago."

He loosened his grip for a moment, obviously stunned by Gina's words. She was able to release one of her hands and, moving swiftly, she clawed at his forearm with her long nails, drawing blood.

"You bitch," he growled.

Gina tried to scramble to her feet, but her busted knee wouldn't co-operate, and he kicked her up the backside. With a yelp, she landed flat on her face.

Her attacker towered over her and stamped down hard on the small of her back.

A sickening crack echoed around the dark alleyway.

Gina lay motionless on the ground, resigned to the fact she was going to die. She closed her eyes.

"Not long now, Georgie."

He rolled her over and straddled her again, but she couldn't feel anything.

She looked into his eyes and gasped. "I know you, don't I?" she said through snot and tears. She definitely recognised his eyes, but where from eluded her.

"You think?" he sneered.

"Yes. Yes, I do. Who the fuck are you?"

"Such a shame you won't be around to work it out."

"But why are you doing this?" Gina asked, as her attacker climbed off her, jumping to his feet.

"You're all sick." Raising his foot, he stamped down on her face.

ONE

I marched past the crowded incident room and headed for the glass-walled office at the end of the corridor.

My boss, DCI Janine Kerrigan, glared at me as I burst through the door. "Jesus, Dylan, haven't you heard of knocking?"

"Sorry, Ma'am, I've been up for hours and I'm not thinking straight." The truth was, I was jittery. So much had happened over the past couple of weeks and this was my first day as Detective Inspector. I was terrified of screwing up.

"That's okay. What can I do for you?" She lifted her reading glasses up onto her head and gazed at me.

"We've found another body, Ma'am. Some kid dragged it out of the Mersey, thinking it was a Guy Fawkes dummy, early this morning. She was lying in the mud flats at the south end of Albert Dock."

"Oh, fuck!" She shook her head, her shoulder-length, straight brown hair swished with the motion. "What do you know so far?"

"She'd suffered severe trauma to the face from what I could see, as well as other injuries. Lauren was called to the scene and is working on her now. We'll know more later, but we believe she's Gina Elliot—a twenty-eight-year-old transgender female. Criminal record as long as her arm when known as George Elliot, but squeaky clean after surgery. Reported missing two days ago by her parents, when she didn't return home from a night out at Dorothy's night club, a popular haunt in Gay Town. There's a chance she's been in the water since then."

"There goes any trace evidence." Janine banged her hand on the desk, startling me.

"This guy certainly seems to know what he's doing," I said.

"I'll get Joanna and Will to do some digging into any exes—the usual. We need to move fast."

"The press will have a field day with this." She held her head in her hands for a few seconds then looked up. "Keep me in the loop. We're bound to take some heat. Looks like we've got someone targeting the transgender community."

"Seems that way," I added.

"As if they don't have enough shit thrown at them. I hope they haven't got their own goddamn serial killer picking them off."

"Tell me about it. Shall I take Layla Monahan with me? It'll be good to have a woman's presence when speaking to the parents. Then, we'll hit the night club once we've got the autopsy results."

"Yeah, good idea, although I'm not sure what you'll find out when you get to Gay Town. You might be met with a wall of silence."

"Somebody's targeting their own, they'll talk, trust me."

"Yeah, yeah," she said, waving me out. "Just keep me informed."

"Gotcha, Ma'am."

"And stop calling me Ma'am. You make me sound like the fucking Queen."

I grinned. "Okay, Janine."

"And about Layla, I've already had a word with her—she's aware she'll be partnering with you now Savage has left."

"Only until Bella's back, I hope?"

"That's ages away yet. We'll sort it out nearer the time." She replaced her glasses and looked back down at the paperwork in front of her.

Clearly dismissed, I walked out of her office and closed the door behind me.

"Listen up everybody," I said once back in the incident room. "There's been another murder. Joanna, Will, can you start digging around for anything you can find on the victim, Gina Elliot AKA George Elliot from 15 Cavendish Crescent?"

"Bloody hell, that's a blast from the past. I knew George Elliot," Will said. "He was a right light-fingered bugger when he was younger—likeable enough though."

"Yes, he had a record for petty theft and burglary, but he's been as clean as a whistle since *he* became a *she* seven years ago. Could you check if there's any connection to the previous victim? I'll send the autopsy results through as soon as we have them in. You all know how imperative it is we pull together so don't let me down. In the meantime, Layla, I believe you're with me."

Layla was seated at her desk in the corner of the room. I sniggered at her pissed off expression. We'd worked together for a while now, but not closely. She'd been partner to my predecessor, Fred Savage, and no doubt thought she should be the one promoted, not me.

Savage had suffered a serious heart attack the week before last while chasing a suspect and his doctor advised him to give up work or he'd be dead by the end of the year. Hence why I'd been promoted out of the blue, much to the surprise of everyone—me included.

"If I must." She rolled her eyes as she got to her feet and sauntered over to me. I found her appearance more suited to the catwalk than keeping criminals off the streets—statuesque and beautiful, she could have had her pick of professions, but she was good at her job, and had worked her way up the ranks faster than most.

"Yes, you must," I said, feeling a little irritated. My usual sidekick, Annabella Frost, Bella to her friends, was on maternity leave. We'd worked side by side for the past six years, only apart when she had her daughter, Lily, four years ago. Now, with a new title and new responsibilities, I wasn't sure I had the patience to break in a new partner as well. This was going to be a long six months.

I was aware the rest of the team didn't think I should've been promoted either and I knew it would take a while for me to win them over. I'd been their equal one day and their boss the next, although Tommo, Pete, and Heather had never shown any desire to be promoted. I had a feeling Will and Joanna would be up for the challenge, but it was Layla who was the competitive and hungry one.

"No problem," Layla said, a fake smile plastered across her pretty face.

Ignoring the sarcasm, I carried on. "First stop is to visit the parents. It won't be pleasant but having you there will be a huge help. Afterwards we'll call in to see Lauren, then on to Dorothy's."

"Oh, wonderful," she replied, in her cute Welsh lilt. "I'll get to spend the afternoon watching you flirt up a storm with the local pretty boys, will I?"

"If I didn't know better, Monahan, I'd swear you were a bigot." I loved to tease her and push her buttons. It was so easy.

"Not funny, Dylan."

"I'm kidding," I replied. "Jesus, have you got a pickle shoved up your arse today? What's the matter with you?"

"If you must know, my separation papers arrived this morning."

I winced. Me and my big mouth. "I'm sorry, Layla. I didn't realise things were that bad between you and Max."

"I'm not stupid enough to think I can compete with that bitch he's shacked up with."

"Don't put yourself down. If he can't see what a good thing he had with you and the kids, then he doesn't deserve any of you." I might have been overstepping the boundaries, but she needed a friend. I put my arm around her and pulled her towards me. "Come on, let's get going, maybe we can cram in a quick cuppa before we head to Dorothy's later and you can tell me all about it."

The two storey, red brick, detached house was immaculately kept with impressive floral borders leading to the front steps.

A tall, stocky man with salt and pepper hair answered the door, a frown on his face. "Yes?" he asked.

"Mr Elliot?"

The man gripped the edge of the door and nodded.

I pulled out my warrant card and introduced myself and Layla.

"Is it Gina? Did you find her?"

The sound of thundering footsteps rushing down the stairs threw me for a second. Moments later a slightly built woman, with vibrant pillar-box-red hair that looked like a wig, pushed the man aside. "Have you found her?"

"Are you Mrs Elliot?"

"Yes. Just tell me. Have you found my daughter?"

"Maybe we could step inside for a second." I eyeballed Layla and was relieved when she stepped forward, putting her hand on the older woman's arm.

Moments later, seated on the burgundy floral lounge suite, all eyes once again were turned to me.

"It's bad news, I'm afraid."

Mrs Elliot let out an inhuman wail, causing Layla to gasp. The man moved sideways and pulled his wife into his huge embrace. She sobbed hysterically.

Mr Elliot stroked his wife's hair and, taking a deep breath, he turned to face me again. "Go on."

"A body was found in the Mersey this morning. We believe it's your daughter, Gina."

"No! No, please no." Mrs Elliot continued to howl.

I hated having to do this. It was the worst part of my job by far.

Layla looked away. I could see she was poking at the corners of her eyes.

"What makes you think it's her?" he said.

"Going by the description you gave when you reported her missing, and the tattoo on her arm, we're pretty certain." I removed my phone from my pocket. "I have a couple of images here. Can you confirm this is Gina's tattoo and necklace?" I handed the phone over.

Mrs Elliot's heartbroken sobs confirmed we were right.

Half an hour later, Mrs Elliot had calmed down somewhat and agreed to take Layla to see Gina's bedroom.

I took the opportunity to ask her husband a few more questions. "Can you tell me when you last saw your daughter, sir?"

"She went out as usual on Friday night. We had dinner together and she was excited about starting her new job today."

"Who was she going out with? Do you know?"

He nodded. "Felicity someone, I don't know her surname. She works—worked with Gina at the post office."

"Which post office is that?"

"The main sorting office in town."

I nodded and wrote the name down in my notepad. "Did your daughter have any enemies that you know of?"

He shook his head. "Not that we were aware of, but she would rarely tell us anything for fear of upsetting us. Her Mum has been sick—breast cancer, and she's just getting over the ravages of the chemo."

That explained the wig. "I'm sorry to hear that, sir. Understandable she'd keep something like that from you under the circumstances. Did she have any trouble when she first made the transition from George to Gina?"

He shrugged. "You know what people can be like, especially around here. There was a lot of nastiness initially, but Gina didn't let it bother her—she often said the relief she felt more than made up for any negativity. She would shrug it off and it wasn't long before everyone that mattered accepted her as Gina. Anyone who met her recently wouldn't even know George had ever existed."

"Do you have a recent photograph of Gina, Mr Elliot?"

He got to his feet and picked up a photo frame from the sideboard. "This is a couple of years old, but it's a good likeness."

"Thank you, I'll take a copy of it and bring it back."

"Don't bother. We have it on the computer."

I nodded and removed the photo of Gina standing beside a yellow sports car from the heavy frame. "She was pretty," I said. "Did she have a significant other—either as George or Gina?"

"Gina was a lesbian which I don't understand to be honest. I thought when she told us she wanted to be a woman it was because she fancied men, but apparently it doesn't always work that way."

"Were you unhappy with your daughter's lifestyle choices?"

"No, not at all. It broke my heart to see my child so miserable. He was always on the wrong side of the law. I suspected he'd end up getting into more serious crimes if he'd stayed as he was. I'd have agreed to anything to make him happy. Being Gina made him happy."

I nodded. "So, did she have a girlfriend?"

"No. Not for a long time. George had a daughter with his first girlfriend when they were still at school. Lisa, our granddaughter, lives with us now. She's twelve this year. I don't know how we're going to tell her..." He broke off and placed a shaky hand against his lips. "I'm sorry."

"Don't worry. Take your time."

Mr Elliott coughed and shuffled in his seat. "Where was I? Oh, yes. I'm sure she dated, but she never brought anyone home or told us about anybody special."

Layla and Mrs Elliot re-entered the room. Layla was pale with dark circles under her eyes.

"So, what will happen now?" Mrs Elliot asked, sitting down next to her husband and reaching for his hand, back in control.

"Somebody will need to formally identify her, of course. But that can be done tomorrow if you're feeling up to it."

"I'd rather do it today. There's still a chance it may not be Gina." She was back in denial.

I glanced at Layla and smiled sadly before turning back to the couple. "We are quite certain, Mrs Elliot. But I understand you wanting confirmation. As soon as the autopsy has been performed, somebody will be in touch with you."

"Is there anybody you'd like us to call?" Layla asked.

"No. It's okay, love. I can manage." Mr Elliot smiled sadly.

"Fuck, that was intense," Layla said, once we were back in the car.

"I know. I hate having to tell any parent their kid is dead, never mind brutally murdered—Bella usually takes over, she always knows what to say."

"And you brought me along because you thought all women were bound to be the same?" She grinned.

"No. But it is common knowledge women are better at that kind of thing than most men."

"Not me. I was well out of my depth in there."

"Yeah, I could tell. You looked worse than Mrs Elliot when you came downstairs. Had something happened?"

"Not really. She showed me Gina's bedroom and it felt strange and more than a little wrong to be going through a dead person's private things. Her book opened on her pillow, dirty undies thrown into a pile behind the door, half-drunk cup of tea on the dresser—I felt like an intruder."

"But you saw nothing out of the ordinary?"

She shook her head. "The room looked pretty normal to me, if not overly girly for the victim's age." She paused and turned to look out of the window. "So, where are we going now?"

"Maybe we should do a detour to the post office. Gina was meant to go out with someone called Felicity on Friday night."

"I believe you're looking for me," The woman approaching us must've been well over six feet tall. Her fine blonde hair fell in a tumble around her broad shoulders. The strong jawline and the shape of her brow told me she was also transgender.

"Are you Felicity?"

"Yes." She shuffled nervously. "What's this about?"

I flashed my warrant card. "DI Dylan Monroe and DS Layla Monahan. Shall we take a seat?" I smiled, indicating the red plastic chairs dotted around the staff room we'd been ushered into by the receptionist.

Felicity glanced at us, her forehead furrowed. "So?"

"We're here about Gina Elliot. Can you tell me when you saw her last?"

"Gina? Why? What's happened? She was supposed to start her new job today but didn't show up."

"Can you just answer the question please, miss?"

"Erm." She shook her head, clearly panicked. "Friday. Yes, Friday night at Dorothy's. Why?"

"Did you spend the entire evening together?"

"No. I had a headache. I left after one drink. Gina was hanging around for the open mic—she sang the same old songs every week and I wasn't in the mood. Has something happened? I tried to call her when she didn't turn up this morning, but her phone was off."

"When you left the bar, did you see who Gina was with?"

"We always hang around with the same crowd of people. We meet up every Friday although I couldn't tell you their full names. Please, tell me. I need to know."

I glanced at Layla before turning back to Felicity. "Gina's body was found in the River Mersey this morning."

Once the initial shock had worn off, Felicity gave us the Christian names of the people they were with at Dorothy's on Friday.

I handed her my business card. "I'd appreciate you letting me know if you remember anything that might be important."

She stifled a sob and nodded.

"What are the chances of that?" Layla asked when we returned to the car.

"What?"

"A couple of trannies working in the same place."

"Birds of a feather flock together, or so they say. And for the record—they're transsexual or transgendered, not trannies, thank you very much. Now, come on, let's see what Lauren has to say." I turned the car around and headed for the hospital.

On the ground floor of the Central hospital, I knocked on the glass door and pasted on a smile. "Have you been here before?" I asked Layla.

"No. Savage used to deal with this sort of stuff on his own."

I always thought it was strange how Savage kept his sidekick mostly office based. "Brace yourself then," I warned.

"Why? Because it's gruesome?"

Forensic Pathologist, Lauren Doyle, looked up from her desk and rolled her eyes. "Come in," she said.

"Yes, that and the fact she's a grumpy old bugger who loves pulling my chain," I said, under my breath before opening the door. "Hey, Lauren, how are you?"

"I was okay until about thirty seconds ago."

"Aw," I said, pulling my best sulky face. "You're not pleased to see me then?"

"When am I ever pleased to see you?"

We were good friends really, but both enjoyed a bit of banter. "This is my colleague, DS Layla Monahan."

"Pleased to meet you," Layla added, stepping forward to shake her hand. "I've heard a lot about you."

"Oh, I bet you have," she said, grinning. "Now what can I do for you both?"

"We're here about Gina Elliot–any news?"

"I finished up a little earlier and will email the full report shortly. To cut a long story short, she's a mess. Broken back, shattered kneecap, stamp injuries to one side of her face, the fingers of her right hand have been cut clean off."

"Shit," I said, casting a glance at Layla who looked sickened.

"That's not the worst of it," Lauren said. "Come on, I'll show you." She led us into the adjoining room and pulled back the sheet covering the body on the examination table.

Layla gasped and began dry retching. "Sorry." She retched again. "Sorry."

An inappropriate rumble of a giggle began in the pit of my stomach and I had to fight to suppress it. Every time she made the terrible retching sound, the harder it was for me to maintain a professional appearance.

"I'm so sorry," Layla said for the last time before racing from the room.

Lauren shook her head, clearly unamused, which made the child in me want to bark out a laugh all the more.

"Should we get on?" she snapped.

I nodded, not trusting myself to speak.

She picked up a Ziploc bag from a metal dish at the side of the table and handed it to me. "This had been fitted just like last time."

I examined the contents and my stomach muscles clenched. "Fuck!"

Layla returned holding a wad of toilet roll to her mouth. "Oh, my God," she said, gripping the back of the chair. Her face drained of colour.

"Exactly," Lauren said. "A prosthetic penis was in place, just like on the last victim, but super-glued this time."

"So, we've definitely got ourselves a serial killer then?" I inspected the bag.

Lauren nodded. "Without a doubt, although technically we

can't declare it's a serial killer until there have been at least three victims, but in this case, I'd stake my career on it."

I rubbed my temples.

Lauren continued. "However, this time, the killer has excelled himself."

"How so?" I dreaded what she was going to say next.

"Take a look for yourself." She beckoned us down the bottom of the table and lifted one of Gina's legs.

I couldn't believe what I was seeing. The lips of Gina's vagina had been crudely sewn shut with a length of red wool.

TWO

We headed to a greasy spoon café and ordered two coffees to go. Taking our drinks outside, we sat on a rickety picnic bench.

Unsurprisingly, neither of us had much of an appetite. The sight of the killer's handiwork had left an indelible impression in my mind. The sickening brutality of Gina Elliot's murder lit a furnace of fury in my belly. I'd get the animal responsible and make sure he spent the rest of his life behind bars.

This case was proving to be the most harrowing I'd ever worked on. Murder of any kind is the worst of crimes, but these latest killings were too close to home.

Layla was quieter than usual. She made no secret she didn't like seeing dead bodies—especially ones that had spent a couple of days bloating in the river.

"That was pretty traumatic wasn't it?" I asked.

She rolled her eyes. "I'd rather not think about it—talk about embarrassing. I wanted the ground to swallow me up."

"I thought it was hilarious if you want the truth. I almost combusted with the effort of keeping it in. Lauren would've rapped my knuckles with a surgical hammer if I'd laughed."

She stifled a grin which briefly lit up her face.

"Are you okay? I know you've just thrown your ring up, but you've been pretty quiet all day."

She shrugged and took a sip of her coffee.

I felt for her. Going through divorce proceedings at thirty-one, especially when there were three children involved, must be devastating. I wanted to wrap my arms around her, but technically, we weren't close friends.

"Talk to me," I said.

"What about?" She seemed distracted.

"How about you and Max for starters, and why, today of all days, you turned up for work?"

"What am I going to do at home besides stare at the four walls and wonder where my marriage went wrong?"

"Max left you, remember?"

"I know that," she snapped.

"Then it's not your fault–it's his."

"I don't want to talk about it anymore, Dylan."

"But what will you do?"

She drained her coffee cup then stood up from the table. "I've got a kickboxing class tonight and I'll take my frustrations out on my sensei." She began to walk away.

"Where're you going?"

"I just need five minutes to clear my head, do you mind?"

"No, take as much time as you need. In fact, if you're not up to it, I can go to Gay Town on my own."

She glowered at me. "I can still do my job, you know."

We entered Dorothy's, Liverpool's oldest gay bar, and waited for our eyes to adjust to the dimly lit interior after the glaring sunshine outside.

We headed towards the bar and I noticed many pairs of leering eyes following me.

I scanned the area looking for CCTV cameras and could only see a couple—one covering the bar and the other the stage.

The place was huge. A single bar stretched from one end to the other. A butch lesbian was at the far end pulling a pint of beer, and a pretty boy with crazy hair and multiple piercings stood serving closest to us. He gave me the side eye and continued to serve the guy propped up against the bar.

As a fully paid up homosexual, I was no stranger to the gay scene, but wasn't a fan of this particular place. Everything about it, even down to the sparkly silver wallpaper and video screens showing old Kylie and Madonna videos, screamed camp. It was also a haunt for drag queens, and, although an acquaintance of mine was a drag queen, they terrified me.

"I bet you love it here," Layla teased, knowing full well I wasn't *that* kind of gay.

"Yeah, it's my favourite place in the whole world." I rolled my eyes.

"What is it with you?" she asked. "You're out and proud, but you're so weird about it."

"So?"

"You don't like anything that's considered remotely feminine, which I find odd."

"Just because I'm gay, doesn't mean I know the routine to YMCA or have every fucking Abba album on vinyl. Have you ever thought it's other people who are weird for assuming we're all the same?"

"Oooh! Touchy today, aren't we?"

"For your information. This case has me rattled, and whatever I think about my place in the gay world, somebody has it in for a community I'm a part of." My anger was rising. "This isn't just a case to me. I actually care about these people too."

"Nobody's saying people don't care."

"Really? Two women are dead, Layla, and yes, the papers will report it, but rather than show sympathy to the victims, they'll dig up every little piece of dirt they find and make them out to be some sort of deviant who deserved their fate. It's not right."

"All right," she said. "Take it easy."

"Why should I?" Suddenly I was feeling I had to speak up for the victims. "They were transgendered, not easy prey for some sicko. Imagine how you'd feel if you were forced to live your life as a man. These women were braver than most by choosing to be true to themselves."

"I wasn't suggesting anything, but I get it's difficult for some people to understand. And besides, what if it's nothing to do with their gender? There could be more to these deaths than you realise."

"They were both transgender women. That's your common denominator right there. It's obviously somebody with a grudge against the transgender community. Especially attaching a prosthetic dick to them both. That's premeditated. Somebody took the time to get their hands on those things. It's not as if you can find them in every corner pound shop."

I ordered two shandies and then headed to a quiet table where we could size up the room.

"Give me a minute, I need to pee," she said.

I watched as Layla walked to the other end of the bar and into the toilets.

Feeling conspicuous, and unsettled, I dug in my pocket for my phone and dialled the station. Will answered.

"Will, it's me."

"Hey, boss."

"The autopsy results should be in now. We've just left

Lauren and she suspects we're dealing with a serial killer," I whispered.

"Really?"

"Yeah and he's a sick fucker. Wait till you see the details. Don't look at the images on a full stomach."

"That bad?"

"Brutal. Gina Elliot spent Friday night in Dorothy's—the same place Jade Kelly was last seen alive. Could you check out the CCTV cameras in the area, see if you can pick anything up between here and Cavendish Crescent on Friday night?"

"Leave it with me, boss. I've been doing a bit of digging too. The GPS on Gina's phone pinged several times on Friday. It looks like she was in the bar till just before midnight and then the phone was on the move at a walking pace. The last ping was recorded at 2:17am on Saturday morning at Columbus Quay."

"That's fantastic. You should easily be able to find something on the CCTV there, especially now you have the exact time. Great work, Will."

"Hope so, and thanks. I'll let you know."

I ended the call as Layla slid onto the seat opposite and filled her in on what Will had said while we sipped our drinks.

"So, what now?" she asked.

"Do you want to try to schmooze the barmaid? She's not taken her eyes off you since we arrived."

"Me?" Layla replied, shocked. "I'm straight!"

"So what? She doesn't need to know that."

She rolled her eyes and got to her feet.

I handed her the photo Mr Elliot had given me and followed behind.

"Hello." The barmaid winked at Layla.

I pressed my lips together, highly amused.

Layla opened her wallet showing her warrant card. "I wonder if you can help me."

"Dunno about that. Depends." She eyed us suspiciously.

"Do you recognise this woman?" Layla placed the photo on the bar.

"Yes. I know her—she's a regular. What of it?"

"Do you recall seeing her on Friday night?"

"Nah. I *was* working, but the place was heaving. We have Drag Queen Cabaret every Friday night. What's this about?"

"We'll need to access your CCTV."

She nodded. "Good luck with that."

"Why?"

"You'll need to speak to Chris Turner. He's the manager but he's not here at the moment. Has something happened to her?"

Layla shot me a quick look before nodding. "I'm afraid she was murdered after leaving here on Friday."

The barmaid gasped. "Jesus Christ!"

"Exactly," Layla said.

"That's the second one, isn't it? Is it a serial killer?"

"It's early days," I piped up. "And we'd appreciate you keeping it under your hat for now."

"Here's my number in case you think of anything we should know." Layla handed her a card.

Once we were out of earshot, I nudged her in the ribs. "Thought you were straight?"

"I am!" she hissed.

"Tell that to your admirer, she thinks she's on a promise."

"Sod off. No, she doesn't."

"How much do you want to bet she'll ring you before the weekend?"

I opened the door and indicated for Layla to go ahead of me.

She bobbed under my arm and smacked straight into the barman from earlier who was on his way back inside. "Sorry," she said, bending to help pick up the pile of leaflets he'd dropped.

I picked a couple up too and the brightly coloured image on the front caught my eye.

CALLING ALL DRAG QUEENS

Are you Liverpool's fiercest Drag Queen?

Is your lip-syncing worthy of an encore?

Do you have the sass to become our most FAB-U-LOUS of performers?

If you answered yes, then get ready to lip-sync for your mother-tucking life.

WE NEED YOU TO AUDITION!

Where? Dorothy's Function room
When? Thursday between 9 and 11pm

"Fancy applying?" The barman winked at me.

"No. Not for me, mate." I handed the leaflet back to him.

"Keep it." He wiggled his eyebrows at me. "You might change your mind, you're certainly pretty enough."

I felt my cheeks heat up and couldn't help but notice Layla's beaming grin.

"See you Thursday, perhaps." The barman blew me a kiss before vanishing through the door.

THREE

Layla continued to tease me all the way back to the station.

"You could so do it, though. I could see you in a massive wig with a face full of makeup, fluttering your eyelashes." She howled laughing.

"I see your earlier black mood has lifted—at my expense, might I add."

"You've got to admit, the thought of you in a frock is pretty funny."

I shook my head but could feel a smile tugging at the corners of my mouth.

"Guys, I think I've found something." Will waved his hand at us as we breezed into the open office. He and Joanna were seated at the same desk.

"What is it?" I said.

Layla and I rushed over to them.

"Based on the GPS info from Gina's phone, I checked CCTV footage and there's a white Transit van that appeared at both crime scenes." Will turned the screen slightly for us to see the grainy image.

"Really? And?"

"We were able to make out the number plate, but it's been deregistered."

"Who was the last registered owner?"

"A Greg Martin, from Southampton. I've contacted Hedge End station and they're looking into it for us."

"Okay, great. Could you see the driver at all?"

Layla straddled a chair and leaned forward.

"Nothing in the first one but we managed to get this off the second." He opened another screen which showed a pixelated image of a slim guy dressed in black with a cap pulled down low covering his face.

"Oh, that's a waste of bloody time then," Layla said, irritably.

I ran my fingers through my hair in frustration. "I feel like he's taking the piss out of us."

"That's what Savage thought," Joanna said.

"I need to read Savage's notes. I would've done it last week, but we thought the murder had been a one off and I had it on my *to do* list this week anyway."

"Tell me about it," Will said. "We had absolutely nothing to go on and had come to the conclusion it was a random murder."

"Are you up to date on the case, Layla?" I asked.

"Mostly, but I'll go through everything again with you if you like? It can't hurt."

"Great. I'll just go and catch up with the DCI. Fancy making me a cuppa?"

"What did your last slave die of? Oh, sorry—she didn't die, did she? When's the baby due?" was Layla's snarky reply.

"Don't worry, boss. I'll make you one," Joanna offered, heading to the staffroom.

"Will, could you contact Dorothy's and get hold of a copy of their CCTV footage from Friday night? The manager is called Chris Turner."

"On it, boss."

I headed up the corridor, knocked on the glass door and waited for Janine to beckon me in.

"How did you get on, Dylan?" she asked.

I filled her in on the morning's events. I knew Savage didn't always give her a blow by blow account, but it felt right to ease myself in gently.

"And no-one saw her leave the club?"

"Her friend, Felicity, told us she'd left Gina at the club with a crowd of their mates, but she didn't know their full names. Will's getting onto the manager of the club now as he wasn't there earlier. Will also discovered a Transit van on the CCTV close to where each of the victims were found but sadly it's not registered to anybody. We've got Southampton checking out the previous owners for us."

She nodded and got to her feet. "Yeah, Will told me earlier. We need to get into the bar when it's busy and find out who the last to see her alive was. Somebody must've seen something." She walked out with me and we went into the staffroom.

"You want a coffee, Janine?" Joanna asked, reaching for another mug.

"Would love one, thanks, Jo."

Moments later, both Will and Layla joined us.

"I've left a message for the manager. If I've not heard anything in an hour, I'll head over there," Will said.

"Did Dylan tell you what he intends to do on Thursday?" Layla handed Janine the leaflet from the bar.

I rolled my eyes and glanced at Will who was already laughing—Layla must've told him.

"Really?" Janine said.

Joanna sat down and leaned over to read the leaflet too.

"No, not really!" I shook my head in mock disgust.

"I think it would be awesome." Layla winked at me. "An undercover cop stroke drag queen. You could call yourself Juliette Bravo."

"Ho, ho, ho. So funny I forgot to laugh." I glared at her.

"You know, it's not such a bad idea," Janine said.

"You are joking—aren't you?"

"Lauren Order," Will cut in, laughing openly now.

"Hansy Kuffs," Layla said, having full on banter now at my expense.

"Cunt Stubble," Joanna said, trying to stifle a giggle.

"Now that's a good one," Janine said, giving her a high five.

"Don't encourage them," I said.

"I've heard you're a gambling man, Dylan. Is that right?" Janine continued.

I shrugged. "Depends on the odds."

"You got a quid on you, Will?"

Will rummaged in his chinos and handed her a pound coin.

"Okay. We'll flip for it." Janine balanced the coin on her forefinger and poised her thumb ready to flip it.

"For what?" I said, my voice raised a few octaves.

"Heads you audition, tails Will does."

"Piss off! I'm not bloody doing it!" Will jumped to his feet.

It was my turn to laugh. "Come on, Will. You'd make a lovely woman. I have a couple of drag queen mates who can give you some makeup tips." I couldn't help but take the piss. He deserved it.

Janine flipped the coin and it spun in the air, then she caught it and slapped it onto the back of her hand.

She revealed the coin and Will let out a sigh. "Thank Christ for that," he said.

"Heads it is!" Janine laughed. "You'd better contact your mates for those makeup tips, Dylan."

"I'm not doing it!" I said, still adamant.

"Oh, yes, you are. We've got a killer to catch."

FOUR

Seated at my desk, I sifted through the stack of Savage's files and found the one I was looking for close to the top.

Layla appeared beside me. "Sorry. It was only a joke."

I ignored her and opened the folder.

She pulled up a chair. "Read it out loud."

I sighed, more than a little pissed off with her. "You didn't need to do that, you know."

"It was a joke, Dylan. How was I to know Janine would jump on the bandwagon?"

"Whatever. You knew exactly what you were doing, and I don't appreciate it, to be honest." I turned back to the matter in hand. "Let's get on with this, shall we? The first victim was twenty-eight-year-old Jade Kelly—born Jason Kelly in Birmingham. Jason moved to Liverpool with his mum after his dad died when he was fifteen. He had his gender reassignment surgery in Thailand three years ago. As Jade, she lived alone in a basement apartment in Liverpool, worked at John Lewis on the makeup counter and was last seen in Dorothy's arguing with a man. According to witnesses she threw her drink over him. The man turned out to be her ex-boyfriend, Darren Wilkes. Why do I know that name?" I turned to my computer and tapped in his details.

"He's a convicted drug dealer—a right dodgy fucker who lives on Wapping Quay and drives a top-of-the-range Audi R8 Spyder," Layla said, as Darren Wilkes' image filled the screen.

"Ah, yes. Now I remember, he's got previous convictions for dealing in under-the-counter hormones and is notorious on the gay scene."

"I was present during his interview when Savage brought him in. He's a nasty piece of work. But he had an alibi. He picked up someone by the name of Rebecca Preston after Jade stormed out of the bar, and she vouched for him."

"What had they been arguing about?" I asked.

"We never really got to the bottom of it. He fobbed us off with some bullshit story, but the fact is he has a cast-iron alibi and we can't touch him."

I returned to Savage's file. "Jade was found in the early hours of Saturday morning approximately the same time as Gina was dumped in the water. She'd been beaten and dumped in the Mersey. Like this latest victim, a prosthesis was discovered during her autopsy, but Savage wasn't convinced it had been placed there by the killer or if Jade was wearing it herself. He thought she might have regretted the surgery. But now we know the killer put it there to show he knew about her past." I rubbed at my temples, feeling like my head was about to explode. "To me, the disrespect shown to the victims by the placing of a prosthesis is one of the most disturbing parts of both murders."

"What drew you to that conclusion?"

"Let's work on the assumption the killer knows his victims are transgender. With Jade he places the one thing on her she went through hell to get rid of, and with Gina, he goes one better and stitches the vaginal opening closed, then glues a prosthesis there. I believe our killer has a loathing for the transgender community, and if we can discover why, it might help us crack the case."

"I didn't think of it like that," Layla replied.

"I might be wrong, but we also need to find out if we have anybody on file who was refused gender reassignment surgery."

"What good will that do?"

"Our killer could be somebody who holds a grudge because he or she is still stuck in a body that repulses them."

"Maybe."

"But first things first. We need to get the team looking through historical cases involving attacks on transsexuals or transvestites in the area, and while my brain is in top gear, find out if anybody local sells these prosthetics, and if we get no leads, we need to try online stockists."

"That'll take forever, Dylan. Plus, we don't have the manpower."

"Then we all pull double shifts. Simple as."

"I've got kids at home."

"They've got a father, haven't they?"

"Woah! Hang on a minute."

I realised I'd gone too far considering our earlier conversation. "Layla, I'm sorry for overstepping the mark. Your personal life is none of my business, but there are two women lying dead in the morgue and that is my business, so we do what we have to before there's another murder."

"We don't know for sure there will be another."

"Come off it, Layla. You know better than that. There'll be more, and right now he's ten steps ahead of us." My head started to pound. "Clever little bastard didn't leave a shred of DNA evidence, so we need to be exploring any avenue we can think of."

"Yeah—it's bloody frustrating having nothing to go on."

"We have the Transit van. Let's hope we get somewhere with that."

Later that afternoon, Will received a call from Chris—the manager of the bar.

"Well?" I asked once he'd hung up.

"He's happy with us viewing the CCTV footage. I've arranged to call in there tomorrow morning."

"Great—heard anything about the van?"

"No. Nothing. I'll chase it up now."

I placed the last of Savage's files in the cabinet. He didn't have too many open cases and the ones he did have were common knowledge within the team so there was nothing I wasn't up to date with apart from the Jade Kelly murder, which would make life a little easier.

Layla and Joanna had left for the day. They were both family women and I figured once we got a few more leads we'd be working all hours, so I suggested they head off early.

Closing my computer down, I stretched and yawned. I hadn't climbed into bed until well after midnight and then received the call about Gina at the crack of dawn. I wouldn't be up late tonight.

Will hung up his phone and walked back over to my desk. "Apparently the van was scrapped after an accident. He had the receipt to prove it. He's going to email a copy through to us. The scrap yard's here in Liverpool."

"You beauty!"

"I thought that might put a smile on your face," he said.

"Do you fancy heading over there now?"

He looked at his watch. "It's after five. I can try to call them—see if anybody's there?"

"Nah. Not likely, to be honest. I'll go with Layla in the morning."

"Fancy a pint to celebrate your first full day as DI?" Will asked, shrugging into his jacket.

"I would, mate, but I told Bella I'd take her a Chinese takeaway. She's fed up."

"I bet. Never mind—I should be getting home anyway. Rachel will be late tonight, so I could earn myself some brownie points by making dinner. Give my regards to Bella anyway."

"You old softy." I grinned. "But if I could ask a favour?"

"Sure."

"I've been thinking about the prosthetics left on the victims and wonder where they're coming from. Any chance you can do some digging. I think you have the report from Lauren with the images."

"I'll do what I can, but hopefully they weren't bought online, or that will be a nightmare."

"We're due some good luck, so let's hope they're from a local stockist."

"Yeah. In fact, I'll get cracking now and come back with an answer as soon as I can."

"What about cooking dinner for Rachel?"

"I'll pick up Chinese on the way home too."

"Good man," I said, slapping him on the back. "But don't stay too late. I don't want your Mrs complaining about you working late."

FIVE

I walked to my car—pleased Will seemed a little more accepting of my position. We were two detectives down with an already heavy workload and now a possible serial killer to catch. I planned to speak to Janine tomorrow about replacing mine and Bella's vacancies on the team.

I was still finding my feet, desperate to do a good job, but felt out of my depth. Although baffled by the case, my instincts told me this was more than just a hate crime. Why would somebody specifically target the transsexual community? I hadn't worked out a motive yet, but one thing I was certain of, there would be further deaths, and each more brutal than the last.

As promised, I picked up a takeaway and headed to Bella's with enough food to feed an army. It was what I needed—a few hours spent pigging out and gossiping with my best friend.

Rain had been threatening all afternoon, and as I pulled up outside Bella's place, the heavens opened.

Grabbing the brown paper bag full of food, I rushed up the path.

Bella must have been waiting for me as before I had a chance to knock the door opened.

"Aren't you a sight for sore eyes?" I said.

"Hello, stranger." She wore a pair of Minnie Mouse pjs and her usually straightened brown hair was piled into a messy knot on the top of her head. "Come in."

"Haven't you bothered to get dressed today, you lazy cow?" I teased.

"Nope. It's just you and me for dinner and I've been curled on the sofa eating junk-food and binge watching *Breaking Bad.*"

I walked into the hallway. Spotless as per usual. I always wondered how she found the time to keep such a clean house.

"Where's Lily?"

"Out with my sister somewhere," she replied. "That food smells divine. Go straight through to the kitchen, the plates are ready."

"Still a glutton, I see."

"Oi, cheeky, I'm eating for two, you know?"

"Just kidding."

Five minutes later, we were seated side by side at the table, open cartons of Chinese food everywhere.

"This is just what baby needs," Bella said, hand resting on her enormous stomach.

"Don't blame it on the baby. I've seen how much food you can put away."

She shovelled a forkful of chicken fried rice into her mouth, chewing voraciously. "You know me too well, but today's junk food is the first I've eaten for a week. My sister only eats an organic, plant-based diet and if she finds out I've eaten this, I'll never hear the last of it."

"Ugh," I said. "Give me a curry any day of the week."

"Exactly, and as soon as this little one makes an appearance, she can get back on the train to Manchester, she's driving me mad."

"I would've come to stay with you, you know that?"

"From what I've seen on the news, you've got enough on your plate right now."

I didn't want to talk about work, and dreaded telling her I had a new, if only temporary, partner, but since she brought it up… "It's pretty sick stuff, Bells."

"Is Layla working out okay?"

"Shit," I said. "You're supposed to be on maternity leave. How did you know about her?"

"I do have *other* friends on the force, you know?" She laughed and shook her head, before another forkful of food disappeared. "And besides, it makes sense. Both of you were left without a partner so I knew Janine would make this call."

"I know. I just feel guilty that's all."

"Guilty. Why?"

"They offered me the promotion, not you. And now I've got a new partner."

She placed her fork on the plate. "Hang on a minute, Dylan. I didn't even want the promotion, and as for Layla, it is what it is."

"But we both know if you hadn't been about to go off on leave, I wouldn't have stood a chance in hell."

"Piss off. You're just as good as I am, if not better."

"You're just saying that because you're my best friend."

"You're probably right." She rested her head on my shoulder, chuckling to herself.

"I don't know why I like you so much," I joked.

"Listen, you got that job because you're damn good at what you do," she said, reassuringly. "The others are just pissed off because you beat them to it. Fair and square I might add, so cut yourself a little slack."

"They've not been too bad, to be honest. Layla was a little

grumpy, but I think that was more to do with her and Max. Did you know they were getting divorced? The separation papers came through this morning."

"No. Really?"

"Yeah. He's got another woman, apparently."

"The dirty bastard, I hope his dick drops off."

I laughed. "Why do men do that? Layla's stunning."

"It's not all about looks, you know. She might be a nightmare to live with." Bella shoved her plate away and exhaled, leaning back in her chair.

"Hey! Aren't you supposed to be on the woman's side?"

"Yes. And I am. But I'm also realistic and can see it from both sides. Just because Max had a good-looking wife doesn't mean everything else in his garden was rosy. She can be a little snippy when she wants to be—just saying."

"Bitchy!" I grinned.

She shrugged. "No, not really. I might not be her greatest fan, but she's a good detective. Look how fast she was promoted."

"You know me, though. I've never been the type to welcome changes—I get too set in my ways."

"Things will settle down in a week or two and it will become the new norm. And as for Layla, I'm pleased you have somebody to work with, but as soon as I'm back, she's gone. Got it, boss?"

"Don't start that shite," I said. "We're a team, you and me, and the sooner you're back, the better."

"Well, this little one," she said, rubbing her bump affectionately, "will make an appearance any day now, then the countdown is on."

"Have you heard from Simon?"

"He's due home on leave next week."

"Oh, good."

"I don't know if I'd prefer to have had the baby by then,

which would enable us to spend the entire time as a family, or if I want him there for the birth."

Simon, a soldier in the British Army, was on his second tour of Afghanistan.

"Well, you know I don't mind being your birthing partner if not. So long as you don't mind me seeing your foofoo, that is."

"I don't suppose I'll care once I'm in there, legs akimbo. I'm not looking forward to that part."

"I should have bought you a vindaloo." I grinned. "That would've shifted you along."

"Why didn't I think of that?"

"All joking aside, I am happy for you, but can't wait for you to come back."

"Me neither," she said. "Those last few months on light duties bored the arse off me."

"You had ankles like an elephant—an eighty-year-old would have outrun you."

She glowered at me, as she poured a glass of apple juice, then smiled. "You're a cheeky sod. Now enough about work and my fat ankles," she declared. "Tell me more about your day?"

"Well, talk about foofoo—you'll never guess what Janine wants me to do."

"Go on."

"She wants me to go undercover and audition as a drag queen on Thursday at Dorothy's."

Bella squealed and began choking on a mouthful of juice— she had to spit it back into the glass. "You're kidding! Oh, that's the funniest thing I've heard in ages. You'd make an awesome drag queen."

"So everybody tells me."

"You would. Remember that fancy dress party where you went as *Bubbles DeVere* from *Little Britain*. You were bloody hilarious."

"That was different—I'd had a skinful of ale."

"No, I don't agree. As soon as that outfit went on you morphed into her. Yes, you got a bit sozzled later on, but you were right into it before that."

I shrugged. "I've not agreed to it yet."

"Why does she want you to do it anyway?"

"Blame bloody Layla for that. She picked up a leaflet for auditions and mentioned it to Janine who thinks it's a great idea. Apparently, I'll hear more gossip as an insider. You know how tight-lipped that community is, but they can be right old gossips behind closed doors."

"You have to do it, if it means getting a nutcase off the street."

"I know, but..."

"Hey, you might like it. Maybe you'll double as a drag queen on the weekends? We'll need to think about a name."

"The team already came up with one, but they can kiss my arse."

"Go on."

"Cunt Stubble."

I couldn't help but join in with her raucous laughter.

Once we'd calmed down and dried our eyes Bella turned to me and tried to be serious. She failed miserably. "What about Val Quaeda?"

Another bout of hysterics followed.

"Patty O'Doors," I squeaked, pointing at her patio.

"Sue Doku." She picked up the puzzle book from beside her on the table with one hand, wiping the streaming tears from her cheeks with her other.

I couldn't breathe. This was just what I needed after the day I'd had.

The sound of the front door opening had us up on our feet and rushing to clear away the containers of congealed Chinese food before Bella's sister caught us. We weren't fast enough. Sounds of Penelope and Lily approached the kitchen.

Trying to distract her I jumped forwards, blocking the doorway with my six-foot two frame. "Penny, how nice to see you." I kissed her on the cheek and bent to chuck Lily under the chin.

"Hi, Dylan. Good to see you too, but call me Penelope, please."

"Sorry," I said, turning and raising my eyebrows at Bella.

Bella pressed her lips together, clearly amused.

"What's that awful smell?" Penelope said, marching to the window over the sink and opening it wide. A gust of damp air rushed in.

"That's my fault. I brought Chinese food for us all." I could never get over how different Bella and her sister were—like chalk and cheese.

Penelope pulled a face. "We already ate at my friend's house. Thanks anyway. So, how's your love life? Met the man of your dreams yet?"

"I've been seeing a guy called Steve, but nothing serious. Besides, what man is gonna put up with the hours I work?"

"Every pan has a lid," Bella said.

I rolled my eyes. "Now you sound just like my nan."

"Seriously, Dylan, you do need to find a better work life balance."

SIX

Layla pulled up next to her mother's car on the driveway of the four-bedroom home she'd bought with Max seven years ago. They'd purchased it off plan from a developer and had been the first family to move onto the brand-new estate. They'd been so happy back then—the perfect family, some might say. She detested the place now.

She leaned back into the seat and closed her eyes, needing a few minutes to herself before facing the tribe.

A fierce rapping on the window caused her to gasp and jump up, her heart beating rapidly.

Her mother peered in, motioning for her to wind down the window.

Layla groaned and pulled the keys from the ignition before opening the door.

"Hi, Mum. I was just taking stock."

"Hello, love. I was hoping you'd be back early. I'm off out tonight."

"Who with this time?"

She tapped the side of her nose. "None of your business, young lady."

Layla frowned. "Do you ever date the same man more than once?"

"There are plenty of fine-looking younger men out there who like a woman with experience, so why should I limit myself to just one?"

"You've just turned sixty, for Christ's sake."

"So what? You should take a leaf out of my book, it's moreish."

"I'll pass, thanks."

"Your choice. The kids have been fed. I ordered pizza. There's plenty left over if you're hungry."

"Thanks. I hope you keep a list of the men you're meeting somewhere. There are plenty of nutcases roaming these streets, believe me."

"Yes. I'm sure you'd have no trouble accessing any dating site I use—you are a detective after all." With that, she climbed into her car and backed from the driveway.

Her mum had helped with childcare since Kyle was born thirteen years ago. Max worked away a lot and couldn't be relied on even back then. She lived a mile down the road and, until recently, used to sleep over during the week. That was until her friend filled out her profile on a dating site. Since then, she couldn't wait to get home most nights.

Once her mum's car was out of sight, Layla headed inside.

In the hallway, a thunderous noise startled her, and she suddenly found herself flying backwards into the wall.

"Jacob!" she cried, rubbing her arm. "That bloody hurt!"

"Sorry, Mum. Are you okay? I didn't expect to see you there. Kyle was chasing me."

"How many times do I have to tell you, no running inside?"

Kyle appeared at the top of the stairs. "Mum, will you tell

him? He just unplugged the PC while I was doing my English assignment."

"Jesus, you two. Can't you let me get in the door before you start your bloody arguing?"

"He's a dick!" Kyle growled, throwing a purple pencil down the stairs at his brother's head.

"Stop that! And less of the language. No wonder your grandmother couldn't wait to get out of here—you're getting worse, the pair of you."

Jacob taunted his brother, but Layla pushed him down the hall. "That's enough. Go and watch telly for a bit."

"Hi, Mum. How was your day?" Joshua said, springing to his feet as we entered the living room. "Shall I make you a coffee?"

She smiled at her youngest son. Although just twenty-four minutes younger than Jacob, the difference in them was vast.

"Shall I make you a coffee?" Jacob mimicked, nastily.

"You could take a leaf out of your brother's book, Jacob." She turned back to Joshua. "Yes please, Josh. You're a lifesaver."

Layla plonked down heavily on the sofa and sighed.

Since Max left, she no longer got any enjoyment out of being at home. Not only had he taken her confidence and self-respect, but he'd replaced it with hatred, disgust, and scepticism. Apart from laughing at Dylan today, she couldn't remember the last time she'd cracked a smile, never mind felt genuine happiness. How could he do what he'd done to them all? It wasn't as though he was a young horny kid. He was almost forty, for God's sake.

Jacob grabbed the remote and changed the channel, flicking through impatiently just like his dad used to. They were so like him, which saddened her all the more. Max's betrayal affected every one of them. Kyle was on school report for fighting—one more issue and he would be excluded. Joshua seemed withdrawn, as though he had the weight of the world on his twelve-year-old shoulders, which didn't surprise her—Josh was super-sensitive.

But Jacob worried her the most. He had an evil streak that had only surfaced once his dad left. She'd caught him stamping on the neighbour's baby rabbit. He denied he'd killed it of course, saying he'd found it like that, but Layla didn't believe him.

"I've brought you some pizza too," Josh said, handing her a plate and placing a mug of steaming coffee on the side table.

"Thanks, love." She patted the sofa beside her. "Come and sit here, tell me about your day."

"Tell her you're a faggot," Jacob snorted.

She glared at him. "Last warning, Jake. Be nice or get to your bedroom. I'm not in the mood for your smart mouth today—I mean it."

Jacob stormed off up the stairs.

"You okay, son?" She turned back to Joshua.

He nodded sadly. "I'm sorry about him, Mum. He's a tit."

"Don't you be sorry, baby. It's not your fault."

"I know, but he doesn't mean it. He thinks he's being funny."

"How did you get to be so smart?"

"I take after you." He grinned.

She pulled him towards her and kissed the top of his head. "Lucky you." She laughed.

SEVEN

I felt as though I'd only just closed my eyes when the alarm sounded. I groaned, hit the snooze button, and pulled the pillow over my face trying to shut out the light from the huge bay window. I never closed the curtains, there were four of them and they required far too much fiddling with to get them to hang right, but the downside was the sun streamed into the bedroom every single morning.

After hitting the snooze button twice more, I dragged myself out of bed and into the shower—determined to have an early night tonight.

Half an hour later, dressed in navy slacks and a pale blue shirt, I downed the last of my coffee and headed out the door, dialling Layla's number on the way to the car.

"Yes, what is it?" Layla answered, sounding flustered.

"Sorry, Layla, I meant to call you last night and tell you I'm going over to the scrap yard to find out what they did with the van. You coming?"

"I'm just waiting for Mum to arrive to sort the kids out then I'll be there, text me the address."

"No hurry. In fact, it's not far from your place so I'll swing by and pick you up if you like?"

"Erm... Okay." She didn't sound too sure.

"Put the kettle on, I'll be there soon."

I pulled into the housing estate twenty minutes later. I'd picked Layla up from there for the Christmas party last year, but I'd never been inside. This particular housing development was too rich for my blood. On a police salary there was no way I could afford to live here, but I didn't know much about Max's income or financial situation. All I knew was that he was co-owner of several local businesses in Liverpool and Manchester. I looked around again and couldn't help but think there had been some dodgy dealings going on. "You're a jealous bugger," I said to myself.

Layla opened the front door wide as I approached. "Sorry, Dylan, I'm running late. I don't know what's keeping Mum. I've called her about six times already."

"Really? Is that normal? Do you want me to shoot over to her house for you?"

"No, it should be okay. Come in and have a coffee, I'm sure she'll turn up soon. She's usually early if anything."

As I stepped inside, a teenaged boy dressed in black trousers and white shirt appeared. He had a school tie hung loosely around his neck and dragged a grey blazer along the floor behind him. He turned and sneered at me. "What do you want?"

Taken aback, I looked at Layla who turned scarlet and glowered at the brat.

"Jacob! Carry on like this and you're grounded. Now hurry up and sod off to school, you'll have to get the bus." She shook her head at me as though she was at the end of her tether.

Jacob shoved past me and up the stairs, the sneer still firmly in place.

"Bad time?" I said once he was out of view.

"Is there any other? Seems to be getting worse instead of better." She led me into the kitchen.

Another boy, who looked identical to the first got up from the table and placed a cereal bowl in the sink.

"Joshua, meet Dylan, my boss."

"Hi, Dylan." Joshua smiled, extending his hand for me to shake.

I vaguely remembered Bella telling me Layla had twins, however, apart from the facial features, these boys couldn't be more different. "Pleased to meet you, Joshua." I shook his hand firmly.

He kissed his mother's cheek, picked up a schoolbag from the back of the chair and headed for the front door. "See you later," he called.

Layla placed the filled kettle on the stand and wiped her hands on a tea-towel. "Aren't you waiting for Jacob?" she called after him.

"He won't get on the bus with me. He has his own friends."

"How about Kyle?"

"He's gone already. Charmaine called for him when you were in the shower."

Layla exhaled loudly and shook her head as she followed him out. I felt sorry for her.

Finding a couple of mugs on the draining board, I set about making two cups of coffee.

"You didn't need to do that," Layla said, once she reappeared. "We can get going now, if you like?"

"No hurry. And besides, you look frazzled. Did you even get any sleep last night?"

"A bit. I wouldn't mind but I could barely keep my eyes open all evening but as soon as I hit the sack, I was wide awake."

"Stay on the sofa then. That's what I do. At least you might get a few hours shut-eye that way." I handed her a steaming mug.

"I might try that tonight. Can't hurt, I guess."

We sat opposite each other at the dining table.

The sound of someone charging down the stairs startled me, and Jacob arrived again in the hallway. He grabbed his bag and stormed out the door.

Layla sighed. "He's a worry, that lad."

"Seems a handful. Won't his dad step in and help?"

She snorted. "You must be joking—he's a waste of space."

"He's still their dad and he has a responsibility to help out. I wouldn't give him a choice if I was you—the cheeky bastard."

A few minutes later, the front door suddenly opened, and a classy looking woman entered. "I'm sorry, love. I can't believe it, but I slept in. Where are the boys?"

"They've already left. They're old enough to get the bus now anyway, but I was just worried about you, that's all."

"Don't worry about me, chick." She turned to me and raised one of her eyebrows. "Oh, hello. I don't think we've met. I'm Pixie."

"Dylan," I said, taking her offered hand in mine.

Layla scowled and jumped to her feet. "We've got to get to work, Mother. I'll speak to you later."

"Oh, really?" Pixie frowned. "Can't you spare a few minutes?"

"No. I'll see you later." Layla kissed her mother's cheek and headed for the door.

"Nice to meet you, Pixie," I said, before following Layla.

"Sorry about that," she said, once we were in the car.

"About what?"

"My mother. She's a right nympho lately."

I braked hard and barked out a laugh. "A nympho?" I asked, sure she'd got her words mixed up.

"Yes. Since she joined a dating agency, she's bloody sex mad —she has a different guy every night!"

"You're kidding!" I spluttered.

"Honest, I'm not. She's embarrassing."

"I think it's a hoot. She's an attractive woman, and she's obviously enjoying herself. Good on her."

"You wouldn't say that if it was your mum."

I laughed again as I thought about my own lovely mother— obsessed with bingo and crosswords, she wouldn't look twice at another man.

"So, where are we going?" Layla dusted off her trouser suit and inhaled deeply as though leaving her problems at home.

"Will called the last registered owner of the van and he'd scrapped it, apparently. The scrap yard is here in town."

"Ooh! Let's hope for a solid lead."

Ten minutes later I parked on the road beside a huge auto recycling sign. We strolled into the vast yard and located the reception.

A scruffy-haired young lad grunted some form of greeting at us as we entered, then went back to staring at the computer screen. I was certain he was doing nothing more important than checking his Facebook page.

"Is the manager about, please?" I asked, flashing my badge.

That got him up on his feet. "Nah! He won't be here till later. Can I help?"

"We're trying to locate a Transit van that was sold to you as scrap several months ago."

He was suddenly devoid of all colour.

I glanced at Layla to see if she noticed his body language. Her eyes narrowed, and she nodded.

The lad cleared his throat and bounced on the balls of his feet. "What van?"

I gave him the number plate details. "And here's a copy of the receipt. Do you recognise that signature?"

"No. This isn't one of our receipts. We always print ours on letterheaded paper." His shifty expression and fidgety fingers told me he was lying. But why?

I took a chance. "Funny, because you match the description of the person who bought the van, to a tee," I lied.

The guy stiffened and eyeballed the door. I sensed he was considering making a run for it.

"Just tell us who you sold it to."

"Aw, man! I'm gonna be in deep shit." He began to blubber.

"Why? Tell us what happened."

"Some guy brought it in one Saturday morning, I was here alone. There was fuck-all wrong with it, so I made up a fake receipt and bought it myself. It had no tax or MOT, but only had minor damage—I knew I could make a killing."

"So, you sold it?"

He nodded, his face crumpled in a seriously ugly cry.

"Who to?"

He shrugged. "I don't know. I didn't do any paperwork. The guy said he was a traveller and wanted something he could convert to sleep in. He paid cash and drove it away the same day."

I looked at the receipt. "So, eight months ago—would you have CCTV footage from back then?"

"I don't think so, man. It's not a very up-to-date system."

"Tell me about the buyer. What did he look like?"

"Late fifties, early sixties. He had an accent and wore a leather jacket and an old-fashioned hat. He was a gypsy, a traveller—he said he intended to do it up to sleep in. I didn't think it would be a problem. Please don't tell my boss—he'll sack me."

"Sorry, buddy, but you've broken the law—getting the sack is the least of your problems right now. What's your name and address?"

EIGHT

Will took a deep breath, descended the steps, and walked into the unknown.

He'd never been inside a gay bar before, especially one as renowned as Dorothy's.

He was surprised the subterranean bar was as big as it was.

He felt the eyes of strangers boring into him.

Why the hell did I volunteer myself for this? He thought.

Walking to the bar, a young guy approached.

"Can I help yer?" He had a broad Mancunian accent.

Will held up his credentials. "DS Will Spencer to see Chris Turner."

The barman's eyes lit up. "Are you here about the murders then?"

"I'm not at liberty to discuss that. Could you please let Mr Turner know I'm here?"

"Sure thing, handsome."

He minced away to the other end of the bar.

Will shuddered and scanned the room, trying to ascertain where the CCTV cameras would be located and only spotted two. Something told him he wouldn't find what he needed on the footage.

Turning back to the bar, he caught the eye of a weedy, older looking camp guy with the complexion of an Oompa Loompa.

"Ooh, look, girl," the man squealed to his equally effeminate, orange tinted companion. "Fresh meat."

Will's face flushed, embarrassed by the unwanted attention.

He glowered his disapproval and was met with the fluttering of eyelashes.

The man blew him a kiss.

The attention shouldn't have surprised him. He wasn't a bad looking guy–shaved head, stubble, rugby player build, thighs like tree trunks. He was a catch but didn't have a gay bone in his body.

A man seemingly in his fifties walked towards him on the customer side of the bar and offered a smile. The first thing Will noticed were the spectacles on a chain around his neck. It put him in mind of the old comedian, Larry Grayson.

"DS Spencer."

"Yeah," Will muttered. "That's me."

"I'm Chris Turner."

Will held out his credentials. "Thanks for seeing me, Mr Turner. I do appreciate it."

"Oh, it's my pleasure, ducky, but call me Blanche, all my friends do."

Ducky. What the fuck? "Erm, okay," he replied, still unsure of what to call him. "Do you have the footage ready for me to view?"

"Yes, all ready. If you'd like to follow me to my office." He led the way. "Can I get you a drink, or maybe a bite to eat?"

"Just a lemonade."

Chris turned to the barman. "Mayday, love, bring a lemonade and a strong black coffee through to my office as soon as you can, please."

"Gimme a few minutes, Blanche."

"Mayday?"

"Yes, ducky–don't ask. Now, where were we? Oh yes, I'm afraid we only have footage from two of the cameras."

"Which ones?"

"The stage area and the bar near the main entrance."

"Main entrance?"

"Yes. There is a side entrance too. Not many punters use it, but it's always open."

"Shit."

"I've put in a request for all the cameras to be fixed."

"Okay. Nothing we can do about it now, but if you don't mind, I'll need your help."

The office was dingy and cluttered. It wouldn't have surprised Will if it had been converted from a broom cupboard. An old-fashioned video recorder sat on top of a TV screen–hardly state-of-the-art.

Chris gestured to the nearest chair. "You sit there and do what you need to do."

"Thanks, but before I look through the footage, I need to show you a couple of pictures of the victims and see if you recognise either of them."

"It's nothing gory is it, ducky? I don't have the stomach for that."

"No, not at all. Just photos for identification purposes."

Will opened his file and retrieved the two photographs, placing them on the desk in front of Chris.

"Those poor girls."

"Do you recognise either of them?" Will asked.

"I'm sorry to say I do."

Will picked up one of the photos. "Can you tell me who this is?"

"Her name is Gina Elliot. She was a regular in here. Lovely

girl. I can't believe somebody would hurt her." He pulled a silk handkerchief from his pocket and dabbed at his eyes.

Will picked up the other image. "And this person? Is she familiar to you at all?"

"Yes, she was all over the news a few weeks ago. And I told the other officer I recognised her."

"Was Jade Kelly a regular too?"

"Yeah, but she didn't come as often as Gina."

Will put the photos away. "Thanks."

"I hope you catch the bastard and string him up by his balls."

"So do I. And the sooner the better."

"You think there will be more murders?" Chris shuddered.

"I'd bet my life on it. This is one sick bastard and unless we catch him, and fast, he'll strike again."

Chris gulped.

Mayday brought the drinks in and set them down.

"Thank you," Will said.

"Gimme a shout if you need filling up," Mayday said with a wink.

Will nodded then guzzled the lemonade back.

For nearly an hour they trawled through the footage.

"That's Gina, right there," Chris said, fingering the screen.

"Are you sure?"

"Yeah, that's her. I remember clearly, she told me she'd only bought the dress that day." He waved his hand regally.

"Great. Do you know who she's with?"

"I don't know them well, but it's usually the same old crowd. Trannies tend to stick together."

"So, it's well known they're all transgender?"

"Oh, yeah, ducky. Nobody cares in here. Anything goes, you know."

"That's good to hear."

"Gina was pretty well known anyway."

"Oh?"

"Yeah, she loved to get up and do karaoke in between the drag acts."

"On the night in question, did she get up on stage?"

"Oh, yes, without a doubt."

They trawled through more footage, and sure enough, Gina took to the stage. He couldn't hear what she was singing as there was no audio, but she was there.

She sang a couple of songs, took a bow, and left the stage. They flicked through the remaining film, but Gina wasn't seen again.

He would need the CCTV footage from the streets, both entrances, hopefully they'd be able to see who she left the bar with.

The footage had been recorded on an old VHS tape, but in this instance that came in handy.

"Do you mind if I take this with me? I'll make sure to return it to you in due course."

"Ducky, if it gets this monster off the street, you keep it."

"Well, thank you for your help this morning. If you hear of anything else, please call me?" Will handed over his card.

"Of course." Chris ejected the video cassette from the machine.

"Thanks, err, Blanche."

"Get that animal off the streets, DS Spencer. These girls have been through enough."

"I promise we'll catch him." He picked up the tape and exited the office.

"Those stairs there." Chris pointed towards the pool table. "That's the other entrance. Feel free to go out that way."

"Got you."

Will walked up the stairs and made a note of the street name.

He called the office, requesting the CCTV footage be sent to him urgently.

Later that afternoon, Will finished looking through the footage he'd requested.

"Damn." He banged his hand on the desk.

"Problem?" Dylan approached.

Layla turned in her chair.

"A fucking big one. I just checked the CCTV from both entrances at Dorothy's..."

"And?"

"She left via the side exit–alone."

"Did anybody follow her?" Layla asked.

"Not that I can see, but I'm waiting for more footage so I can track the route she took from the bar and hopefully see if we can ascertain where she met her attacker."

"Good thinking." Dylan said. "Keep me informed."

"Oh, boss, before you head off. I meant to tell you I got a hit on those prosthetics."

"You're kidding?"

"Nah, I struck lucky earlier. Apparently, there's a place not far from Lime Street Station–pretty seedy by all accounts but they stock this particular line."

"Did you speak to anybody there?"

"Just a brief call with the shop assistant but he didn't know too much or wasn't giving anything away. He said the store manager..." He looked at his notes. "... a Damien Robinson, would be back around 4pm so I said I'd head over and speak to him in person."

"Sounds like a good start, but if you don't mind, you focus on the footage and I'll ask one of the others to head over."

"I can do it if you want," Layla volunteered. "I'm finishing in a minute, and it's easy for me to swing by on the way home. You just need to give me the address for the place, Will."

"Are you sure?"

"Yeah, it's not a problem."

"Great, that's one thing off the list."

Will handed her a piece of paper. "I'll fill you in tomorrow morning if that's okay, unless I get something concrete that needs immediate action."

"Fine by me," Dylan said. "Thanks guys, keep up the good work."

NINE

I'd just finished the morning briefing when Janine pushed open the double doors, her face scarlet with rage.

"Good morning, Ma'am," I said, cheerily.

"Dylan. My office. Now!" she snapped, then turned on her heels and left the way she came.

"On my way."

Joanna looked worried. "What's that all about?"

"No idea, but I'd better go and find out."

"Good luck."

"Thanks." My phone buzzed and I checked the screen. It was a message from Layla.

Running late.
Heading to sex shop.
It was closed last night.

I rushed down the corridor and knocked on Janine's office door.

"Come in," she bellowed.

I took a deep breath and pushed the door open, ready for the onslaught that was obviously about to be delivered. "Ma'am."

"Sit," she barked.

I took a seat opposite.

She tossed a newspaper across her desk. It landed in my lap. "What's this?"

"Read it and see for yourself."

I grimaced upon reading the headline.

SERIAL KILLER TARGETING TRANS COMMUNITY.

"Shit. Where have they got this from?"

"Keep reading." Her face was twisted in rage. "A high-ranking officer confirmed to Chris Turner, the landlord of Dorothy's, that we suspect a serial killer is targeting the trans community. Do you know how many calls I've had since this... this rag hit the stands a few hours ago?"

I continued to read, astounded the reporter had made so many links without confirmation. What the reporter had actually written wasn't so far off the mark. "This is all speculation."

"Can you say that for a fact? Didn't Will spend some time with the landlord? What makes you think this hasn't come from him?"

"With respect, I know my own team." I was pissed off with her attitude and accusatory tone.

Her eyes widened, clearly surprised by my response. "I sincerely hope so, for your sake."

"Permission to speak freely, Ma'am."

Janine leaned forward. "Go for it."

"I'd be surprised if any member of the team would be stupid enough to confirm to any outside source what we suspect. However, the guy has been questioned about two of his customers. It wouldn't take a rocket scientist to put two and two together."

"I want him brought in for questioning."

"For what reason?"

"I want to know where he got this information from."

"That's fine, but have you forgotten you've got me auditioning for him tomorrow? He's bound to recognise me."

My words seem to cool the fire within her. "I didn't think of that. But remember, three or more murders before we have to confirm a serial killer. If he strikes again, then what?"

"Then we deal with it, just like we always do. We'll get the bastard, mark my words."

"I don't share your enthusiasm, Dylan. In fact, I'm dismayed at the lack of progress you've made so far."

"I disagree."

"Really?"

"Yes!" Her snotty attitude had pissed me off and I wasn't going to sit here and let her berate me and my team without merit. "And as you gave me permission to speak freely, I will."

Janine cocked an eyebrow.

"The team have been working with whatever evidence the killer has left behind which is bugger all, might I add. Plus we're two officers down, but you don't want to recognise any of that. They are a loyal and dedicated bunch, and they're working their arses off."

"How far has that got us? We need action, Dylan."

"Action? I've only been on the job for two days! Two days! I'm trying to find my footing with the team and get them onside and you storm into *our* office, bark orders at me like I'm a dog, and leave me to deal with the fallout later on."

She was about to interrupt but I raised my hand.

"Seriously, Janine. How do you expect the team to respect me when they see my superior can't even pretend to?" I paused to take a breath. "Savage might have put up with you speaking to him like shit in front of everyone, but I won't. Not under any circumstances. If you want a yes man, you're looking at the wrong guy." I stood up, ready to take my leave.

She leaned back in her chair, her face flushed. "Have you quite finished?"

"Apparently." Right then, I didn't care if she demoted me. I wasn't about to be spoken down to by her, or anybody, and if she didn't like it, tough.

"Then sit down and allow me the chance to speak."

"Fine."

"Maybe I was a little hasty earlier in apportioning blame, but top brass are breathing down my neck. The trans community are getting nervous and shit rolls downhill, and right now, it's heading my way. The buck stops with me, so I need answers, and fast."

"I get that, but respect works both ways, Ma'am. The team will do what they have to do, but back them into a corner and treat them like shit and they'll give what's expected and nothing more."

"Noted. It won't happen again."

"Good. Now let me fill you in on what we have so far."

Half an hour later, I was sat at my desk when Layla arrived. It wasn't good news by the look on her face.

"How did it go at the sex shop?"

"Dead end, I'm afraid."

"Dammit." I felt deflated. "What happened—wrong store?"

"I don't think so," she replied. "Apparently, that store is the only stockist of this particular item for thirty odd miles."

"So we can reasonably assume the location is correct."

"Yeah, I'd say so. Anyway, I spoke to Mr Robinson, the manager, a right little gob-shite he was too. He confirms they do stock them, but also says he sells lots of them, mainly for hen parties, he thinks."

"That doesn't give us much to go on. Any in-store CCTV footage available?"

"No go, I'm afraid. The place is an absolute dump inside."

"Shit!" My hopes of finding a suspect were dashed. "Have they had any multiple purchases?"

"Yeah, some Polish bloke bought several of them a while back, but he doesn't remember anything else about him."

"By any chance does our Mr Robinson know how the items were paid for?"

"Cash, he seems to recall." She opened her notebook and read quickly. "Reckons he doesn't get much call for card paying customers—these things show on bank statements and most visitors to his store would rather the wife or girlfriend didn't find out what they were purchasing."

I held my head in my hands. "So we have the store they were purchased from at least. Speak to Will and see if there is any street cam footage we may be able to take a peek at."

"Got it."

"While you're all here," I said to the room. "I suppose I'd better get this out of the way and I don't want any wise cracks."

Everyone stopped what they were doing and looked at me.

"I've decided I'll do the audition at Dorothy's tomorrow. I must be bloody crazy."

The reality of what I was doing hit home. I was going to stand in front of God knows how many strangers, in a frock, wig, and full make-up, then lip-sync to a song I hadn't even chosen yet. Added to that, I didn't have a clue what I was doing. I'd never dressed as a woman and wouldn't know where to start.

I decided to call Bella.

TEN

Bella picked up after a few rings.

"Hiya. I need your help."

"What's up?"

"No smart remarks, but I'm auditioning at Dorothy's tomorrow."

"Oh, my God," she squealed. "You're kidding me?"

"No, I'm not, but shut it for a minute and listen. That mate of yours, you know, the camp one, is he still doing drag?"

"Roy? Yeah, why?"

"Do you think he'd be up for helping me?"

"I don't know. I could call him and ask."

"Would you?"

"Yeah, but I'll have to tell him the truth about why you're doing it, but don't worry, I trust him with my life."

Later that evening, I sounded the horn and glanced at the front of Bella's house, waiting for signs she'd heard me. She appeared in the doorway wearing a bright orange, full-length wool coat, and looked even bigger than she had on Monday.

"Jesus, Bella, are you gonna fit in the passenger seat? Maybe you should climb in the boot?" I said through the open window as she approached the car.

"Shut it, or I'll sit on *you.*"

I feigned terror and then laughed. "So where are we meeting Roy? At his house, I hope."

She eased herself into the passenger seat and closed the door before turning to me. "Nope. Afraid not. He's at the town hall rehearsing for this year's panto."

"You mean there'll be other people there?"

She grinned. "A few, maybe. Don't worry, you'll be fine."

"Bloody hell, Bella. I'll be a frigging laughingstock."

"Oh, stop whinging. As if anybody will give a toss about you putting a bit of slap on. They do it every night."

I shook my head before pulling away. "I have a bad feeling about this."

Less than five minutes later we parked up outside the Town Hall and I followed Bella inside. I wasn't happy about this. In fact, the more I thought about it, the more I hated the idea.

"Daaaaarling!" Roy's booming voice startled me. He suddenly appeared wearing a gaudy yellow kimono, his face totally devoid of make-up and no wig on—which I'd never seen before—he'd always been either dressed as a guy or fully made up as a woman when I'd seen him in the past. This look was half and half. What bit of hair he had was scraped back, and he had some fine mesh cap holding it in place.

"Hi, gorgeous," Bella said, holding her arms outstretched to him for a hug.

"Goodness, Bella, you're huge!" Roy said, kissing the air just above each of her cheeks.

"Oi, you," she giggled, patting his pert backside.

"You know what I mean. Shouldn't you be in hospital popping that little sweetheart out by now?"

"Not long to wait, I hope," she said, stroking her bump.

"Right, Dylan, darling. I hear you're ready to embrace your feminine side and need my help?"

"All in the name of the law." I grinned, unsure what Bella had told him.

"Then follow me, I can't wait to get my hands on that delectable jaw line of yours."

I cringed. Roy had been a friend of Bella's from school and she'd tried to set us up on a date many moons ago, but, although he'd been more than keen, I didn't fancy him. I was into manly men and didn't relish the idea of being up close and personal with him one jot.

He led us through a series of corridors to a small dingy-looking room at the back of the building. "Here we are, darlings. Take a seat. Bella, you'll have to perch on the edge of the coffee table. There's not much room in here, I'm afraid." He reached for a small aluminium case. "Now, I've gone through all my old make-up and pulled out a selection of everything you'll need. Give it back to me when you've finished as it costs a small fortune."

"Are you sure? I don't mind buying some, but I wouldn't know where to start, to be honest." I sat on the only chair in the room.

"I'm always buying new stuff so it's fine. Now, do you want me to apply your makeup, or would you like me to show you how I do mine and you copy me?"

"I'd prefer to do my own, if possible." I smiled, relieved I wouldn't have him intruding too far into my personal space.

"Okay then, darling. You have quite the five o'clock shadow. When did you last shave?"

"This morning." I rubbed my prickly chin.

"Well, we can go over the top of it this time, but when you're doing this for real, you'll need to shave as close as you can, capiche?"

I nodded, glancing at Bella who had a silly grin on her face. I sighed, praying it wouldn't take too long before I could get out of there.

"Okay. First things first. You'll need a wig cap." He handed me a brown piece of nylon that reminded me of fishnet stockings. "Put it on, like this." He patted his head.

Reluctantly, I did as he asked.

Bella sniggered, and I shot her a warning glance.

"Okay, great. Now, we need to apply some aftershave balm. It has a lot of glycerine in it, which will help prevent your skin drying out." He squirted some cream into his palm before handing me the bottle, then slathered it all over his face.

I did the same. I hated the feel of it, and this was just the beginning. God help me!

"Next, we need a good primer to fill in the pores. Just cake it on." I watched as he squirted a dollop into his palm before focusing mainly on his nose, forehead, and chin.

He handed me the bottle and I did the same.

"What we need to do next is the colour correct. You're not gonna like this and you'll think it's silly but it's necessary, I promise." He took a large lipstick-like tube and began to cover his chin and upper lip with dark terracotta coloured makeup. He looked like he had a ginger beard and moustache when he'd finished, then he drew two half-moons in the same colour under his eyes.

"Really?" I glanced at Bella, thinking they were taking the piss.

She shrugged.

I took the makeup stick and proceeded to do the same.

"Honestly, you won't see it once we've finished. But you need it under your foundation to counteract the colour of the five o'clock shadow." He looked comical and it was a huge effort not to laugh.

"I never expected so much went into applying makeup," I said, feeling a change come over me as I preened myself in the mirror.

"These are just the basics. You should see what some queens do. They can take literally hours to put their faces on. Right. Once you've done that, we need to apply foundation. I usually use a medium coverage on the top part of my face and finish my five o'clock shadow with full coverage makeup." He poured some beige liquid onto his fingers and spread it roughly all over the upper part of his face, right up to his hairline.

I tried the same, being a little more frugal with the liquid.

"You'll need more than that," he said, taking the tube from me and squirting a good dollop onto my fingers. "If you're going to do this right, less is definitely not more in this case —capiche?"

I nodded again and, cringing, covered my face with the gloopy stuff.

"Perfect. See how lovely your complexion looks already?"

"Let me see?" Bella said.

I turned to show her.

"Wow! I might try some of these techniques myself. Your skin looks a-ma-zing."

I turned back to the mirror just as Roy was dabbing the full coverage foundation onto a cotton bud, then he dabbed it all over the terracotta goatee area. "Here you go. You do the same." He handed me a cotton bud. "This is too intense to use your fingers— we need to blend it in with a brush, like this."

"I'm never gonna remember all this," I said, more worried than ever.

Roy smiled. "I'll write some notes for you once we've finished."

"Thanks, mate. Although I'm still not convinced I'll even be doing this—it's too far out of my comfort zone, to be honest."

"Wait till you get your full face on, you'll feel different again. It's liberating."

"Maybe for you. You're into all that but I'm not."

"We'll see."

My face felt strange as the foundation began to dry. I was impressed at how even my skin tone looked. There was not a hint of the terracotta makeup.

"We need to apply a layer of powder now. I know what you're thinking—applying makeup before the concealer is crazy, right? But it works, I assure you."

"You're right, that's exactly what I was thinking." I eyed Bella who barked out a laugh.

He pulled out a huge brush and dabbed his entire face before handing it to me to do the same.

I had to admit I was shocked at how fantastic I was beginning to look. Although quite happy with my physical appearance as a man, I'd never thought of myself the least bit feminine, but I looked bloody gorgeous. I pouted at myself in the mirror and Bella screeched hysterically.

"See, your inner goddess is emerging!" Roy said, proudly. "Now, concealer. I use my fingers for this step and blend it with a sponge afterwards." He squeezed a blob of lighter beige makeup onto the back of his hand before dabbing it on under his eyes with his little finger and blending it in with a sponge. "Look, no dark shadows! It's fabulous, isn't it?"

I nodded, and did the same, really getting into it.

"Now more powder, but not too much."

With each layer, my skin looked even more flawless than the last.

"Contour next. And, darling, if you like what you see now, you'll be creaming in your panties shortly!"

More hysterical laughter from Bella, but I was too serious, scared to crack my beautiful porcelain-like face.

Taking a large brush he dabbed it into some brown powder and, with sweeping strokes, created two hollows underneath each cheek bone. "Your turn."

Just when I thought I was completely finished, he insisted I put pale highlighter along the length of my nose, finishing with a dab on the tip, resembling an exclamation mark, and more highlighter under and over the top of my eyes. By the time we got onto the eyeshadow, I was morphing into a woman. The way I held my head up and the pout of my lips added a whole new dimension to my personality. Eyeliner and mascara was topped off with false eyelashes, which were a bastard to master, and then the lipstick was the finishing touch. Stunning.

"Just wait until I show you what's next." Roy excitedly bounced from the room returning moments later with a huge baby-pink wig. "Now, you must promise to look after this as it cost a blummin' fortune." He proceeded to place the wig on my head.

I didn't recognise myself. Turning and pouting in the mirror I examined myself from every angle. It was remarkable. My own mother wouldn't recognise me.

"I have several older costumes you can borrow, I need my newer ones for my own act, but there's nothing wrong with them."

"Are you sure? I can't tell you how grateful I am for all your help. If I can return the favour, you name it and I'll do it."

"Just kill it. Go out there and knock 'em dead. Oh, and tell me where you'll be. I'd love to be there for your debut."

"Not a chance, sorry. Top secret, I'm afraid." The last thing I wanted was for him to show up at my audition and subsequent debut performance—I'd die.

"Shame. I'd pay good money to see you. But I think you're ready. What size shoe are you?"

"Men's size ten."

"Ooh! You may be in luck—hang on." Once again, he left the room and returned with a pair of ridiculously high heels. "You may need to practise walking in these. Come on, have a go."

"Nah, it's okay. I'll practise at home."

"Come on, Dylan," Bella urged. "Don't be shy."

"I'm not shy."

"Do it, then."

Scowling, I slipped off my comfortable shoes and socks before sliding my feet into the strappy silver sandals.

"How do you have such smooth skin on your feet?" Bella exclaimed. "Mine are like sandpaper."

I shrugged. "Dunno. Never thought about it." Once I had the shoes fastened, I tottered to my feet. "This doesn't feel good." Catching sight of myself looming majestically in front of the mirror, all pink hair and flawless complexion, I forgot about my balance and moments later, wobbled off the heels and crashed to the floor in an unsightly heap.

Bella's hysterical laughter was mixed with a series of groans and then the sound of something being spilled onto the floor. "Oh, shit, my waters have broken!"

ELEVEN

"I need to get to hospital, Dylan. You'll have to take me."

"Are you kidding me, Bella? I can't be seen in public looking like this." I pulled the heels off and reached for my shoes and socks, not wanting to stand in the puddle in bare feet.

"Then you'd better learn how to deliver a baby, and fast, 'cos it's coming."

Roy dithered like an old woman. "Ooh, dearie me, look at the mess. Baby juice all up me tights."

"I'm sorry," Bella added, panting.

"Right, ambulance." I decided. "Roy, do the honours, will you."

Bella let out a huge wail.

Roy flapped about. "Oh, God, she isn't gonna give birth in here, is she?"

"If you don't dial the bloody ambulance, then yes, she might."

"Right-o, flower. I'm on it." He dashed from the room.

"He'd be no good in a crisis," I said.

"You're right. I just hope he isn't faffing about on the phone because it's not gonna be long."

"You've only just gone into labour, Bella. Surely, there's loads of time."

"This baby wants out," she wailed again. "Help me get my knickers off, will you?"

"Oh, God. Oh, God." Now I was panicking when I should have been helping her.

"Calm down," she said. "I've done this before, remember." She edged her knickers down to her ankles.

"I'm sorry." I knelt down and picked her underwear up, wrapped them in a wad of tissue I found by the sink, and shoved them into my pocket.

Roy reappeared. "The ambulance is on the way now. Five minutes tops. Let me see." He crouched down and peered up Bella's skirt, his face scrunched into a grimace. "Looks like a car crash down here, darling."

I stifled my laugh.

"Cheeky bastard," Bella replied. "You've probably never seen a fanny before."

Roy ignored her comment and stood upright. "Have you ever seen that old eighties movie, *Predator*?"

Bella glowered at him.

I had no idea where he was going with this but answered anyway. "Yeah, why?"

"Don't you see the resemblance?" He was deadpan in his delivery.

I bit my lip because I could see the similarities, but I daren't laugh as Bella would have taken my head off. "Roy, shut it before she throttles you with those stockings," I warned. "Help me get her outside."

"No!" Bella screeched. "What if they don't get here on time? I don't want to have the baby on the pavement, for fuck's sake."

"Alright, but let's get closer to the front door for when they do arrive."

Roy grabbed Bella's orange coat and handbag while I slid my arm around her back and led her towards the exit.

When we reached the foyer, I eased Bella down onto a leather armchair.

Roy dropped her belongings beside her. "Right-o, darlings, I must love you and leave you. Good luck popping the sprog out, Bells."

"Hey!" I said. "You can't leave us. What if the baby comes?"

Just then, I heard the sound of an approaching ambulance and I almost wept with relief.

"There you go," Roy said, backing up the way we'd just come. "Give me a call. I can meet you again tomorrow to go through the other stuff if you like?" And then he was gone.

"Come on, Bella, let's get you outside now, they're here." I pulled her up onto her feet.

She suddenly held herself rigid and groaned gripping my hand hard.

"Yikes, Bella," I said, prizing her fingers apart. "Aren't you supposed to pant, or something?" I made panting sounds like I'd seen on the telly.

She thumped me on the shoulder.

Once the pain eased, we proceeded through the door just as the ambulance pulled up outside.

The two paramedics wasted no time and had Bella in the back of the ambulance in a flash.

"Can I come with you or should I take my car?" I asked the male driver.

"Suit yourself, pal," he said, a stupid grin on his face.

I suddenly remembered that not only was I wearing a face full of makeup, caked an inch thick, but a candy-floss pink wig as well.

"Don't leave me, Dylan," Bella cried.

Humiliated, I climbed in beside her just as another contraction kicked in. "Don't worry, I won't be going anywhere."

The doors were closed, and we sped off in the direction of the hospital.

"What's the show you're doing?" the female paramedic asked once she'd sat down beside us.

"Beg your pardon?" I asked, confused.

"I'm presuming you're in a show."

"The makeup," Bella said, calm again.

"Oh, no. I mean... well, I don't usually dress like this, but..."

"None of my beeswax, love," she said with a wink, causing another bout of giggles from Bella.

"Glad you're still able to laugh at my expense, missus." I pulled the wig off and shoved it into Bella's bag.

Bella's laughter suddenly turned to groans as another wave of pain creased her.

"That'll teach you for laughing at me." I grinned, then flinched as Bella tried to punch my arm again.

By the time we got to the hospital there was barely a break between contractions. The paramedics wheeled Bella in on a gurney and handed her over to the duty midwife, Ursula, a tall, skinny Polish woman.

She eyed me with amusement. I could tell it wasn't every day a younger, hotter version of Eddie Izzard made such an entrance.

Bella almost broke every bone in my hand as I walked beside her on the way to the maternity unit.

Stifled laughter and stupid grins were all that greeted us from the gawking onlookers we passed along the way.

I blew a kiss to a particularly butch-looking biker dude and he flushed scarlet and rapidly turned away.

Once in the delivery unit, several midwives set about preparing Bella for the birth. I was moved from pillar to post, getting under their feet.

"I'm going to try to get this muck off my face, Bells—I'll be back in two ticks."

In the throes of another contraction, Bella didn't seem to care, so I ducked out of the room in search of a bathroom.

It wasn't until I saw my reflection I remembered the fishnet cap on my head. I whipped it off and stuffed it in my jacket pocket alongside Bella's knickers.

I peeled off the eyelashes and they also went in my pocket. I spied a soap dispenser on the wall and pumped three squirts into my palm, before adding a bit of water. I covered my entire face with the lather, but it was useless. This muck was industrial strength, designed to defeat the sweltering heat of stage lights and a few squirts of liquid soap weren't going to budge it. I gave up and rubbed as much off as I could with a couple of paper towels.

"Where've you been?" Bella cried when I re-entered the room. Her face had contorted into something that resembled a she-devil.

"Just to the loo. Are you okay?" I was relieved most of the nurses had gone. Only Ursula remained, and she was fiddling with Bella's nether regions.

"I am now but please don't leave me again."

"I won't, babe. I promise."

The midwife stood upright and snapped off a pair of latex gloves. "Eight centimetres," she said. "It shouldn't be too long now."

Another midwife entered pushing something that looked like an oxygen tank."

"Oh, good," I said.

"Can you ring my sister?" Bella asked me. "Tell her I won't be home, or she'll be worrying."

"Of course, I'll go out and do it now."

"No! Don't go. Call her from here."

I glanced at Ursula for approval and she nodded. "Okay then, Bells, I'll stay." Pulling my phone out of my jeans pocket, I dialled Bella's home number and stepped to the side of the room.

"Penelope speaking."

"Hi Penny, it's Dylan. I'm at the hospital with Bella. She's in labour."

"Really? Is she alright?"

"She's fine. It came on pretty quick and the midwife seems to think it won't be long now. I'll call as soon as there's any news."

"Great. Give her my love and tell her not to worry about things here. I've got it covered."

"Thanks Penny, er, Penelope, I mean." I hung up and returned to Bella's side, surprised to see her attached to the oxygen mask. "What's that for?" I asked Ursula.

"It's pain relief—gas and air," she said. "We don't have time to administer any other pain meds. Your baby will be here soon."

"Oh, it's not my baby," I said. "We're just friends."

Ursula gasped. "Really? Then maybe you should stay at the top of the bed," she said disapprovingly as she pulled down the sheet to cover Bella's modesty.

"Oh no, here comes another," Bella cried, writhing about on the bed in agony.

"Pant, Bella," Ursula said. "Do it with me." She began huffing.

Bella joined in until the pain subsided.

"Maybe you can rub her back—that sometimes helps," Ursula said to me.

"Of course. Sit forward, Bella, so I can rub your back."

"I don't want you to rub my fucking back. I don't want you to touch me."

Shocked by the venom in her voice, I stepped away. "Okay, suit yourself, I'm only trying to help."

"I'm sorry, Dylan." Tears filled her eyes. "I didn't mean it. Don't be mad at me."

"I'm not mad." I took her outstretched hand once again.

She winced as another contraction started. "Something's wrong. Please help me," she pleaded with Ursula. "Something's really wrong, I'm certain of it."

Ursula checked the monitor and turned a dial. The room was suddenly filled with a gentle thrum. It took a second for it to register it was the baby's heartbeat. "Your baby's doing fine, Bella. Don't worry, everything's perfectly normal."

"I don't wanna do it. I can't do it, Dylan. Oh, my God, please, someone, please help me."

TWELVE

I was out of my depth. Bella's cries got louder, and her nails dug deeper. I was relieved when Ursula told us it was time to push.

"Right, my love. As soon as you feel your next contraction, I need you to bear down as though you're having a poo."

"No way! What if I poo? I don't want everyone to see my..." She gripped my hand as another wave of pain washed over her.

"Push, Bella," Ursula urged.

Bella did as instructed; her face turned a deep shade of purple.

"That's it. Good girl," Ursula said.

I took a leaf out of her book. "That's it, Bells, push that bowling ball out."

Bella huffed out a laugh and pushed again.

"Okay. Stop now," Ursula said. "Wait for the next contraction, you're doing really well."

"I don't feel like I'm doing well," she sobbed.

"What? Of course you are." I stroked her forehead.

She grabbed my hand with hers and threw it off. "Don't touch me," she yelled in my face.

"Okay, okay. I'm sorry."

"Right, Bella are you ready? Let's make this pain count." Ursula folded the sheet back.

Five minutes later, Bella squeezed a wrinkly baby boy from her foofoo.

"You did it, Bells," I said, suddenly overcome with emotion.

Ursula cut the cord and wiped some thick white mucus off the baby's body before placing him on Bella's tummy.

Tears flowed freely down her face. "He's perfect," Bella said, totally besotted with her baby boy. "Isn't he beautiful, Dylan?"

I hesitated. "The face only a mother could love." I laughed. "He's a bit wrinkly, and his nose looks as though he's gone ten rounds with Mike Tyson."

Bella snorted. "Did you hear your uncle Dylan," she cooed at the fidgeting bundle.

Another midwife entered. "Gosh, you don't waste time, do you?" she grinned. "Let's have a look."

"Okay, Bella. I need you to deliver the placenta," Ursula said.

"Here, let me take the baby. I need to clean him up and weigh him anyway," the other midwife said.

Bella reluctantly handed the baby over.

"Do you have a name yet?" the midwife asked.

Bella glanced at me. "I need to check with Simon first, but I was thinking I'd like to call him Dylan."

My breath hitched in my throat and I felt my eyes filling again. "Really?"

She nodded and allowed her own tears to fall.

"That means the world to me," I said. "And I was only kidding. He's a gorgeous baby—just perfect."

THIRTEEN

The bedside alarm clock shook me awake. I reached across and hit the snooze button.

Squinting to see the time, I groaned upon the realisation I'd only managed to get about two hours, and could quite easily have called in sick, rolled over, closed my eyes and slept the entire day.

The alarm sounded again. Unable to deal with the ringing, I knocked it off the cabinet, forced myself out of bed and stumbled half-awake to the bathroom. A few minutes later, the hot jets of the shower pummelled my skin. It felt good and dragged me kicking and screaming into the land of the living. I scrubbed at my face again, hoping to have eradicated all trace of makeup, but even when dry, dressed and ready to leave, I could still see a hint of dark eyeliner. Hopefully, nobody would notice.

I arrived at the station just before 7am, parched and dying for a large mug of strong black coffee.

Already counting down the hours until home time, I strolled down the long corridor towards my office, otherwise known as the incident room. I pushed the doors open surprised to see some-body there so early.

"Morning, boss," Will said, far too jovially for this ungodly hour of the day.

"You're in early," I replied. "Did you shit the bed or something?"

He laughed. "I've got a shed load to do and wanted some peace and quiet before the rest of the team showed up."

"Seems we had the same idea. Is Janine in yet?"

"Yeah," he replied. "She popped her head in about half an hour ago."

"How did she seem?"

"Chirpy," was all he said.

"Well, that's something at least. I'll pop down and show my face. Do you want a coffee on the way back?"

"Yeah, if you don't mind."

"Cool, won't be long."

I turned away.

"Oh, and boss, one more thing before you go." He was smiling.

"Yeah," I said, turning back. "What is it?"

"Nice eyeliner," he croaked before bursting out laughing.

"Piss off, Will."

I stomped off, leaving him in fits of giggles.

Rushing into the toilet, I checked my reflection in the mirror. "Shit!" It was obvious, but I didn't have time to waste this morning. What was the old expression about suffering for one's art? I'd spend the day as the butt of never-ending jokes, but it beat scrubbing my skin raw.

I was in and out of Janine's office in five minutes and, luckily, she didn't mention anything about the eyeliner, if she even noticed it at all.

Grabbing two coffees, I made my way back to the incident room and handed Will his.

"Cheers, boss."

"So, what you got on today?"

"I'm looking into the travellers–see if we can track down who bought the van, but I won't lie, it's not gonna be easy."

"Do what you can."

"I have a few leads."

"Oh, yeah?"

"There's a large community that were settled just outside of St. Helens a few weeks ago. Seems they've moved up towards Manchester way and have taken over a parking lot behind an abandoned service station. I'll take a drive up and see what I can find out."

I rolled my eyes, knowing how much carnage the travelling community usually left behind. Their lifestyle wasn't for me, but I certainly respected their choices. I just wish they could be a bit more respectful of the places they took over. "Let me know, and if I'm not up to my eyes in it, I'll go with you."

"No worries, boss. If you're too busy, Joanna can come with me."

"Perhaps that might be the better option as I can cover some other stuff I didn't get around to doing yesterday."

He grinned again.

"What's so funny now?"

"Is it true you were in full makeup when Bella gave birth to the little fella?"

"Fucking hell, Will, news travels fast around here. How did you know she'd had the baby?"

"She's good mates with my Rachel."

"Oh, yeah, I forgot that." Nothing was sacred in this place.

"So?" He cocked an eyebrow.

"What?" I didn't want to give him anything else to laugh about, but as Bella had already dropped me in it, what could I do?

"Is it true?"

"Kind of, but keep that to yourself, or I'll be a laughingstock."

I could have throttled Layla right at that moment. It had been her bright idea for me to audition in the first place. I really didn't want to do it, but when lined up against two dead women and the possibility of further murders, it seemed churlish of me to refuse. Playing dress up and lip-syncing to some long forgotten disco classic wasn't going to kill me.

He sipped at his coffee then looked up. "You're the boss."

"Yeah, right, like that'll stop you taking the piss when the rest of the team get here."

I came back from lunch, stuffed up to the eyeballs after an all-you-can-eat *Pizza Hut* buffet, to find a gift-wrapped box on my desk.

The room was deathly silent.

"What's this?"

"Just a little something to celebrate your promotion, boss," Joanna said.

"Guys, you didn't have to do this," I said, touched. I ripped the wrapping paper off and pulled open the box, aware of the sniggers ringing out around the room. "Very fucking funny," I said, as I lifted a personalised bronze desk nameplate up to read the words *Detective Inspector Drag Queen* etched into it.

Roaring laughter shattered the silence. I had to admit, it *was* bloody funny and I laughed right along with them, positive if the shoe had been on the other foot, I'd have willingly played along too.

"It was nothing to do with me," Layla said, looking pale and drawn.

"Are you okay?" I asked, concerned for her, once the laughter had died down and everybody had gone back to work. "You don't look too good."

"I'm fine," she replied. "Not much sleep last night."

"I know how you feel, but is there anything I can help you with?"

"Not really," she sighed. "Max came around last night with his new girlfriend."

She appeared to be at breaking point. Max had always seemed the decent kind, so rubbing Layla's face in his infidelity didn't sit right with me, and I vowed to tell him so if our paths ever crossed again. "The insensitive pig."

"It didn't go well, which is no surprise really, and the kids were heartbroken. I wanted to kill him, Dylan." She stifled a sob. "How could he do this to me, to all of us?"

"I don't know what to say because nothing will make any of this right, but maybe you should call it a day and go home, get some shut eye while the kids are at school and come back with fresh eyes tomorrow."

"The kids didn't go to school–none of them, they were still too upset this morning and I didn't have the heart to make them go. Mum's looking after them, which has thrown a spanner in the works for her plans."

"Apart from it interrupting her love life, what does she make of the situation?"

"She was there when Max arrived last night and she went mental. I had to hold her back."

"And the girlfriend?"

"Eh?"

"His new girlfriend."

"Oh, yeah, her." Tears formed in her eyes. "Do you mind if we change the subject because I don't want to get upset in front of this lot?"

"No, not at all, but go home if you want to. It's fine." We really couldn't afford to lose another staff member, but what use was she if she was just going to be moping around all day?

"I'll stay for another hour or two if that's okay? I'm eager to know what Will and Joanna find out from the travellers."

"Okay," I answered, "but I can call you at home if you're gone by the time they get back."

Halfway up the M62, Joanna looked at her watch and frowned.

"This will be a total waste of our time, Will."

"You think so?"

"I know so," she replied, huffing. "This lot will clam right up as soon as they see our badges. They stick together through thick and thin. And if our killer is one of them, no way will they give him up easily."

"I'm not sure you're right, Jo. Not this time anyway."

"Why?"

"Would anyone want this lunatic living amongst them? No, I think if somebody knows something, they'll spill."

"Bet you twenty quid we come away with nothing." She smirked confident she'd win the bet.

He kept his eyes on the road. "Deal."

Ten minutes later Will turned the car into an abandoned parking lot. Caravans and other vehicles could be seen for hundreds of yards.

"What an absolute shit hole," he said, frowning.

"Was there ever any doubt as to what we'd find here?"

"Something tells me you're not too fond of the travelling community."

"I've got nothing against them personally, Will. It's just this." She gestured at the mess all around her. "They think they have the god-given right to settle anywhere and expect us hard working taxpayers to foot the bill for the clean-up."

"I see what you mean."

"Make sure you lock the car," she said. "Though we'll be lucky if it still has four wheels when we get back."

"Gotcha," he said leading the way. "Let's start over here. He looks like the friendly sort."

Joanna cast a glance and spied an unkempt, bearded guy who looked to be in his fifties, drinking from a can of lager. "If you mean him, I wouldn't bank on it."

Will readied his credentials. "Sir, would you mind if we spoke to you for a moment?" He held them up for the guy to see.

"You got a warrant?" The man spat out a mouthful of chewing tobacco, right at their feet.

Will stepped back. "No, but—"

"Then I've nothing to say to either of you."

"Look," Joanna said, already annoyed. "It's just a few questions."

"And like I said, I don't wanna talk to you, or him. You won't find much help around here so get in your car and go back the way you came."

"I'll be the judge of that Mr...?"

"Man," he replied with a smile.

"Your name is Mr Man?" Joanna asked. "Very funny."

"Well, Mr Man," Will said, cutting in. "Who's in charge around here?"

He laughed. "Do you think there's some sort of Gypsy King who will grant you an audience? Get fucked, the pair of yer." He hacked up a ball of phlegm and spat on the ground again.

"How would you like to spend a night in the cells?" Will stepped forward. "It can be easily arranged, or perhaps, I could call for back up, see what you lot are hiding?"

His face paled. "What do you wanna know?"

Joanna grinned. "Funny how amenable you lot can be when threatened with the law."

"I can tell you haven't been laid in a while," he said.

"You cheeky..." Joanna's face twisted in outrage and looked as though she was about to slug the man.

Will stepped in before things took a turn for the worse. "Jo, why don't you wait in the car for me?"

Joanna glared at them both before stomping off.

"I'm looking for the owner of a van," Will said once she was safely at the car.

"What van," he asked. "I don't know nothing about no van, so save your breath."

Will opened his file and retrieved a photograph, shoving it under his nose. "Does that ring any bells?"

He glanced down at the photograph. "Not a sausage."

"Look properly," Will ordered.

"I said I didn't recognise it, so looking at it again won't change that."

Will wasn't amused, but maybe Joanna was right when she said they'd come away with nothing to show for the drive there.

"I'd like to speak to a few of your friends, see if they know anything."

"Go for your life, but I can say for certainty, nobody will recall a thing. Terrible memories, us lot, we're renowned for it."

"Yeah, something tells me you're right. But, all the same, I'm here now, so there's no harm in me looking around and speaking to a few of, what was it you said, your lot."

"They won't like you snooping around, throwing accusations."

"I haven't accused anybody of anything, yet."

I picked up my phone. "Hi, Will, any joy?"

"A complete waste of time, boss. Nobody knows anything and even if they did, we'd be the last people they'd tell. We did have a good look around and couldn't see the van parked up though."

"Well, for what it's worth, thanks for trying–at least we can cross that off the list.

"Righto. Jo and I are heading back now."

"Okay, I've got to get ready for the audition tonight. I'm just going to make a quick call to Layla, then I'm off to collect Bella and baby Dylan from the hospital."

"Baby Dylan–how cute," Will teased in a baby voice.

"Shut it," I replied, ending the call.

I scrolled through my phone and found Layla's number.

"Hi," she said upon answering. "How did it go?"

"It didn't. They found nothing," I replied. "So, stop worrying."

"Okay. Thanks for letting me know. My head is spinning with it all."

"Mine too. Are you feeling any better?"

"Much. Thanks, Dylan. I'll see you later at the club."

"I'll set up a *WattsApp* group for you and Will so we can communicate. Don't acknowledge me, whatever you do."

FOURTEEN

I raced over to Bella's house to collect the car seat.

After my knock went unanswered, I slid down the side of the house and rummaged under the rocks beneath the huge oak tree in the back garden for the spare key.

Handmade banners covered in welcome home messages, and balloons filled the wide tiled hallway. "Penny? It's only me," I called out, concerned a crowd of people might be about to pounce out from every hiding place to surprise me.

There was no response.

I located the baby seat in the cupboard underneath the stairs and was on the road again minutes later.

The car-parking gods were with me as I found a vacant space right outside the hospital's main entrance. I was quite excited to see my little namesake again, and, after parking, I walked briskly to the lift.

"You took your time!" Bella startled me as I stepped out into the corridor.

"Oh, hello. What are you doing there? Have they kicked you out already?"

"No, you twit." She laughed. "I was just stretching my legs. I've been ready for hours and was beginning to think you were never gonna get here."

"Some of us have a job to do, you know."

She took the car seat from me. "Thanks for this."

"Where's baby? I'm dying for a cuddle."

"In the ward, fast asleep."

I fell into step beside her and we headed to the only empty bed in the ward.

Baby Dylan was squeaking and snuffling in his bassinet on the far side of the bed.

"Hello, you," I said, pulling the white cotton sheet down and away from his face. I gasped out a breath as I gazed into his midnight-blue eyes for the first time. "Oh, gosh, Bells, I love him."

"He is pretty special, isn't he?" She also bent over and became all doe-eyed, clearly besotted with her little man.

"Have you managed to speak to Simon?"

"No, not yet. I left a message—he'll probably call me tonight."

"Are you okay? You seem a little stressed."

Bella sighed and moved towards the bed, slumping down on it. "I'll be better when I get home—I miss Lily. Hospitals get all my nerves on edge."

"Well, what are we waiting for, then? Let's go."

Ten minutes later, we were in the car, heading towards Bella's house.

"So, how come Penny didn't bring Lily in to see you?"

She shook her head. "I don't know. I've not even heard from her. I guess she's waiting for us to get home. Did you see them when you called in earlier?"

"No. They weren't home. I had to root around for the spare key."

"Really? That's odd."

"Odd?" I glanced at her, puzzled.

"Yeah. If they'd gone out, why didn't they come to see me?" She seemed hurt.

I didn't want to spoil the surprise that Penny and Lily had clearly been working on all morning. A few more minutes of thinking her sister didn't give a shit wouldn't kill her. "Haven't a clue, but I'm sure she's got a good reason."

She exhaled noisily and turned around, leaning between the seats to get a look at the baby. "Did you call Roy?" she asked when she turned back.

"Not yet."

"Dylan! Bloody hell. Your audition's tonight, isn't it?"

"Yes. I'm well-aware of that. I'll call him in a minute."

"Don't think you're getting out of it. Laughing at you in those heels caused my bloody labour."

"I'm not trying to get out of it. Why would you say that?"

"Because I know you, DI Monroe. I'm going to call Roy now." She pulled her phone from her bag and moments later Roy's voice boomed from the speaker.

"Bella, darling, how did it go?"

"Hi, Roy. I have a beautiful baby boy. I hope we didn't leave you too traumatised."

"I did sink an extra couple of cocktails last night, if I'm honest. My nerves were hangin' out, but congrats on the sprog though. I'm thrilled for you."

"Thank you."

"How's that partner of yours? Is he still planning to come by for round two?"

"That's the reason I'm calling. He'll be popping by shortly if that's okay? Time's running out."

"Looking forward to it. I can't wait to see him all dolled up— the man has bone-structure to die for."

I cringed and shook my head at Bella, not wanting him to know I was listening.

She grinned. "Okay gorgeous. Be kind to him."

"Oh, don't worry. I'll handle him with kid gloves."

Bella ended the call and burst out laughing. "I think he has a crush on you."

"Oh, don't, for Christ's sake—that's all I need." I pulled up to the curb outside Bella's house.

The front door suddenly swung inwards, and Penny and Lily flew out and down the path towards us.

Bella cried out, dropping to her knees, and dragging Lily into her arms. "There you are, my gorgeous girl! I've missed you so much!"

"We've beened to buy a present for my baby brother."

"Have you? I bet you're dying to meet him, aren't you?"

"Yes!" Her eyes lit up as she remembered.

Penny rubbed her hands excitedly. "We've been waiting for ages."

I wanted to say she hadn't been waiting that bloody long— they weren't even home earlier, but I didn't. "Right, I'll get going then if you don't need me for anything else. I'd rather get Roy over and done with and then I might be able to get some much needed practice in those heels."

"Roy?" Penny wiggled her eyebrows.

"Nothing like that, cheeky!" I shook my head at her as I leaned into the back of the car and unclipped the baby seat. "Come on, little fella. You're the man of the house until your daddy gets home."

Penny pounced on him as I lifted the seat out of the car.

I grinned at Bella who pressed her lips together in amusement.

"Here, you're gonna need this." Bella dug in her bag and pulled out the pink wig.

"Gee, thanks."

. . .

Ten minutes later, I pulled up outside the town hall. I wasn't really feeling this and still hadn't decided if I was going to go through with the audition or not.

Roy, dressed in a purple velour tracksuit, his face devoid of makeup, appeared as I stepped from the car. "Here he is, the Wirral's answer to Dame Edna." He kissed the air above both of my cheeks.

"I don't have a lot of time, Roy. Can we rush through the basics? I'll take my time getting ready when I get home, I promise."

"Suit yourself." He stomped up the steps and into the foyer as though I'd pissed him off.

I followed him to the same room as last night.

By the time we closed the door, he appeared to have got over his snit. "I nearly died when Bella almost dropped the sprog on my dressing room floor. I don't know how you could've gone to the hospital with her—I couldn't get away fast enough."

"Do you think I didn't notice?" I laughed.

He shook his head. "Sorry. Okay, do you want to go through the makeup again? We can do it fast."

"No. I'd rather not. I'll watch some *YouTube* videos at home. But I'd appreciate any other tips."

"Okay. I have a couple of outfits picked out for you to choose from, but I guess the main question is what look are you aiming for? I mean, are you looking to be a camp queen or a glam queen? Because your audience will judge you accordingly."

I shrugged my shoulders. "I don't get you."

"Think Joan Collins or Marilyn Monroe—pardon the pun, I know your surname is Monroe." He chuckled. "Which do you prefer?"

"Definitely Joan Collins. Sophisticated, demure. I'm not the sex kitten type."

"Right, in that case I have the perfect outfit for you. The next thing you need to master is the art of female impersonation. I mean you might have cheekbones to die for but if you walk like a trucker, it will spoil the overall effect. So you need to think of the performance as a whole. Some drag queens are prized for their hair and audacious appearance, whilst others are considered legends for simply being beautiful and exotic. But overall, you need to be unique if you want to stand out."

I nodded, trying to take it all in, but chickening out a little bit more as every second ticked by.

"Now, I know you're nervous about me turning up at your audition, I promise I won't—but tell me, where is it being held?"

"Dorothy's."

"Thought so. Right, Chris Turner, AKA Blanche, is a complete sucker for redheads, so we need to change your wig. The pink number won't go with what I have in mind for you anyway. I've got the perfect outfit, did I already mention that?"

"Once or twice." I grinned.

"Now, at Dorothy's, the audition is basically lip-syncing to your favourite song. There's no cold performance or chatting required. But be warned, Blanche is fierce in there and will kick you off the stage if you're shit."

"That's a comforting thought." I was more nervous than ever.

"Just a word of advice, if you do get the gig and the crowd starts hollering when you're on stage, tell 'em to feck off, but make sure you have something funny lined up to talk about."

"Such as what?"

"Daily observations usually go down well, something everyone can relate to. Even crude toilet habits get a few laughs."

"Fuck! I don't have anything like that." What the hell had I got myself into?

"Oh well, Ducky, never mind. Like I say it's not essential. Any more questions?"

"Thousands, but none I can think of right now."

"You'll be fine, I promise. Just remember to shave or wax every inch of your body—the bits on show, at the very least. And depending on if you want to use tape to secure your tuck, it will be far less painful to remove if you're bald down there." He pursed his lips and glanced at my nether regions suggestively.

I placed a protective hand over my groin area. "I'm not shaving down there! Are you mad? There's only so much I'm willing to do for my job."

"Is this to do with those dead girls? I did ask Bella but she wouldn't say much."

"Yeah, it is. But this is all top secret." I hoped he could be trusted to keep his mouth firmly shut. "So please, keep shtum or you'll find yourself in handcuffs." As soon as the words escaped my lips, I knew he would find some innuendo in it.

"Ooh, don't tempt me."

I raised an eyebrow.

"Just kidding, darling. My lips are sealed, err—what will you call yourself?"

I thought back to all the stupid names we'd come up with the other night and shook my head. "What's your stage name? I've forgotten."

"Betty." He curtsied. "Betty Swallocks at your service."

I grinned. "Do you have any suggestions for me?"

Roy rubbed at his jaw and looked me up and down. "You look like an Avaline to me."

"Avaline?"

"Yeah, Avaline Saddlebags. Kinda catchy don't you think?"

"I guess that'll do."

Roy sighed. "Get this audition out of the way and you'll feel much better."

"I hope so."

"Promise to call me and let me know how it goes?"

"Will do. Oh, and just one more thing I need to ask. You mentioned tucking your bits away earlier."

"Ah, you want a lesson in tucking your meat and two veg?"

I nodded, feeling my cheeks pink up.

"I'm glad you asked that. Now, if you've never done it before this will sound awful, but it's really not. Firstly, you need to pop each of your testicles back up into your abdominal cavity."

"What?" I jumped to my feet in horror.

Roy guffawed. "I told you, you wouldn't like it, but it's really quite painless. There are two natural pockets either side of your penis, you just pop them in there and then the scrotum and penis can be tucked underneath and secured with a gaff."

"What the hell's a gaff?"

"Like an industrial thong."

"Fuck that! I'm not doing it." I shook my head rapidly. "Not a fucking chance."

He shrugged. "Okay, that's your choice, but I do suggest you do some form of tucking, even if you just use a pair of pantyhose. It really makes a difference how you hold yourself and helps create the illusion. But the dress I have in mind for you requires nothing too drastic. Perfect for a drag virgin."

"Very funny."

"It is funny. You see, most men who want to come out as a cross-dresser or drag queen have experimented for years behind closed doors—stolen their sister's bras and knickers, maybe even bought their own lingerie to wear under their jeans. I've never known anybody do this from scratch before. And if you want my honest opinion, I don't think you'll pull it off. Even though you looked shit hot last night, being a woman isn't all about looking pretty—it's about having confidence and sass. You need to make it as easy on yourself as possible, in my opinion."

"I agree. So what do you suggest?"

"Well, hip pads, butt pads and chicken fillets used to be all the rage—but luckily for you, thin is in at the moment and I'd be inclined to stick with this for now."

"Sounds good."

"Okay, let me go and get your outfit and see what you think." He left the room.

My stomach dropped when he reappeared carrying a sequined emerald green dress with a bustle. "Aw, come off it. Don't you have anything less... less... just less?"

"Drag queens don't do less. Less is definitely not more in my world—trust me."

"How did I know you'd say that?"

"Are you going to try it on?"

"I won't, if you don't mind. I'll just get going and do it at home."

"Suit yourself. You'll find practically everything you need online but if you get stuck call me. I don't even mind helping you get ready later."

"No!" I shook my head. "Sorry to snap but it's going to be bad enough as it is."

"Well, if you change your mind, you know where I am. But remember, don't be subtle. Go for it! What do you have to lose?"

FIFTEEN

The approaching audition weighed heavily on my mind. I had images of a panel of Shirley Bassey impersonators booing me off the stage.

"What the hell have I got myself into?" I said aloud, looking at the ghastly frock hanging on the back of my living room door.

I looked at the clock–4:52pm. It seemed far too early to get ready, but I needed plenty of time to get my slap on, and practise tucking my bits away. If I was going to do this, I should give it my everything. I couldn't be precious about it. After all, I had a damn good reason for doing this in the first place–there was a killer to catch and a few minutes of me feeling uncomfortable wasn't going to hurt. I just hoped I'd get through, but then I'd have the nerves of opening night to worry about, flouncing around that stage in Dorothy's while a gaggle of drunken, screaming gays sang along to some song of yesteryear.

That was another problem. I'd sat in front of my laptop since I got home, trying to decide what to lip sync to. Even though I was old school and preferred *iTunes*, *Spotify* had become my new best friend as I trawled through playlists searching for the right song.

Finally, I'd narrowed it down to two. *No More I Love You's* by Annie Lennox, which was a slower number and *Man! I Feel Like a Woman* by Shania Twain, which was a foot stomping anthem I wasn't convinced I could carry off, especially in six-inch stilettos.

My thinking was, do the slower number as I was less likely to go arse over tit and make a fool of myself. I just had to pass the audition. Then I would have time to rehearse a faster number in the heels. I knew I could do it. I just needed to make sure I looked the part too.

On the way back from Roy's earlier I'd popped into Boots and grabbed a couple of pairs of tights. No way was I shaving my legs. I wasn't the hairiest of people anyway; I didn't have any hair on my chest to worry about, and what I did have on my arms and legs were fine and fair. Two pairs of tights should cover what was down there.

I knew I should eat but my stomach was in knots so decided against it, choosing to practise putting my face on instead. Grabbing my laptop, I searched drag makeup tutorials on *YouTube*. It looked easy enough, and I confidently stood in front of the mirror after memorising what I needed to do. But it wasn't easy, far from it, and by the time I'd finished, I looked like Hatchet-Face from that old John Waters' comedy, *Cry Baby*.

Staring into the mirror, there was nothing passable or presentable, and panic set in.

I called Bella. She answered right away.

"I'm shitting myself, Bells."

"Why?"

"I just had a practice run with the makeup and look a mess. I'm not sure I can do this."

"Yes, you can, don't worry. I'm sure you don't look that bad."

"If you could see me now, you wouldn't be saying that."

"Send me a pic and let me judge for myself."

"No chance."

"Go on, I won't laugh."

"Okay," I replied, knowing it was a mistake. "No laughing."

"I promise I won't."

"Hang on." I took a selfie and hit the send button. "It's on the way but show nobody. Do you hear me?"

"It just came through–hang on."

The line went quiet, and then I heard it, the snorting noise, and I knew she was trying to stop herself from laughing. "Bella, are you there?"

"Yeah, I'm here," she said after a few seconds.

"What do you think?"

"Erm, you look... okay."

"You're a lying bitch," I snapped as she lost it completely and dissolved into riotous laughter.

"I'm sorry, but you've got to admit, you look bloody funny."

I stared at myself in the mirror. The words dog's dinner sprung to mind. No way would I be taken seriously unless I was going for the comedy angle. "What am I going to do?"

Trying to control herself, she coughed a few times and said the one word I'd been thinking. "Roy."

"Do you think he'll come over and help me?"

"You haven't got much choice right now."

"He did say to call him if I needed help."

"Do you want me to call? I know you're wary of him."

"No, but thanks. The guy will be doing me a favour so the least I can do is ask him myself."

"It will all be fine, and you know I'd be there to support you if I didn't have this little man to look after."

"How is the little cutie?"

"A dream. Much quieter than the little miss upstairs."

"Is Penny still there?

"Oh, yes, she's decided to stay on until Simon comes home next week."

"You heard from him, then?"

"Yeah, about an hour ago and he confirmed his ten-day paternity leave had been authorised. I can't wait to see him. He's so excited and told me to say thanks for looking after me. He agrees there is no better name for baba."

I felt honoured. "I might tear up if you carry on."

"See, all that slap has brought out your feminine side.

"Piss off, Bells." I looked in the mirror and cringed. "I'm going to get something to eat, then I'll give Roy a call."

"Let me know how it all goes. I won't go to bed until I hear from you."

"Will do. Give the kids a kiss from me."

I ended the call and grabbed the wet wipes from the coffee table.

After a large, strong coffee and two slices of toast, I scrolled through my phone and dialled Roy's number.

"Speak," he said upon answering. He didn't sound pleased to have been disturbed.

"Hi Roy, it's Dylan."

"Oh, hello, darling. I thought I might hear from you but wasn't expecting it to be so soon."

"Sorry, but I'm having a crisis and need your help."

"What time is your audition?"

"They are seeing people between 9 and 11pm."

"Text me your address and I'll be there tout de suite."

"Eh?"

"Straight away, darling. Straight away."

"Oh," I replied, thankful for the translation. "I can pick you up, if you prefer? Where are you?"

"That might be better. I'll text you my address now and throw this cuppa down my neck while I wait."

"Thanks, Roy."

"Anytime, darling."

Five minutes later I was heading towards Gay Town. Why wasn't I surprised he lived in the midst of all the action?

SIXTEEN

"Thanks for this, Roy, I really appreciate it."

"Ah, don't worry, ducky. It's all in a day's work."

I admired my reflection, looking less Hatchet-Face and more Glamazon. My lips pouted as I turned my head from side to side. "If you'd seen how awful I looked..."

"I did–Bella sent me the pic."

"That bitch." I had to laugh. "I told her not to show anybody."

"We all start somewhere," he said, sipping delicately from the only china cup I had in the place. "But, just to be on the safe side, I'll come to the audition with you. Blanche and I go way back, so you're more likely to get through if I butter the old trout up."

"I'm not sure..."

"Darling, try not to worry so much, or you'll start to sweat and your face will peel like a mask."

"I still don't know what I'm going to do."

"Have you even chosen your song?"

"Yeah, I'm down to a choice of two."

"Tell me what they are."

I confirmed my choices.

"Go with the ballad, definitely."

"Are you sure?"

"Yes, darling. You can do a lot with a weepie, and the queens will be bawling their eyes out, trust me."

"I wish I was as optimistic."

"Right, get those heels on, crank up the stereo and let's see what you got."

"You're joking?"

"If you can't do it in front of me, how you gonna do it in front of a panel?"

"Oh, God." Suddenly this idea didn't seem like such a good one.

I prepared the music and drew the curtains, not wanting my neighbours to see anything.

"Okay, take a deep breath, find your inner shemale and let's get going. We have an hour, tops to make you as good as you can be."

I took a deep breath and hit play.

"Well, darling, it was better than I expected, but I'd suggest smaller steps. You're still a bit wobbly on those heels and my nerves were hanging out watching, so keep it simple."

"You think?" I felt better after a run through.

"Maybe a few more sweeps of the arm, a few chest bangs, you know, just like Celine Dion does, and you could be pretty good."

"Got it."

"Right, let's start again, from the top."

"Again?"

"Yes, and then again and again. Practice makes perfect, darling, and don't you forget it."

"If you're sure?"

"Do you think Madonna steps on stage without knowing what she's doing?"

"I haven't given it much thought," I replied, not being a fan.

"And five, six, seven, eight..."

I hit play again and gave it my all.

Roy dabbed the corner of his eyes with a handkerchief.

"How was that?"

"You moved me, darling."

"I did?"

He blew his nose. "Behind that macho bravado of yours, there's a bloody good little performer lurking."

"Wow, I'm shocked you thought I was good."

"Practice, you see, Now, come on, it's time to go. If we get there a little early, you might get in first."

———

"That was so embarrassing," I said, as we pulled up outside Dorothy's.

"I found it quite entertaining."

"You would." I was in a filthy mood.

"Not many people can say they pulled up next to a man in full drag." He tittered to himself.

"I didn't even give it a moment's thought about driving here in all this get up."

"You're here now, so shut up moaning and get in there and give it some welly."

Hesitantly, I climbed out of the car, slipped my usual shoes off and straight into the high-heeled sandals.

"I'm shitting myself."

"Just do what you did in your living room and they'll clap like you're the resurrection of Marlene Dietrich."

"Are you still coming in with me?"

"Wouldn't miss it, darling."

We made our way inside. The bar area was packed to the rafters, and loud music pumped out of the speakers. One of the doormen directed us to the function room. The place was deserted save for two effeminate guys and a very butch woman who were sitting behind a makeshift judges desk.

I whispered to Roy. "What now?"

"Get yourself over and tell them who you are."

"Okay." I walked slowly, but confidently, over to them.

"We haven't seen you before," one of the male judges said. "What's your name?"

"Avaline Saddlebags," I replied. "And I'm here to audition."

"What song are you doing, luvvie?"

"*No More I Love You's* by Annie Lennox."

"Interesting," the woman replied. "I'd have pegged you as a Kylie fan."

"Love her," I lied, "But nobody should mess with perfection."

"Quite right." the middle guy nodded. "I'm Blanche, and this is Daphne." He turned to his left. "The bit of fish to my right is Norma."

"Nice to meet you all."

"Likewise," Blanche said peering behind me. "Ooh, as I live and breathe, is that Betty Swallocks over there?"

"Yes, that's right." I turned and smiled at Roy.

"Bloody hell, I almost didn't recognise him without his face on. Now give me a few minutes to sort the music and then we can get cracking. If you want to grab you and Betty a drink, I'll give you a wave when we're ready for you to start."

"Thank you." I made my way to the bar. Roy followed and sat on the stool. "What you having?"

"My nerves are shot to pieces, darling, so I think I'll have a..."

"What can I get you," the cute barman asked.

"Gin Sling for me, and my mother here, will have soda water and a straw since she's driving."

Mother, I thought. I'll bloody have him when we get out of here.

"No problem," he replied. "I'll be right back."

I only had the chance to take a sip of my water before Blanche called me over.

"Break a leg."

Break a leg was supposed to be good luck, and I'd need all I could get. "I will in these fucking heels," I replied, feeling sick.

I walked towards the judges. "Stand on the X, dear." Blanche pointed to the middle of the dancefloor. He turned to the barman. "Hit it."

A spotlight came on, almost blinding me. I didn't move. My legs felt like lead weights.

The familiar bars of the song's opening kicked in. Do be do be do do do oh oh.

My mouth began to move, and I was off, feeling the music flow through me as though I was singing the words myself. Annie's vocals pulled me deeper into the song, pushing me to perform like my life depended on it.

Conscious of the heels, I took graceful steps, and clutched my chest to convey the emotion I felt inside. A few waves of my hand at appropriate moments enhanced my performance and for that moment in time, I felt like a star.

Making eye contact with the judges, I held them in the palm of my hand as I moved around in the spotlight. The final bars of the music rang out and it was over. I took a bow, like the Prima Ballerina delivering her final performance of Swan Lake.

I looked to the judges, awaiting their critique.

Blanche stood up, and I could see pools of tears in his eyes.

"Brava Diva," he cried, clapping like a demented sea lion.

The other two judges and the barman joined him in his rapturous applause.

But Roy was noticeably silent, too busy crying into his handkerchief.

I was in!

I dropped Roy off at home and changed back into my own clothes, leaving the frock and heels there. Thankfully Roy had some makeup remover that cut through the cake in seconds, removing any trace of Avaline.

Once back in the car, I called Bella as promised.

"I'm in," I said as soon as she picked up the phone. "They loved me."

She squealed with delight. "Oh, my God, Dylan, I wish I could've been there to see you in action."

"Well, you couldn't," I replied. "You'd only put me off, plus you have a newborn baby to look after, don't forget."

"What did you sing at your audition?"

I laughed. "I didn't *sing* anything, Bells."

"You know what I mean?"

"I lip synced to *No More I Love You's* by Annie Lennox."

"Ugh," she groaned. "That's a bit bloody miserable, isn't it?"

"I haven't mastered high heels yet so going with a ballad was the safest option."

"Yeah, I suppose, but still..."

"It was all about getting myself in, so that's what matters."

"I get it, so when is your debut performance?"

"Tomorrow—and I'm shaking just thinking about it."

"I bet Roy was a godsend."

"Yeah, he was, and thanks for sending him that pic of me, by the way."

She snorted laughing. "Sorry, but I couldn't help it. It's my new screensaver."

"Get stuffed, Bells."

"Just kidding."

"Yeah, right. That's just the sort of thing you would do for a laugh."

She chuckled again.

"All joking aside, I couldn't have managed without Roy and he's even agreed to help me prepare for tomorrow night."

"He's a sweetheart," she cooed. "What are you going to perform?"

"I was thinking of doing *Man! I Feel Like a Woman*, but I'm not so sure now."

"Oh, go on, do that one–the gays will love it."

"Aren't you forgetting something?"

"What?"

"I'm not doing this because I hanker for a career as a drag artist."

"I know, I know, but you could meet some hottie who fancies a cock in a frock."

I wanted to laugh but decided against encouraging her any further. "I've got enough going on. This on-off thing with Steve is doing my head in."

"You gotta keep your options open, Dylan."

My complicated love life was the last thing I wanted to discuss. "I'm going. I need to be in the office for a briefing first thing in the morning."

"Okay, but pop by after work if you want, I'm making a huge pan of Thai Green Curry and I'll only eat it myself and end up like a big fat pig if you don't come and share it with me."

"Won't Penny eat any of it?"

"Ha," she scoffed. "Lady Penelope won't eat anything I make, remember?"

"Oh, yeah. I'll swing by if I get the chance."

My phone buzzed as I hung up. It was a text message from Steve.

How's things?
Not heard from
you in a few days

> ***Been busy.***
> ***Just on my way***
> ***home. Fancy***
> ***sharing a kebab?***

Sounds good–see you soon

SEVENTEEN

When the alarm sounded, I groaned and pulled the pillow over my head. It had been another sleepless night. I'd tossed and turned until the early hours worrying about tomorrow's performance, or should I say today's performance seeing as today was already here.

"What time is it?" Steve said, startling me. I'd forgotten he'd come over last night.

"Time to get up," I moaned.

"Ten more minutes, plee-ease?" He snaked his arm around my waist and pulled me close to him.

I considered it. Steve wasn't usually affectionate in the cold light of day and I kinda liked it.

"Do you want to grab a pizza tonight?" he asked.

"Can't, sorry. I'm busy. Maybe tomorrow night?"

Thinking about tonight again made my nerves jangle. I'd agreed for Roy to attend the show, since he'd already seen my audition, I had nothing to hide from him anymore, in fact he'd been a huge help. He was due to meet me here at 7pm. He also said he'd organise the outfit and wig. I had nothing to worry about, apparently. Yeah right!

But, before that, I needed to put in a full day at the station.

I pulled the pillow from my head before dragging myself out of bed.

I pushed the doors open, ready for the onslaught from my team but, to my surprise, not a word was said.

"Morning, boss," Will said. "How was it?"

"Terrifying, but I'm in."

A grin spread across his face. "Oh, I can't wait to see that." He clapped his hands, bringing the room to order. They all turned to look at him. "Listen up everyone..."

"Will..."

"Our new boss is now the star of his very own drag show at Dorothy's."

Everyone burst out laughing.

"Fuck off, the lot of you," I shouted.

"What's all the racket?" Janine said as she stepped through the door.

A hush fell over the room.

"Just this lot taking the piss, sorry," I said.

"Anything I should be made aware of?"

"Not really."

"Go on," Will urged. "Tell her."

"Tell me what?" She eyed me with curiosity.

I figured I might as well get the ribbing out of the way now. "I got through my audition."

A wide smile lit up her face. "Really? That's fabulous!"

"Yeah, and no wise cracks either."

"Well done, Dylan. That's what I call going above and beyond."

"It was strictly a one-off performance."

"Hmmm," she replied. "Then let's hope you find what you're looking for, or you might find yourself signing up for a residency."

The team were all ears, but I had a stern warning for them. "I don't want any of you lot there."

Layla suddenly appeared with a bottle of water in her hand. "That's a bit daft, Dylan."

"You think?"

"We need to be there to interview everyone who knew George—"

Rudely, I cut across her. "Don't you mean Gina?"

"Yeah sorry, but you know what I mean—I need to be there, and I think a few others do too."

"Agreed," Janine said. "I wish I didn't have a prior engagement, or I'd be there myself." She tried to keep a straight face. "So, what name did you decide on?"

I was dreading that question. "I haven't, yet."

"Come on, don't tell lies," she urged. "We'll find out, eventually."

I should just get it out of the way. By tomorrow, a number of them would've seen me all dragged up. They'd be taking pictures and would have all the ammunition they needed to make my life hell. "I decided on Avaline."

"Just Avaline?" Janine enquired. "Just the one name like Madonna or Kylie?" She tittered.

"Not quite."

"Come on, Dylan," Layla said. "Just tell us and get it over with."

"Alright," I snapped. "I'm gonna call myself Avaline Saddlebags." I could feel my face burning up with embarrassment. "Are you all happy now?"

I was greeted by a moment's silence before the place erupted in hysterics. Even Layla laughed, which was good to see, despite the fact she and the rest of the room were laughing at *me*.

"Aye aye, Avaline," Joanna teased.

I stuck two fingers up as my phone began to vibrate in my pocket. Retrieving it, I waved at the room to silence them. "DI Monroe speaking."

"Dylan, it's Lauren."

"Oh, hi, what can I do for you?"

"It's just a courtesy call really to let you know the coroner has finally released Jade Kelly's body back to her family."

"About time," I replied, feeling for her parents and siblings. "Do you know when the funeral will be?"

"I don't know any more than that but wanted to give you the heads up."

"Thanks. I'll drive round and see her parents this afternoon."

"Let's hope no more dead bodies turn up in the meantime."

"With a bit of luck–thanks, Lauren, I'll catch up with you soon."

"Gotcha." She ended the call.

I brought the room to order. "Listen up everyone, Jade Kelly's body has been released to her family and I don't need to tell you how they'll be feeling right now, so let's get moving and find this sick bastard before he strikes again."

Janine spoke first. "I'll leave you to it, Avaline–I mean, Dylan, but keep me in the loop." She walked out of the office chuckling to herself.

"Layla, you and I can head round to see Jade's parents."

"What are we going there for?"

"I think it's a good idea if we attend the funeral—"

Layla interrupted. "Oh, I'm not sure about that, Dylan."

"Well, I am." It was happening whether she liked it or not. "I have a hunch the killer will be lurking somewhere."

"Give them at least that day for Christ's sake," she snapped. "They're burying their child. I wouldn't want a load of cops traipsing through if I was burying one of my kids."

"And they'll want us to do all we can to catch the animal that robbed them of their daughter."

Layla's face twisted in disgust. "I'd rather not if that's okay with you. It's disrespectful and I don't want any part of it."

"Suit yourself," I replied. "I'll ask Joanna to come with me– you stay here and get your priorities right because, in this job, there are plenty of things I don't like to do but have little choice about."

"Hang on a minute," Layla stood with her hands on her hips. "I'm damn good at my job, Dylan, and go above and beyond what is expected of me, so I don't find your comments fair."

If she wanted a row, she was about to get one, but not in an open forum where her colleagues could hear. "Interview Room 1," I ordered. An uneasy silence fell on the room. "Now." I stormed along the corridor and into the interview room, waiting for her to arrive.

Layla was thirty seconds behind me. "Reporting as ordered, *sir*," she sniped.

This behaviour was so unlike her. "Come in, close the door and take a seat."

She sat down, and for a moment I thought I saw a flash of hatred in her eyes. "Is this really necessary?"

"What do you think?" I asked, a contrary tone to my voice.

"No, I don't."

"Then we're at odds straight away," I said, trying to remain calm. "We may have been thrown together as partners, but I'm still your superior, and I will not tolerate any of my officers refusing to carry out a reasonable request, especially in front of the rest of the team, do you understand?"

"I do understand, but believe you're in the wrong on this occasion, *sir*."

Sir, I shook my head, disappointed she would refer to me that way just to prove a point. "I happen to think otherwise, but feel free to raise a grievance and air your concerns if you think I'm not doing my job properly."

Her face flushed at the suggestion. "I'm not a snitch."

"That doesn't matter to me. If you think I've overstepped my boundaries, you're well within your rights to flag it with my superiors, but right now, my concern is your attitude—"

"I don't have an attitude."

"You're usually very easy to work with, and without going into specifics, I am aware things are happening in your personal life, but it can't be allowed to impact your role here."

"I wasn't aware my personal life *was* impacting my job."

"You refused to accompany me to the Kelly's without justifiable cause. Apart from your personal opinion, that it is disrespectful—" Layla made to interrupt, but I held up a finger to silence her. "You'll get your turn to speak, but so we're clear, the fact Jade Kelly is lying in a funeral home after being mutilated is far more important to me right now, and I would have hoped you'd see it my way, but obviously not."

"Are you making this reprimand official?"

"I'm hoping once I step out of this office, the matter is forgotten, and you come to your senses and do what is necessary to catch this killer. Unless, you're going to tell me you can no longer do your job effectively, then I'll have no other choice but to make it official."

"I can do my fucking job, Dylan."

I wasn't used to this level of animosity, but I didn't want to wade in guns blazing because I did care about her, which was another reason for me conducting this meeting in private. "Then do it and leave your conscience at the door because our killer certainly doesn't have one."

"I'm trying..." Tears filled her eyes. "But it's hard..." She lowered her head, obviously not wanting me to see her cry.

I felt like an absolute twat. "Layla, it wasn't my intention to upset you, or to make you cry." Shit, I thought, pulling out a pack of tissues from my pocket and offering one to her. "Come on, this isn't like you."

She took the tissue and dabbed at her eyes. "I'm sorry, Dylan."

"Hey, you don't need to apologise to me, Layla, I just need to know you're with me on this and I can rely on you."

"I am, I promise." She sniffed up. "I just need to get my shit together. And you can rely on me."

"Is Max still giving you hassle?"

"He wants the kids to start staying weekends with him..."

"And the new girlfriend will be there too, I assume?" If that was the case, I could see why she was so upset.

"It's not happening, Dylan, over my dead body." She stifled a sob. "We didn't ask for this, but everything is about him, how *he* feels, how *his* life has been turned upside down." Her voice rose a few octaves. "But what about me, and our kids, eh? Aren't we important?"

"Yes, you all are." I knew it was a rhetorical question but felt the need to say something anyway.

"He didn't care about us when he made this decision. We just have to live with the aftermath."

I reached over for her hand, but she pulled away. "I'm so sorry, Layla. It must be awful for you all."

"I wouldn't wish how I was feeling on my worst enemy, but there's no end to it, not when Max turns up out of the blue with these demands, upsets the kids, then swans off leaving me looking like the bitch."

"Have you been to see a solicitor yet?"

"Over custody?"

"Yeah."

"No, not yet."

"I know it's none of my business, but you need to, especially if his actions are upsetting the kids."

"I really thought everything would be okay, you know, that he would get all this out of his system, and the Max I fell in love with would come back to me, then we'd put it behind us."

"Life isn't always like that, Layla, but I think you need to take some time off, if only to process what's happening."

"I don't want that, Dylan." She looked into my eyes. "Not rattling around home, surrounded by memories of what I used to have. Please, I need to be in work doing something useful."

"Okay, but if the time comes when you do need to step aside for a while, promise you'll come straight to me?"

"I promise," she replied.

"Okay, but for today at least, you need to go home, forget about Dorothy's tonight. Have a few glasses of wine, and just relax."

"No way, I went home early yesterday. And I'll be there tonight, I've already arranged for my mum to watch the boys."

"Okay, sounds good to me, if you're sure."

She stood up. "I am. I'll go and powder my nose, then I'll need to apologise to everyone for making a show of myself."

"You don't need to apologise to anyone, Layla. We all have our moments and they'll understand. You know they're a good bunch of people and have your back, just like I do."

"Thanks, Dylan," she said with a hint of a smile.

The incident room was deserted when I returned, and I found

Will and Joanna in the staffroom. "Pour me a coffee while you're at it, Jo. I'm still not awake yet."

"Today's the day, hey, boss. Are you excited?" she said, reaching for another mug. She poured out a strong-looking brew, just what I needed, and handed it to me.

"Thanks. And no—don't remind me. Changing the subject, do you mind coming to see Jade Kelly's parents with me this afternoon?"

"Of course, I will. Is Layla alright?"

"I'm here," Layla said, suddenly behind me. "And yes, I'm fine. I'm so sorry for having a meltdown. I've just got a lot on at the moment."

Joanna hugged her friend and Will winked at her.

"Get a coffee down you, Layla. I want to go and have a chat with Jade's ex—the drug dealer."

"You mean Darren Wilkes?" she said.

"Yeah, that's him. Are you up to it?" I wanted to tread lightly.

"Yeah, I guess. Although he did have an alibi for Jade's murder. He was with some other bint from the club."

"I know, but I just want to acquaint myself with every aspect of the case. We're obviously missing something."

"Not necessarily. The killer could just be extra careful."

"How often do we see that, though? I mean really, every time a crime is solved how often do we say, oh, of course, why didn't we see that, it was plain as the nose on my face? Hindsight is a wonderful thing." I turned to Will. "Can you do me a favour?"

He nodded as he bit on a slice of buttered toast.

"Can you trawl through the CCTV footage from the night Jade was killed? See if you can spot the van anywhere else now we know what we're looking for."

"Already on it, boss."

"I'll just check my emails, Layla, then I'll be ready to go."

I took my coffee through to my desk and flicked open Jade's

file, stopping at Darren Wilkes' details. The scummy prick didn't have a job yet he lived in a penthouse apartment on the waterfront and drove a top-of-the-range Audi—go figure. Why do they think they can get away with blatantly breaking the law? He didn't even have the sense to create some sort of cover story.

Twenty minutes later, we left the station just as the heavens opened. We darted between the parked cars to my vehicle and hurriedly jumped inside.

The streets were filled with commuters and people going about their daily school run or heading to work.

"Why is it all the dickheads hit the road as soon as it starts raining?" I said, pulling onto the high street and heading to the other side of town.

We drove the rest of the way in silence.

"How are you feeling?" I asked.

"Like shite." She shook her head and looked out of the window.

I pulled up outside the flash penthouse apartment building and whistled. "Crime certainly does pay, Layla. I take it all back."

"It does in this case. The guy seems to have a Teflon-coated hide, I'm telling you. He's a smug git, but wily—I'll give him that."

I cut the engine and pulled the collar of my jacket up around my ears. "You ready?"

Layla bobbed her head and darted from the car.

I followed on her tail and we stopped only when we were under the cover of the entrance overhang.

"Shit, I'm soaked," I said, brushing myself off.

"Tell me about it."

I glanced at her and grinned. "Yeah, I think you managed to get even wetter than me. How is that even possible?"

She rolled her eyes heavenward and didn't even crack a smile. Suddenly the door swished open and a young businesswoman dressed to the nines in a lime green suit and black stilettos burst out, battling with an umbrella.

Jumping forward, I put my foot in the door and turned to smile at Layla, pleased with myself.

"Hey!" the woman turned on us, clearly unhappy.

I held my badge up and she closed her mouth and backed off.

Once inside, we entered the lift and hit the button for the top floor. Moments later, the doors opened up to a swanky hallway that housed several huge potted palms and stylish artwork. We knocked at the door.

Darren Wilkes had the exotic good looks of an Arabian prince, with flawless skin, designer stubble and sleek black hair scraped up into a man-bun. He wore nothing but a pair of tight, black, designer boxer shorts. "How the fuck did you get in?"

"Mr Wilkes, I'm DI Dylan Monroe and this is my colleague—"

"I know who the fuck she is. What do you want this time? This is harassment, do you hear me?"

"Loud and clear, Darren. I can call you Darren, can't I?"

He exhaled noisily and spun away from the door, leaving it swinging open.

"I guess that means, 'Come on in, detectives...' Oh, don't mind if I do." I wiggled my eyebrows at Layla before following him down the hallway and through to the wide, open-plan kitchen/dining/lounge area. The views from the huge picture window were spectacular overlooking the River Mersey.

Darren had his back to us as he filled the coffee pot from the instant hot water tap beside the sink. While he was preoccupied, I paced the highly polished floorboards, impressed at how clean and tidy everywhere was—he clearly employed a cleaner.

"So, come on, spit it out. What do you want from me this time?"

"May I?" I nodded at one of the modern box-shaped, grey marl sofas.

"Whatever, mate. Just spit it out then piss off."

I took a seat and Layla sat beside me.

Darren perched on the arm of the sofa opposite.

"I know you've already been interviewed regarding Jade's murder, but I've recently taken over the case and I just need to speak to everybody to familiarise myself with everything."

"Well, let me tell you, I have a watertight alibi as the last guy discovered."

"So I hear."

"Then what the fuck are you here for?"

"I thought I'd just explained that, Darren." I was being purposefully annoying to try to get under his skin.

He sucked his teeth and scowled at me.

"Darren, can I ask you a question?" Layla shuffled forwards in her seat.

"Ask me what the fuck you like, don't mean I'll answer it."

"Do you know this woman?" She handed him her phone with a photo of Gina on the screen.

"Yeah. Why?"

"How do you know her?"

He shrugged. "Just from the club. She's there every fucking week, singing the same songs over and over. She's annoying."

"Really?" she said. "Annoying enough for you to kill her?"

"What are you even on about?"

"Gina was murdered on Friday night after leaving the club."

He sprang to his feet. "Whoa! Don't start that again. It has nothing to do with me."

"Were you there on Friday?"

"Yeah."

"And do you remember seeing her?"

"I think so. In fact, yes. She was there."

"Did you see her mixing with anyone?"

"No."

"Did you speak to her at all?"

"No, I don't know her to talk to. Just see her about, you know?"

Layla nodded and glanced at me before turning back to Darren. "Do you own, or have access to, a white Transit van, by any chance?"

He shook his head. "Do I look like the sort of bloke who would own a Transit van? Give me a break."

"I take it that's a no then?" I said. "Getting back to Jade—who was it that gave you the alibi?"

"Ask her." He nodded at Layla. "She interviewed her."

"I'd rather ask you."

"Rebecca. I don't know her surname. We spent the night together."

"I see."

"Rebecca Preston," Layla said.

"Yeah, that's right." Darren nodded.

"But don't take my word for it. Rebecca lives above the taxi rank in town and your mate saw CCTV footage of me going in and I didn't leave until the next morning." He smirked and something about his smug expression made me want to smash my fist in the centre of it—rearrange that pretty boy nose for him.

But, ever the professional, I got to my feet and smiled. "Right, that will be all for now, Mr Wilkes. We'll be in touch if there's anything else. Good day to you."

"Tosser!" Layla said under her breath once we were out of earshot.

"Who me?" I chuckled.

"No, that other tosser back there. He makes me so mad."

"Me too. But it's only a matter of time before he slips up."

"So you think he's our killer?"

I shook my head. "No, but he's clearly screwing the system with his dodgy dealings. He'll get what's due to him sooner or later."

"It must be nice living in your ideal world. A place where the baddies get caught and the goodies reign supreme. Do I need to remind you, this is the real world, Dylan? Shitheads get away with stuff all the time." She scowled.

"For God's sake, Layla. Straighten your face. If you purse your lips any tighter, you're gonna swallow your chin."

Thankfully the rain had stopped, but the clouds hadn't lifted, giving the illusion it was much later in the day.

"Do you mind if we dart around to see this Rebecca woman? I just want to speak to her for myself."

"If you must. But isn't all this a bit of a waste of time? They've both been interviewed and ruled out."

"Just humour me, okay?"

She sighed. "Whatever."

A few minutes later, I parked the car opposite the taxi rank on the high street.

"Have you been here before?" I asked.

She nodded.

"Lead the way then, detective."

Shaking her head, she took off across the road.

"Hang on. Wait for me." I jogged to catch up with her. "Are you pissed off with me?"

"No," she snapped. "I've already told you, I feel like shit. Maybe I'm coming down with something."

I wanted to snap back that she should've gone home, but I didn't.

We walked past the front door of the taxi office and Layla knocked on the shabby, black door beside it.

Minutes later, a short, pretty, blonde-haired woman answered. The timbre of her voice gave away the fact she started life as a male, but she had stunning good looks most women would give their right arm for.

"Hi, Rebecca," Layla said, showing her ID. "Do you remember me?"

Rebecca's face dropped as she looked from Layla to me. "What have I done now?"

"No, nothing. Don't worry." Layla smiled. "We just want to ask you a few more questions about Darren Wilkes. Can we come in?"

She nodded and stepped backwards to allow us access into the tiny hallway and up the steep and gloomy staircase.

At the first landing, Layla continued through a doorway straight ahead.

I paused and glanced around, noticing the small landing led to a further flight of stairs, before following Layla into the small, poky living room.

"Take a seat." Rebecca swept a flamboyant arm towards the shabby-chic leather sofa.

"Thanks, this won't take too long," I said, sitting down beside Layla.

"So, what's Darren done this time?" she asked.

"What makes you say that?" I was suddenly suspicious.

"Because she said it was about Darren."

"Yes, that's right. But last time you gave him an alibi. So, with you saying 'what's he done this time' insinuates he's done something again, in which case you must think he was guilty last time."

Her face drained of all colour and she shook her head rapidly. "No. I just meant what is he being *accused* of this time?"

"Really? Nice save."

"I'm sorry, I don't understand what the problem is here."

"The problem is, Rebecca, you gave a known drug dealer an alibi."

"I gave a man an alibi because he came home with me. I don't remember much about that night but your colleague checked the CCTV and was happy he'd been here all night."

My ears pricked up. "So you can't actually vouch for him being here yourself?"

She shook her head. "I never said I could. He was here when I went to sleep and he was here when I woke up. End of."

Layla suddenly jumped to her feet. "Do you mind if I use your bathroom?"

"No. Not at all. It's up the next flight of stairs, the first door on the left."

"Thanks." She moved fast. I suspected she was going to be sick and hoped she made it in time.

Rebecca turned back to me. "What you said about Darren Wilkes being a drug dealer—wasn't it murder he was being investigated for?"

I nodded. "Yes, that's right. But he's dealing too. I'd steer clear of him if I were you."

"I'll bear that in mind."

"Very wise." I got to my feet, wondering where the hell Layla had got to. "Thanks, Rebecca. You've been very helpful."

"Have I? I don't know how. I didn't do anything."

"Oh, on the contrary. You were more than helpful."

Layla returned looking a little worse for wear.

"You ready?" I said, easing myself past her and down the stairs.

We arrived back at the station and Will met us in the corridor. "Bingo, boss. I've found the van on the outskirts of town just as you said we might. I've sent the footage to IT to see if they can make the image of the driver any clearer."

"Good. Have you alerted ANPR?"

"Yes. Hopefully the next time he takes the van onto the motorway, the Automatic Number Plate Recognition cameras will nab him."

Layla scowled again and shook her head storming past him into the incident room.

"What's up her arse?" Will said.

"I suspect she thinks we put too much faith in the system."

We followed behind her.

"Come on then, Layla. What do you suggest we do?" I asked.

"This individual is one step ahead of us at each turn. We can't underestimate him. Think about it—if we wait until the van is out and about again it probably means another murder is in process and that's far too late. We need to catch him before that."

Joanna appeared in the doorway. "Janine wants to see you, boss."

I groaned. "Okay, thanks." With a heavy heart and even heavier boots I trudged to Janine's office, preparing for a bollocking.

"Come in," she called as I was about to knock.

"Hi, Ma—erm Janine, you wanted to see me?"

Janine's smile was a welcome relief. "Yes. I want to make sure you're all set for tonight?"

"I am, although I'm trying to put it to the back of my mind right now. I've been stressing about it all night."

"Oops, sorry." She grinned. "Shame I'm busy tonight, I'd pay good money to see you perform."

"Don't you dare! It's bad enough Layla and Will are gonna be there—if I see any more familiar faces you can just forget it."

"Okay, okay, spoilsport. Now, where are we up to with the case? Joanna said you'd gone to interview someone."

"Nobody new. Just the ex of the first victim. But he's already been cleared by Savage."

"So why waste your time? Do you think Savage was wrong?"

"No. I just want to familiarise myself with every aspect of the case. I'd hate to miss something just because I think it's already been covered."

"Good man. I knew we'd made the right decision promoting you."

The familiar feeling of self-doubt settled in the pit of my stomach. We were two bodies deep into a case and absolutely nothing to go on, bar the licence plate of a deregistered van. "Thanks, Janine," was all I said.

"Good luck for tonight. I'm dying to hear all about it. Oh, by the way, do the club management know you're undercover?"

I shook my head. "No. I thought it was best to try to get in organically, that way nobody will be able to blab. I'll arrive and leave in full make-up—hopefully no-one will recognize me."

I pulled up outside the Kelly's home.

"This won't be pleasant," Joanna said.

"I know, but I really think it's important and don't just wanna turn up out of the blue. At least if they give me their blessing..."

"And if they don't?"

"Then I'll still go anyway and watch from the car."

We walked towards the front steps, but our arrival must have been noticed as Mr Kelly opened the door.

"Who are you?"

"Hi, I'm DI Dylan Monroe, and I am overseeing your daughter's case. This is my colleague, DC Joanna Mason, I wondered if we might have a word with you and your wife?"

Mr Kelly scrutinised our identification. "You better come in, but my wife is asleep in bed–losing Jade has hit her very hard."

"That's understandable," I replied as we followed him inside.

He led us through to the kitchen. "Take a seat." He gestured towards the chairs.

"Thank you,"

"Can I get either of you a drink?" he offered.

"No thanks," I replied.

"Not for me," Joanna added.

"So, what can I do for you?"

"I have been made aware Jade's body has been released."

"Yes, we were advised late last night, and Jade was moved to Porter & Sons in Anfield this morning so we can finally start to make funeral arrangements."

"I know it must be a terrible time for you all, but I had something I wanted to ask."

"Go on." He eyed me suspiciously.

"Would you object if my partner and I came to the funeral?"

"For what reason?"

"Firstly, to pay our respects, and secondly, I believe Jade's killer will show up. I'd like to see if I recognise any of the faces present."

"You really think whoever did that to my daughter will turn up?"

"It wouldn't be the first time, and I know how sad the occasion will be, but I want to do all I can to get this animal off the streets and make him pay for what he did to Jade and, of course, Gina Elliot."

"You do what you have to do as long as you remember where you are. I won't relay any of this to my wife. She's been through enough." His eyes glistened with tears. "But if it helps get that bastard, you have my permission." Tears leaked down his cheeks. "Just promise me you'll catch whoever did this to my Jade."

I felt sick to my stomach.

Two women had been brutally murdered and we had no evidence that could lead us to who the killer was.

For anybody in my profession, it was soul destroying having no concrete leads to go on, but tonight, I had to focus on getting my performance spot on otherwise I'd be heckled off the stage by a load of vicious queens.

I ordered a bunch of flowers and a couple of balloons for Bella and the baby on behalf of the team and picked them up after leaving the station. I headed over to Bella's.

Simon flung the door open and pulled me into a rough bear hug.

I still held the flowers and balloons so stood there with my arms outstretched and a huge hunk of a guy wrapped around me. "Easy tiger." I laughed.

"Don't panic, I haven't switched teams." He chuckled. "But I owe you big time." He released me. "Come in, come in. Bella's dying to see you."

"When did you get back?" I asked. "I thought you weren't due till next week."

"This afternoon, I wanted to surprise everyone." He ushered me inside.

Bella was seated in the untidy living room with baby paraphernalia all around her. Gone was the spotlessly organised household and in its place was a scene of delicious chaos.

"I don't have long. Roy's coming round to get me ready for tonight. Plus I need to rehearse."

"Ooh! Get you. You sound like a pro."

"I wish. But I'm really glad Roy's taken me under his wing. His input is priceless."

"I told you years ago you'd love him."

"Yes, but not the way you intended." I laughed, picturing the effeminate, balding man.

"Shame. You two would get on like a house on fire and I'd get my dream wedding."

"You've had your dream wedding."

"Not for me, silly. I meant the dream wedding I've planned for you."

"Not happening, so get it out of your head."

She poked her tongue out at me.

"Have you seen any more of Steve?"

I nodded. "Last night."

"On a school night!"

I goggled my eyes at her, nodding. "And he spooned me this morning."

"Oh, goody. I might get my dream wedding after all."

"Shut up and get your boob out of his face. I need a cuddle before I go."

EIGHTEEN

My stomach was in knots and I wasn't sure I could go through with tonight's performance. After arriving home, I'd practised in the mirror for an hour and I looked ridiculous. There was one positive though; I'd finally mastered the heels.

Roy flounced into my bedroom. "Are you okay, darling? You look a little peaky."

"Why the hell did I agree to this?"

"You'll give yourself wrinkles fretting so much. There's nothing to worry about." He placed a comforting hand on my shoulder. "If you can visibly move that old witch, Blanche, you can win over a load of pissed up queens."

"You make it sound so easy."

"I'm not saying it's easy, but it's not rocket science either. You know the words to the song, right?"

"God, yeah, it's one of those songs I couldn't forget if I tried."

"Anything with a beat and they'll proclaim you the second coming, so chin up, and boobs out."

"Boobs out." I looked down and had to laugh. "This silicone breast plate weighs a bloody ton."

"They take some getting used to but make your silhouette more feminine. And besides darling, it moves the focus from your shoulders." He appraised me once again. "You've got that manly, athletic frame, so anything you can lay your mitts on to make it convincing is a good thing in my book."

"I'm quite impressed with it though–these will look good under the frock." I turned to look at it hanging from the door. A hot-pink sequinned number that I'd have to grease myself into. Thank fuck I wasn't going to be padded out.

"See," Roy said, with a raised eyebrow. "You're already thinking with a more feminine flair."

Shit, I thought. By the time this was over with, I wouldn't know if I was Arthur or Martha. "I'm not so sure about that."

"Well, I am, and I've seen a lot of drag queens over the years, some were fooking awful if I do say so myself, but something tells me you've got the makings of a good one."

"This is a one-off, remember."

"So you keep saying, darling, but I'm impressed, and that doesn't happen often, trust me. You've mastered the heels, and you know what will look good for your body, if only you didn't apply makeup like Ronald McDonald you'd be my perfect protégée."

I burst out laughing. "Cheeky fucker." Surprisingly, I found myself liking Roy more and more. Not in a romantic sense, but he would make a great friend. That would teach me for judging people before getting to know them.

"Does your man know about tonight?"

"Christ, no," I said. "And he's not my man, not really."

"Do you like him?"

"Yeah," I answered.

"Is he good in bed?"

"Too right."

"And do you look forward to spending time with him?"

I hadn't thought of it before. "Erm, yeah, I do."

"Then he's your man, so stop pissing about and sort yourself out. You know as well as I do it's hard to find somebody decent nowadays."

"Yeah, you're right, but let me get my Shania on, sort this case out, then I can focus on my relationship."

"Bollocks to that, darling," he replied. "You'll always be working a case, so stop with the excuses."

I considered myself well and truly told off. "Yes, boss."

"Now, come on, let's get that makeup of yours sorted out, and this time, pay attention to what I'm doing 'cos I can't always be here to wet nurse you."

"It's a one-off, I keep telling you."

"Then you best hope you catch your killer."

I was hopeful, but what if he was right and tonight didn't work out the way I'd planned it to. Shit, I thought. I could be strutting around Dorothy's until this case was solved.

"I might need your help, Roy. People trust you, including Blanche. Maybe you can ask a few questions behind the scenes?"

"Ooh! Like your sidekick? I should've had my police woman outfit dry-cleaned, I could've gone in character with you as Cagney and me as Lacey."

"Thank fuck you didn't." I grinned.

It was a nightmare getting into the car and getting out was even worse wearing the wig.

In the end, I had to abandon it, and put it back into place once I arrived at the club.

"Will this thing stay on?" I asked, nervously.

"Don't fling your head about and it'll be fine."

"I'm lip syncing to Shania so I can't exactly stand still."

"Don't worry. I've got the wig glue here. If I have to, I'll Sell-otape it to your head."

That wasn't a comforting thought, but we were already there, so it was too late to back out. Roy fixed my wig in the shadows at the back of the carpark.

"Blanche told me to use the side entrance. It's closest to the dressing room, apparently."

He gave me a final once over. "Perfect. I'll see you inside when I get back. I'm going to get my glad rags on." Roy kissed the tip of his finger and placed it on my lips. "Break a leg, darling."

"Thanks, Roy, for everything."

"My pleasure, now get in there and knock 'em dead."

It was now 10pm. I banged on the metal security door and a burly guy with a shaved head pushed it open.

"Name," he growled, holding onto a clipboard like I was asking for entrance to the backstage area of Wembley Arena.

"Avaline Saddlebags," I replied, feeling a right tit saying it to a complete stranger.

He looked up and down the list. "Oh, yeah, there you are. Straight down the corridor and turn left. The other girls are already here."

"Thank you."

He tapped me on the arse as I slid past him. I could feel his gaze lingering on my rear. "No problem, sugar tits."

I cringed. Bella's words came back to haunt me. A cock in a frock, I thought. Gross.

Feeling like a lamb leading itself to the slaughter, I turned the corner as the dressing room door opened. A man rushed out of the room and immediately my curiosity was piqued. I was certain it was Darren Wilkes, but wouldn't testify to that in a court of law, having only seen him for a split second before he vanished down another corridor. If it *was* him, what was he doing back here with the talent? And how the hell was I going to make sure he didn't recognise me?

Pulling my phone out of my matching sequinned clutch bag, I found the WattsApp group the team had set up.

Darren Wilkes sighted backstage -the last thing I need. If it looks like he recognises me, arrest him.

Will replied, **Gotcha, boss.**

I stood at the dressing room door and took a deep breath. Pushing it open, a room full of heavily made-up faces stared blankly back at me. The place reeked of cigarette smoke and a thick fog hung in the air. So much for not smoking in public places.

"Hi," was all I could think of to say. But I was met with a wall of silence, making me feel even more out of my depth. Pushing through, I found an empty seat towards the rear of the room and switched the fan at my dressing table on full.

Sitting in this dress wasn't easy, but if I pulled it up a touch, I could just about slide my arse into the canvas chair.

"Eh, love," one of the queens glowered at me. "Turn that friggin' thing down will ya. I'm trying to sort this wig out and your fan's blowing at me like Hurricane bloody Katrina."

The other queens laughed.

"Good one, Mayday," someone else said.

I was more intrigued by the name. "Mayday–that's unusual," I piped up.

"It's 'cos she's always going down," another of the queens cackled.

"Piss off, you old horse."

And they were off with the banter. This was the reason drag queens had always terrified me. So quick was their wit, most people didn't stand a chance. I decided to keep out of it until another approached me waving a piece of paper.

"Here, girl," a half made up queen said, handing me the paper. "This tells you when you're due on stage."

"Oh, thank you," I replied, raising my voice to something less manly. Glancing at the list and seeing my name at the bottom made my stomach flip. Shit, I was closing the whole thing. "I'm Avaline, by the way."

"Oh, we wondered who you were. You're new, ain't ya?"

"Tonight is my first ever stage performance."

"And you're starting out here and closing the show? Who did you bend over for to get that slot?"

"I just auditioned."

She pursed her bright red lips and looked me up and down. "I see."

"What's your name?"

"I'm Anna Bortion."

I wish I hadn't asked. "Nice..." I replied, not knowing what else to say. "Original."

"Who did your face?"

"I did it myself."

"Very impressive for a drag virgin."

"YouTube taught me all I know."

"Hmmm."

I decided I should keep my mouth shut because she clearly

didn't believe a word I said. "Anyway, it's been good to chat, but I need to get myself ready."

"You know you don't need to hole yourself up in here, don't you?"

"What do you mean?"

"You can go into the club and mingle, just use the lockers over there to store your personal stuff. It can get pretty boring waiting back here, and as long as you're back ten minutes before showtime, nobody cares."

"Thanks." I didn't like the idea of milling around back here. It was hot, and stank of stale cigarettes, plus, the less I had to say, the better, and as much as I didn't want to go out on to the club floor looking like this, especially with Will and Layla in attendance, it would be the wisest thing to do. "I think I'll do that—see you later."

"Hmmm," she said once more before slinking away.

Five minutes later, I stepped carefully down the steps at the side of the stage into a packed club.

Darren Wilkes was the first person I spotted, propping up the bar, talking and gesticulating wildly to a small blonde woman. So it *had* been him backstage. As much as I disliked him, I could see the attraction—that sexy, thuggish look he sported so well suited him. But who was he talking to? I decided to take a closer look, but as I approached, he turned and headed for the main doors.

I stood in his place. "Hi," I said. "How are you?"

"Hiya, love," the petite blonde said, turning to smile. "I've not seen you in here before." She had the most beautiful of faces, just like a china doll. Once again, the deep voice gave her away and I guessed she was pre-op. I wondered why she had been talking to Wilkes. Was he up to his old tricks and dishing out black market hormones again?

"First night tonight," I said. "I'm terrified."

"You'll be fine—you're bloody gorgeous."

"Thanks, so are you. I'm Avaline."

"Good to meet you. I'm Kimberley."

"Was that your fella you were talking to? He's hot."

"Fuck, no, that's Darren. You'll soon find out he has a thing for trannies, cock or no cock. Steer clear of him, love, he's bad news."

"Sounds like you've been on the wrong side of him before?"

"A while ago, he sold me some pills, you know the type, and I got myself into a bit of debt and had to pay him off the old fashioned way. He was like a bloodhound—relentless. I was glad to see the back of him. He disappeared for a while but lately he's made a bit of a comeback."

I was chancing my luck. "You don't think he had anything to do with those murders do you?"

Kimberley leaned in and whispered, but the din of the music made it hard for me to hear what she was saying. "Wouldn't surprise me to be honest. Darren's got an evil streak and would think nothing of pulling a knife or giving somebody a back hander. God help anybody who crosses him."

My blood boiled. We needed to get him off the streets. "That doesn't sound good."

"I've been fucked by worse to be honest, plus he has a massive cock and is good in the sack, but once I'd paid my debt off, the best thing to do was give him a wide berth. He wanted a hook up tonight, you know, for old time's sake, but I told him to piss off."

"Good for you." I liked her. She was gutsy. I just hoped Wilkes kept his distance. "Can I get you a drink?"

"That's kind of you. I'll have a rum and coke."

I nodded to the barman, but he'd heard her anyway. I wasn't having anything to drink, especially if it contained alcohol. "You're helping to settle my nerves so it's a small price to pay."

"What time are you on?"

"Midnight."

"Oh, you're the closing act?"

"Yeah, so I believe."

"Then you must be bloody good."

"Or the rest on tonight's bill are shite." My stomach dropped. It hadn't occurred to me that might be the reason I was topping the bill. Maybe I was just the best of a bad lot.

She laughed. "What song are you miming to?"

"*Man! I Feel Like a Woman.*"

"This lot will love that."

"I hope so, or I'm out of a job."

"You'll smash it. I wish I could hang around to watch, but I'm sure you'll be back. You seem like a classy queen which makes a change for this dump."

"Are you not out for long?"

"I'm working tomorrow morning so daren't stay out all night or I'll be late, and I'm already on a written warning for my poor timekeeping."

"What do you do?"

"Nothing special I'm afraid–work in Charlie's American Diner, but I'm on prep duty first thing."

"I could just eat a hotdog now, I'm starving." I'd been so busy, I didn't have a chance to eat.

"Pop into the one by Lime Street station tomorrow and I'll sort you out."

"That's kind of you."

"Not at all, but excuse me a minute, I need to use the ladies. That rum has gone straight to my bladder."

NINETEEN

I spied Layla and Will sitting in the corner sipping their drinks. Apparently, they'd seen me already judging by their faces. They looked totally out of place. I pulled my phone out texted our group chat with one word, *mingle* and a minute later both were on their feet.

Layla sent a WhatsApp message.

Kids fighting.
Sorry, gotta go.

What a shame you'll miss my act. LOL

I know, gutted.

*I'm not – did you get
any leads?*

*Not much. I'll
email everything
to you in the morning.*

Speak tomorrow

I looked at the time–almost 11pm.

There wasn't long to go until show time. I ran through the routine in my head, desperate not to make an arse of myself.

Kimberley had left for home a few minutes ago. I'd enjoyed her company.

I watched with interest as Darren Wilkes stormed out of the club, a bouncer right behind him. Hopefully, Kimberley had hopped into a taxi and was well gone.

Roy appeared, dressed as his alter ego, Betty Swallocks. I hadn't seen him in full drag before, not in person anyway, but could tell it was him by his eyes alone. I was impressed; he certainly looked every inch the star.

"Hiya, Avaline," he said, sounding more effeminate than usual. "Are you ready to blow everyone's panties off?"

"I'm not sure about that."

"Just do what you did in your living room and you'll have them eating out the palm of your hands."

"I've seen some of the others and they're good."

"Same old, darling, same old. They do the exact same routine every week which is why you being here has caused a trickle of excitement mixed with a shitload of resentment."

"Really."

"Oh, yes, the knives are already out and you haven't done anything yet, but once they get a load of how natural a performer you are..."

"Exactly what I didn't want."

"The word is, you got the gig by sitting on poor old Blanche's face after the audition."

I burst out laughing, the idea comical. "Is that how most of them get through?"

"Perks of the job it seems. She promises the silly bitches stardom and they fall for it every single time."

"Sitting on Blanche's face wouldn't be much of a perk for me."

"Nor me, darling, but each to their own. The word is, she's got a tongue like an electric whisk." He looked at the dainty gold watch on his wrist.

I shuddered at the thought of Blanche's tongue anywhere near my arse. "Yeah, wish me luck."

"A star is born," Roy said, waving his arms about. "Anyway, Saddlebags, you best get backstage and prepare yourself."

"Okay, I'm off. Are you waiting around for me?"

"I'm not going to leave you in town looking like that am I?"

"Thanks, Roy. I really appreciate everything you've done. If there's ever anything I can do..."

"Oh, don't mention it." He had a cunning smile across his face. "I may decide to call on you if I have problems casting this year's panto." He walked away leaving his threat hanging in the air.

I turned to find Will. Layla was long gone, so he was flying solo. It didn't take me long to spot him as he was busy chatting to a group of women on another table. I guessed they were Gina Elliot's friends and hoped he'd glean some useful information, or tonight had been all for nothing.

TWENTY

Rebecca curled up on the sofa, glad she hadn't gone out after all. She rarely missed a Friday night at Dorothy's—the social highlight of her week. But she just couldn't be bothered tonight. Instead, she'd legged it down to the shop on the corner and bought a tub of Ben & Jerry's Minter Wonderland ice cream, a huge bag of midget gems and a bottle of prosecco—heaven. Then she watched a few episodes of the *Killing Eve* box set on demand.

At just after 11pm, she heard a strange, set-your-teeth-on-edge, sound. But being above a taxi rank on a Friday night was never going to be peaceful. Standing up, she peered from the window, but couldn't see anything untoward.

Since she was already on her feet, she ran upstairs for a pee and changed into her pink silk pyjamas, considering an early night—she had a big day on tomorrow. A dreaded visit to her mum, who she hadn't spoken to for over six months. Rebecca had lived as a woman for eight years now, and although her mum didn't like it, she seemed to accept her youngest child was now a woman but as soon as she'd told her she intended to have the op and make it official, her mum had hit the roof. She refused to answer her calls or have anything to do with her. But hopefully she'd mellowed by now. Rebecca's brother had organised a birthday party for her mother's sixtieth and she'd agreed Rebecca could be invited! Big of her. Rebecca didn't have a clue which way it would go, but her brothers would be there for moral support. She doubted her mum would cause a scene in front of everyone.

She heard that awful noise again—a screeching, metallic scraping sound she'd not heard before tonight. She couldn't tell where it was coming from, so she headed back downstairs and once again peered from the living room window.

A woman in a long red coat sat on the edge of the pavement opposite, her feet in the gutter, and she was yelling at someone beyond Rebecca's view, although a man's voice was yelling back. Were they playing around or was it a domestic in progress? She really didn't want to know. It had taken her a long time to realise she couldn't solve everybody's problems and to mind her own business, but now she made an art-form of it.

Heading to the kitchen for a cup of hot chocolate, she hoped it would settle her down. She suddenly laughed at herself. Her mother wouldn't believe her if she told her tomorrow. Hot chocolate! On a Friday night? *Yeah right!* she'd say.

Sprinkling the top of the frothy brown milk with cinnamon, she froze. That sound again, but it was closer this time. Peering from the small kitchen window, she gasped. The fire escape ladder from the top floor had been released and now went all the way down to the back alley.

———————

I stood in the darkness, hearing the chatter of the crowd behind the curtain.

What would they make of me? I was terrified and could feel myself trembling.

The DJ spoke, startling me. "Please give a warm welcome to Dorothy's newest star, Miss Avaline Saddlebags."

I plastered a smile on my face as the curtains opened.

The crowd clapped half-heartedly.

The opening bars of the music kicked in. *Let's go girls...*

And I was away, prowling round the stage like I'd been doing it for years.

I was lost in the music and gave it everything I had.

Will stared open-mouthed, seemingly entranced his boss was strutting about on stage in a sequinned frock and sky-high wig. Any other time, I'd have laughed, but I went hell for leather, pointing at him, then blowing a kiss in his direction. That brought him to his senses and I imagined behind the flashing lights, his face beetroot red.

The crowd roared its approval with every kick of my heel or wave of my hand. It really was that easy despite the worry I'd go arse over tit and launch myself headfirst into the crowd. The heels were a bugger to dance in and I was looking forward to freeing my aching feet and squashed toes from their confinement once my performance was over with.

Rebecca couldn't believe it. How the hell had that happened? She'd lived there for almost a year and never even attempted to use the fire escape. What could've caused the ladder to unlock like that?

Sighing, she trudged back upstairs, the last thing she wanted was any Tom, Dick or Harry climbing up and peering into her bedroom while she slept.

Her blood ran cold and a whimper escaped her lips. The

window at the top of the stairs was open, and the curtain blew in the breeze. Surely that hadn't been like that ten minutes ago? Wouldn't she have noticed it?

She pulled the curtain across and climbed out onto the rickety iron cage-like structure and tried to pull the ladder back up, but it wouldn't budge. She figured there must be a locking mechanism, but it was too dark to work it out. Climbing back inside, she closed and locked the window—totally freaked out.

Heading back downstairs, she picked up the mug from the kitchen and took it through to the living room and curled up on the sofa.

"Rupert?"

She leaned forward and shoved the mug onto the coffee table and reached for the remote—turning the TV off. Was she hearing things? "Who's there?"

"Rupert?" The deep male voice sent chills up her spine, nobody had called her that for years.

She squealed and grabbed one of the scatter cushions and held it up to her face as though she was watching a scary movie. What protection she thought it would give her, she had no clue.

"Rupert?" The voice sounded closer this time, just outside the door on the landing.

She lunged at the door and tried to slam it shut but something prevented it closing the whole way. "Fuck off! Whoever you are, just fuck the hell off! I'm calling the police." As she said it she spied her phone still on the sofa.

"I wouldn't do that, Rupert."

A bang on the back of the door made her scream and she began to whimper and shake uncontrollably. Then the door was pushed inwards a few inches. The person was strong—far stronger than Rebecca was. "I don't give a shit what you'd do. Get out of my home! What the hell do you want from me?"

She felt herself sliding forward as the door opened slowly.

Trying to get a grip was useless. The wooden floor and silk pyjamas made it even more difficult to gain purchase. She couldn't hold the door any longer.

Darting for her phone, she managed to press 9 twice before a blow to her right shoulder sent the phone flying through the air before landing with a crash and skittering across the floorboards.

She screamed and turned, lashing out blindly at the intruder who was dressed from head to toe in black—all she could see was his manic brown eyes. "Who the fuck are you, and what do you want?"

On full alert, she kept eye contact and stepped sideways, trying to get some distance between herself and her attacker. She darted to the other side of the coffee table. Reaching for the half-empty mug, she launched it at his head, but it glanced off him, not having any effect whatsoever.

He laughed. "Feisty little bitch aren't you?"

"What the hell do you want from me?"

"You've got nothing I could possibly want, Rupert." He lifted his hand and a huge knife glinted sharp and menacing.

"Don't call me that, you mental bastard." She upended the table in his direction. "Help!" she screamed, praying someone in the street would hear and come to her rescue.

"I'm going to slice the tongue out of your head if you don't shut up." The quiet, calm manner he spoke in freaked her out even more than if he'd been yelling. He lunged for her, but Rebecca was fast and a lot smaller and she darted out of the way, causing him to stumble.

This gave Rebecca the opportunity to get out, past him, but he was close behind. She made the split-second decision to go upstairs not down, remembering she'd locked the front door and the key was in the fruit bowl, in the kitchen. The fire escape ladder was her only way out.

Although a lot bigger than her, he was equally fast and, just a few stairs up, she felt him on her tail. She turned and kicked out at him, feeling she had the upper hand, and if she could get him to fall just a few steps, this could be all the time she needed to get out.

He saw her foot coming and buried the blade deep into her heel. The pain was beyond anything Rebecca had ever experienced before.

They both froze for a millisecond, their eyes locked, then his eyes crinkled at the corners and she realised the crazy bastard was smiling!

Yanking her foot backwards, she turned again, and, this time, the knife sliced through her calf muscle. More intense pain washed over her, but the adrenaline had kicked in and forced her forward at speed.

As she reached the top of the stairs, getting sight of the window, her escape, the blade punctured her right buttock. The force of the blow was so intense she felt it travel right through her and pin her to the floorboards beneath. She couldn't move.

Her attacker then yanked the knife out, climbed on top of her, pressing her to the threadbare carpet. He grabbed her hair and tore her head back, placing the knife at her throat.

She knew she was going to die.

The blade sliced her throat, but she felt no pain.

The last thing she was aware of was him picking up her left foot and dragging her through to the bedroom.

TWENTY-ONE

Blanche glided over, looking like a bulldog chewing a wasp. I guessed her outfit, makeup and hair were meant to be paying homage to Dusty Springfield, but listening closely, I swear I could hear poor Dusty spinning in her grave.

She was full of exuberance and flannel. "You were sensational, Avaline, and the crowd just adored you."

"Thanks." What else was I going to say?

"I knew there was something special about you, the moment I laid eyes on you."

"You're too kind," I said.

Blanche took my hand. I looked down and noticed the costume jewellery. Every finger was adorned with a ring with some gaudy, vulgar-looking stone. "I'd like to offer you a regular spot every Friday night, if you're interested that is?"

I wasn't at all interested, but until the killer was off the streets, working at Dorothy's was the better option. I needed to be where the action was and although I didn't relish the idea of doing drag for the rest of my life, right now I couldn't look a gift horse in the mouth or whatever that old saying was.

"Wow, really? I'm thrilled."

"Good, good," Blanche replied. "Same time next week then?"

"Yeah, sure."

"Leave your contact details with Matt at the bar." She pointed to the handsome barman who had served me earlier. "Free drinks for you from now on." Air kisses were delivered before she flounced off.

I guessed that meant I wouldn't be getting paid with good old cash, but free drinks weren't to be sniffed at.

Roy dashed over. "You're a star, do you know that?"

"Behave yourself," I scoffed. "I only mimed along to a song."

"Oi, don't put yourself down. It takes guts and artistry to do what you just did and get a roar of approval from this smelly lot. You were absolutely fabulous." He sounded a little choked with emotion. "I always wanted my very own drag daughter, but I'll be buggered if I'm lumbering myself with the name Saddlebags..."

"Eh?"

"... No, there's only one thing for it, you'll have to become a Swallocks. Ooh, the Haus of Swallocks, who'd have thought it?"

"I'm becoming neither, soft arse." This drag lark was so complicated. Drag mothers and daughters. What was the world coming to? "You know why I'm doing this. The fact the crowd liked it hasn't changed how I feel."

"Yes, I know, but a girl can dream, can't she?"

"Dream away, Roy." I watched as Will exited the building and dreaded the ribbing, on Monday morning, from him and the team. I wasn't naïve enough to think he didn't capture at least some of my performance with his mobile phone.

"Are you ready to go? My face is melting with the heat in here."

"Yeah, come on," I said. "I'll treat us to an Indian takeaway on the way back to mine." It was the least I could do, and even though there wasn't one slither of sexual attraction, from my side at least, I liked him and enjoyed his company.

"Ooh, not for me, Avaline love, I'd blow a bloody big hole through my mattress if I ate that muck. Gives me shocking wind, you know, anything with spices. I'd never be off the lav."

This time I did laugh. He had a way with words that tickled my sometimes bawdy sense of humour. "*McDonalds* then?"

"That sounds more like it, but we'll have to use the twenty-four-hour drive-thru, I'm not walking in there with you looking like that."

It was quite the performance getting back into Roy's car now we were both in full drag. After banging my head several times on the ceiling, I tore the wig from my head and chucked it onto the back seat.

Moments later, Roy pulled into the drive-thru. "Two Big Mac meals, darling," he purred into the mic.

"What do you want to drink?" The waitress sounded tired and uninterested.

"Orange juice," I whispered.

"Orange juice for both meals."

"Drive to the first window."

The sight of us certainly woke the girl up.

I almost pissed myself at the expression on her face. She didn't know where to look. I was still laughing when we pulled back out into traffic. "Did you see her face?"

"You get used to it after a while, darling," Roy said.

"I never thought about it before to be honest. I'd probably try to keep my face straight too and avoid mentioning the elephant in the room, when really, it's okay to say something. In fact it's pretty hilarious if they don't."

"I know, the funniest reactions tend to be from the manliest of men—bouncers, security guards, the brutes are usually huge and muscle-bound but they act like frightened schoolgirls if you speak to them."

"I really enjoyed myself tonight," I confessed. "Once the nerves had calmed down, I wasn't expecting the buzz I got from it, to be honest."

"I knew you would."

I smiled at him and glanced out the window. A white Transit van was speeding along the side street. "Stop!" I screeched.

Roy slammed his foot on the brake and the car skidded forwards and began turning sideways. The squealing sound was deafening.

"Shit, Roy! Take it easy."

"Why the bloody hell did you do that?" he asked, gripping his chest dramatically. "You almost gave me heart failure."

"Because I saw something. Turn around and go up that street back there. Hurry up, he'll get away."

"Who'll get away? What the heck did you see?"

"The van we've been searching for. Quick!"

Roy, in a panic, was an even worse driver than usual and that was saying something. He proceeded to do a twenty-five point turn before we finally turned into the street. But, by then, of course, the street was empty.

"Hurry up! We can't let him get away. He might be looking for his next victim."

"Bloody hell! I told you I should've dressed as a cop!"

"Just drive, Roy. This could be a matter of life or death."

"You really think it's the killer? Oh, shit! I can't do a car chase —I'll kill us both."

"Pull over, for fuck's sake. I'll drive."

"Oh, no you won't. You're not insured to drive my car."

"Then put your fucking foot down. He'll be over the other side of town by now."

"Don't yell at me, darling. I'm not used to driving fast, and you yelling is making me worse."

I rolled my eyes—stressed to the hilt. As we sped along the street, I suddenly spotted some rear brake lights in the distance. "That must be him.".

But by the time we got to the end of the road, there was no sight of him.

"Left, or right?" Roy asked, flapping his hands in a panic.

"Fuck only knows. Try left."

Roy turned left, but he'd gone back to driving like an old woman.

"Just take me home, Roy." I pulled my phone from my bra and sent a message to Will and Layla.

I spotted the van on Bennett Street. Can't be certain, but I think it was our guy. Lost him. Roy was driving. I'll come back out in my own car.

Will replied.

Sorry, boss, I'm already home. Do you want me to meet you?

Yes please, Will. If Rachel doesn't mind. If I do end up finding him I'd prefer not to be alone.

No problem – meet you at yours in half

an hour.

Once home, Roy helped me remove the outfit and then I dressed in my jeans and T-shirt. Using Roy's make-up remover, I looked more like myself in minutes.

Still a little shaken up, Roy loaded his car and headed off, taking his food with him.

I crammed the burger down my throat, grabbed my jacket, and ran outside when Will texted me moments later. I jumped into the passenger seat of his car, hoping he wasn't as bad a driver as Roy had been. But if he was, at least I'd be able to take over.

As we pulled away, a movement to the side of my gate caught my eye and I spotted Steve standing there looking at Will and me —a suspicious expression on his face.

Shaking my head, I sent him a text.

Sorry, Steve.
Didn't see you.
I'm on police business.
I'll call you in the morning

Steve didn't reply. For fuck's sake, that's all I needed—a jealous stalker guy as a boyfriend, give me a break.

We drove round and around for what seemed like hours, stopping several times at Columbus Quay where the Transit van had been first picked up on the CCTV after Gina's murder. There were definitely no Transit vans to be seen—in fact the streets were practically dead.

"Sorry, Will. I was certain we would find it—maybe I was totally mistaken."

"It's okay, better safe than sorry. I'll go into the station and check the street cameras tomorrow morning."

"Exactly. You may as well drop me off at home and get back to Rachel."

TWENTY-TWO

I slept like the dead until well into the afternoon. It was years since I'd done that and I felt quite guilty.

I reached for my phone. There were several texts from Bella asking about last night's performance and one from Steve.

**I'm presuming we're
still out tonight?**

I considered calling it off, but it was our first official date and I didn't want to give him the wrong message.

**Sounds good.
What time and where?**

**Your call,
I'm easy.**

I did consider making a joke of how easy he was but sensed he was still a little miffed about last night and might not get the joke.

Fancy Italian?

Can do.

Angelo's then – 8.30?

*If we can
get a table.*

*I'll call them
and book.*

I checked my emails—nothing that couldn't wait till Monday morning. I thought I would've heard from Will regarding the CCTV but there was nothing from him—maybe he'd slept in too?

After going to the bathroom, I swapped my bed for the sofa, too exhausted to even get dressed. I felt utterly lazy.

Waking from another nap, I finally replied to Bella, promising to call in tomorrow and fill her in. She seemed happy with that, probably because Simon was still home and keeping her occupied.

The longer the day went on, the more relieved I felt that nobody had reported a dead body or a missing person. Maybe my instincts had been totally wrong about the van after all. I hoped so.

At 8:35pm I entered Angelo's trying to scan the dimly lit room for Steve. The waiter informed me I was the first to arrive as he led me to one of the booths.

It irked me he was late. I wanted to be the one arriving last—not look like I was desperate. How childish was I?

I ordered a glass of lager and browsed the menu.

"Hey!"

Startled, I looked up as Steve slid into the seat opposite me.

"Sorry I'm late," he said, not volunteering any explanation.

"Are you? I didn't notice. I've only just arrived myself. What do you want to drink?" I spewed the words out and wanted to kick myself

"What are you having?"

"Lager."

"Sounds good." He nodded at the waiter who was hovering close by. "Another lager, please."

"So, about last night," I said, wanting to get it out in the open so it didn't ruin the evening. "I didn't see you till I was in the car. We'd had a sighting of a van we've been looking for. Will came to pick me up."

"Will?"

"He's a colleague."

"I see. So who was the *person* I saw leave your house moments before that?"

Shit! It hadn't occurred to me he might have seen Roy. How long had he actually been standing there? Could he have seen me as Avaline? I decided to come clean—otherwise it could bite me in the arse. "Roy, a friend of mine, AKA Betty Swallocks."

"Classy," he said.

"We'd been to Dorothy's."

"The nightclub?"

I nodded. "I performed on stage as a drag queen last night."

His eyeballs almost shot from his head. So he hadn't seen me —that was obvious.

"I didn't know that's what you're into."

"I'm not. I was undercover."

"Really?"

"Someone's targeting the trans community—I don't have much choice."

"Fair enough."

The waiter returned with our lager, putting an end to that conversation. "Are you ready to order?" he asked, taking a pad from his pocket.

"Gosh! No, sorry. Can you give us five minutes?" I grabbed hold of the menu again—my stomach rumbling noisily. "Sorry. I'm starving." I laughed.

His lips twitched. I could tell he was thawing.

"What do you fancy?" I asked.

"You."

That was unexpected. I felt the blood rush to my face. "Okay, I meant food."

"I know what you meant."

Putting the menu down, I scratched my head. "What's happening here? I thought we'd agreed to keep things casual. Why do I feel the goalposts have moved?"

"I know what we agreed, but honestly Dylan, I can't get you out of my head."

"I like your Kylie reference." I grinned, wanting to lighten the mood, but it flew over the top of his head.

"I don't know how you feel, but *I* want more than just meeting up for a quickie once or twice a week. I came last night to tell you, when I saw Betty..."

"Swallocks."

"... Swallocks leaving. Then, moments later, another bloke

turned up. I thought I'd got you completely wrong. That you were a slag, to be honest."

"Gee, thanks for that."

He shrugged, his gorgeous green eyes glinting in the candlelight.

"So what changed your mind?"

"Last night, I thought fuck it, it's not meant to be—plenty more fish in the sea—the usual shite. But this morning, I still couldn't get you out of my head, and decided to tell you how I feel. So here I am, making a complete fool of myself."

I smiled. "I don't know about that, I kinda like it."

"What do you mean?"

I shrugged. "I think I feel the same."

"For real?"

"Yeah, for real."

"I want to kiss you right now."

"Don't you dare! I don't go for kissing in public."

"I'm glad you told me that before I made an even bigger. fool of myself."

I laughed. "But I'm looking forward to seeing how things develop after our first date."

"Can't wait."

"You do know my job must come first though, don't you?"

"Of course, I do."

I nodded. "Good, because that's the main reason cop's relationships don't go the distance. Oh, shit! The waiter's on his way back." I grabbed the menu once again. "Quick, decide what you're eating."

TWENTY-THREE

"Hello, you two," Bella said, pulling the door open. "Come in and go straight through to the kitchen, we're sat in there."

I pushed Steve in first. He bent down to kiss her cheek. "Nice to finally meet you."

"You too."

I followed them in. "How's baby?"

"Fast asleep, thank God. The little bugger has had me up most of the night."

"Oh, no, I bet you're both knackered."

"I'm exhausted, Simon not so much."

"How come?" I asked.

"He can sleep through dropping bombs remember, so a crying baby is nothing."

Steve tittered. "We can look after the little one if you want to get a bit of sleep."

"Thanks, love, but I tend to sleep when little master does."

"Well, we won't stay long," I said.

"Don't be daft, Dylan. We've been looking forward to seeing you, and I'm eager to know how the case is going."

The four of us sat around the kitchen table.

I figured Bella must be bored because she'd baked enough cakes and scones to sink a battleship.

"You'll miss all this, Bells," I teased, winking at Simon.

"Like hell I will," she snapped. "I'm not the Mary Berry type, but tied to the house, my options are limited."

"She'd be back in work tomorrow if she could." Simon shovelled half a buttered scone in his mouth. "Mmmm–delicious."

Bella glowered at him. "You'll have to excuse my husband's manners–he's used to shitting in the desert and wiping his arse on the sleeve of his jacket, aren't you, love?"

"Huh?" He shoved the other half in his mouth.

I snorted. "You two crack me up."

Bella turned to Steve. "If you two ever get married, any mystery soon dissolves." She nodded towards me. "He'll soon be using the toilet when you're in the bath."

I didn't have a response and was thankful when Simon spoke up. "How's the case going? I've seen it on the news–sickening stuff."

There was nothing I could go into detail about, especially with Simon and Steve listening, but told them what I could.

"You know I'm at Dorothy's again on Friday?"

Bella's face lit up. "Oh, I know and can't wait."

"Why?"

"Cos I'm gonna be there, that's why."

"You're bloody well not."

"I wish I could see it," Steve piped up. "But he's barred me from going."

"I'll be there, you mark my words. I've already squared it with Simon. Roy's gonna pick me up and drop me off home. I can't wait to see you do your stuff."

"But you have a new baby. You can't be out 'til that time of night."

"I'm not Cinderella. I don't have to be home by the stroke of midnight," she said. "My gorgeous hubby is returning to barracks soon and has insisted I enjoy a night out, because, let's face it, we don't know when the next one will be."

"How sweet of him," I said, with a snide tone.

"You're such a little bitch," Bella said, playfully slapping my arm.

"I'm not. It's just embarrassing."

"Bollocks," she shouted, before remembering the sleeping baby in the adjoining room. "Will sent me a few videos from your last show—"

"It wasn't a show," I interrupted. "Just me miming to one song."

"You know what I mean. I thought you were absolutely fabulous–even Simon said he'd do you, didn't you love?"

Simon spluttered. "I didn't put it quite like that, Bells."

"Have you still got the video?" Steve asked.

"Yeah." Bella was all smiles. "Wanna see it?"

"No, he doesn't," I protested.

"Yes, he does, miserable arse." She got up and grabbed her phone from the work surface.

I wanted the ground to swallow me whole. "Don't you dare show him."

"Ah, shut up."

As she went to give the phone to Steve, I snatched it from her hand.

"Aw, come on—let me see," Steve asked.

"No. I'm not ready yet." I was adamant he wouldn't be seeing, it. "Anyway, I'm going to check on the baby if you don't mind."

"Suit yourself, Avaline," Bella said.

I stuck my middle finger up and they all burst out laughing.

Monday morning traffic was usually a nightmare and today was no exception. I was less than eager to get into work knowing what was coming. After my performance at Dorothy's I'd be a minor celebrity, albeit fleetingly until all jokes were exhausted.

My thoughts were correct–I already knew Will had recorded my performance and sent it straight to Bella. I wondered who else he'd sent it to.

I'd tried to call Layla all weekend, but she didn't reply. I hadn't heard from her since Friday when she'd told me the kids were acting up. Hopefully, normality had been resumed and she would be in work today.

Walking tentatively into the reception area, Stan, the desk sergeant, turned and sniggered. Here we go, I thought.

"Buzz me through and shut it," I said, pre-empting whatever he had planned.

"Anything you say, DI Saddlebags." He turned away, his shoulders rising and falling in obvious mirth.

I pulled the door open and strolled through the main reception area.

"Hey, big spender," Fiona, a WPC, cackled.

"Hi, Fiona," I said with a smile. "Howd'you fancy traffic duties next week?" That wiped the smile off her face. "No? Thought not."

Not another word was spoken, but as I approached the incident room, I braced myself and pushed the doors open.

It was just gone 8am and the place was a hive of activity.

"What's going on in here?"

Layla walked towards me. "Morning, Dylan."

"Hi. What's happening?"

"I think the team have found a new level of admiration for you after your performance last week."

"Oh?"

"You've earned a huge amount of respect putting yourself out there like that. I think they wanted to acknowledge your sacrifice and get in early, you know, crack on with the case."

I wasn't overly emotional by nature, but I was touched by the gesture, and grateful the place hadn't been decorated with feather boas.

"Well, I appreciate that, but there's something I need to make you all aware of."

"What is it?"

I brought the room to order. "Ladies and gents, can I have your attention, please." All eyes focused on me. "Thanks for getting in early today. I really appreciate your efforts." They nodded. "I'm not sure if Will told you but I'm certain I spotted the Transit van after leaving the club early hours of Saturday morning. My driver tried to give chase, but, let's just say, he's no Lewis Hamilton and we lost him."

"Will did tell us and we're just waiting on the street cams to see if it was the same van you spotted, and if it was, where it went to," Joanna said.

"Fantastic. So, Layla, how'd it go at Dorothy's?"

"I didn't get much before I had to leave," Layla said. "Lots of people knew of her, but they knew no more than us. They're all just club friends and don't socialise outside of that environment."

"Shit," I said.

"Exactly, but it was worth a try."

"Yeah, it was. I'm back at Dorothy's on Friday night so I'll see what I can find out then. Once my alter ego is familiar there, people will be more open to blabbing."

"Are you performing again?" Layla asked.

"Afraid so." I looked around the room. "Go on," I urged. "Get it out the way because you won't get another chance."

"Well, I thought you looked hot," Joanna said.

"A bit butch for me," Will joked.

"And what about you two?" I nodded to Pete and Heather. "Anything to contribute."

Pete shrugged. "Are you sure that was your first time?"

"Yes, definitely."

"Well if it was, you were bloody convincing." Heather shook her head in obvious amazement.

"Well, thanks, but I'm sure the real Shania has nothing to worry about."

Tommo lifted his head up from his computer. "You looked like a decent bit of totty to me. Are you sure it's not a secret calling of yours, boss?"

"Busted. My secret's out." I shook my head, exasperated. "Now can we get back to work, please?"

"What happened with Darren Wilkes in the end?" Layla said.

"The slimy git was at the club chatting up a girl I met called Kimberley. She wasn't entirely complimentary about him and seemed to think he was up to his old tricks. He shot off just after I arrived in the bar. We need to keep a close eye on that one."

"Yeah, agreed," Joanna said. "I'd love to lock him up and throw away the key. I'm still convinced he has something to do with the murders."

"Me too, but we've got jack-shit to go on. We need to carry on with other lines of enquiry until we do. As soon as something comes to light, I'll nail him to the wall."

Just then, PC Jake Mackintosh entered. He blushed. "Sorry to interrupt, but can I have a word, Dylan?"

"Sure, what is it?" I hadn't seen much of him since our brief encounter a few months ago—we'd hooked up after a heavy celebration for wrapping up a particularly gruesome case. "You can say it to the room. Unless..." I felt my face flush, hoping it wasn't something personal he wanted to talk to me about. If it was, I'd just invited him to comment in an open forum.

"I've just taken a phone call from a Mrs Angela Preston. She has reported her son missing."

"And," I quizzed.

"Well, I say son, but it's a bit more complicated than that. Her son apparently identifies as female."

Preston? My blood ran cold as a silence fell over the room. "What's the name of the missing person?"

He looked at his notepad. "A Rupert Preston AKA Rebecca Preston."

"Fuck," I said, jumping to my feet.

Realising I needed a moment to gather my thoughts, Layla took over and began firing out orders. "Will, Joanna, head over there now, you have the address on file. Dylan and I will follow on."

"Jesus," Will said. "You don't think...?"

"I hope not," I said, heading for my desk. "Layla, give Janine the heads up will you?"

"Sure," she said charging towards Janine's office. "I'll meet you out front."

———

"I have a bad feeling about this," I said to Layla once we were in the car.

"It might be nothing. Maybe she's just gone away for a few days?"

"Let's hope. But I just knew when I saw that van there was going to be another murder. I hope I'm wrong, honest to God I do, but I don't think I am."

"Do you know how many white Transit vans there are just in this area alone? I'm not being funny, but without seeing the number plate there's no way of knowing if you were right."

"I just can't shake this feeling, that's all."

Indicating, I pulled into a parking space opposite the taxi rank, noticing a crowd had already gathered.

We approached Will and Joanna.

"Anything?" I asked.

"Not yet. We've knocked a few times and had no response, but someone from the property agency is on their way over now with the spare keys."

"Why didn't you just boot the door in?" I asked.

"What if she's in bed, or ill, or just doesn't wanna talk?" Joanna said.

"And what if she's lying there in a pool of her own blood, Jo?" I went to the apartment door and something definitely felt off. Call it intuition but I had a feeling we were already too late. I pushed the letterbox open. "Hello, Rebecca, can you hear me? This is DI Monroe. Could you come to the door, please?" Then the smell hit me, making my stomach churn. I took a step back before kicking the door open.

"Dylan, what the hell are you doing?" Layla protested. Will and Joanna were standing close behind her. "What if Joanna is right and—"

"She isn't," I said, an overwhelming feeling of sadness washing over me. "But I wish she was."

The smell from the open door wafted out.

Will pulled a handkerchief from his pocket and retched.

"Get the area cordoned off and one of you call Lauren, tell her we need her right now." I headed inside. "Layla, come with me," I called over my shoulder as I ran up the first flight of stairs. The smell was stronger the further into the property we got.

"Don't touch the walls," Layla said.

I was about to ask why when the horror revealed itself to me.

Along the hallway blood spatters lined the wall, and for a moment I had visions of Rebecca terrified, running for her life, the sadistic killer chasing her. "My God," I said.

The colour drained from Layla's face. "Should we wait until the team get here?"

"No," I said. "But if you want to go back, I understand."

"I'm staying with you."

She looked terrible and I was worried this was way too much for her.

The living room door at the top of the stairs was closed. I pulled my gloves out of my pocket and put them on before pushing it open.

There were definite signs of a struggle, but no blood spatters like there had been in the hall. I turned and slowly made my way up the next flight of stairs.

As I reached the top I stood there, open mouthed, gawking at the sickening scene before me. A huge pool of blood soaked the top landing, and a smear trailed from it into what I presumed to be the bedroom.

I forced myself to continue. Stepping over the blood, I entered the room, struggling to take in what I was seeing.

My eyes focused on Rebecca who was lying flat on her back, and, slowly, I scanned her naked and mutilated body. It was like a scene from one of those horror movies I refused to watch. I said a silent prayer, hoping she hadn't been conscious, or aware, when the evil monster delivered his death sentence.

Stepping away, I turned to look at Layla, who was still half-way up the stairs, then I closed the door behind me.

"What...?"

"You don't need to see this." Close to tears, I struggled to swallow my anger.

TWENTY-FOUR

Lauren arrived within the hour as well as the Scene of Crime Officers.

Joanna and Will had returned to the station in order to get the investigation underway.

Layla still appeared spaced out, and I doubted it had anything to do with the death of Rebecca. We dealt with things like this all the time and, although it's never nice, we're programmed to get on with it, otherwise nothing would ever get resolved. I presumed something had happened with Max over the weekend, but our priority right now was to catch a killer and her private life would have to take a back seat. Harsh, but true.

"I'll accompany Lauren," I said. "Do you want to do a bit of door knocking, somebody must've seen something, and the sooner we get a lead to sink our teeth into, the better."

She nodded, clearly relieved.

I pulled on a pair of overalls, bootees and gloves, and followed Lauren inside.

"The body's on the top floor, Lauren."

"Oh, dear." She pointed at the blood spatters up the wall.

"Yes. It gets far worse—brace yourself." In fact I dreaded seeing the body again.

As we reached the top of the stairs, Lauren gasped, shaking her head.

Rebecca's naked body was covered in blood. It was difficult to see where the majority of it had come from.

"That's different to the last two." She pointed to Rebecca's private parts and I was surprised to see she still had her boy bits intact. Red wool stitching ran under the breasts.

"What's gone on there?"

"My guess is, she's had her breast implants removed."

Of course. The killer was putting the victims back to the way they were born. Clearly Rebecca still having a penis had thrown the killer too, which is why it had been left alone—the prosthesis wasn't required.

"Her tongue has been removed too," Lauren said.

"What the...?" Why the hell would he cut her tongue out?"

"Beats me."

"Can you give me any idea when she was killed?"

"Judging by the rigor and lividity, I'd say anywhere between Friday evening and Saturday morning, but I'll have a better idea once I get him to the lab."

"Her, you mean?"

Lauren glanced at the genitals before rolling her eyes. "If you insist."

"I do."

I left Lauren to it and had a quick look around the bedroom and bathroom. I found nothing of interest.

As I stepped out onto the landing, a grating sound caught my attention and made me look through the window. I couldn't believe my eyes. "You've gotta be fucking kidding me," I muttered angrily to myself, shaking my head. How was I going to explain to the team that Savage and Layla had made such a massive mistake? Wilkes' alibi had hinged on the fact he hadn't left the apartment all night and now that had just been blown completely out of the water.

Down in the living room, I took a quick glance around, looking for one thing only—drugs. Namely under the counter prescription drugs. The kitchen drawer didn't disappoint.

I ran down the stairs and stripped off the overalls at the door. Where the hell was Layla? We needed to get going.

I needn't have worried. Layla was standing by the car, talking to someone on the phone. She seemed relieved to see me and ended the call as I approached.

"Anything?" she asked.

"You're not going to believe this," I said, opening up the car and slipping in behind the wheel.

"Go on," she said once she was seated beside me.

"There's a back entrance to Rebecca's apartment."

"Fuck! How did we miss that?"

"Exactly. How did we?"

"But I looked around. I was with Savage during the first interview with Rebecca and I swear I looked around. I didn't see any other door."

"Because it's not a door. It's a window with a fire-escape ladder.

"Oh, my God."

I was quietly seething. If we'd known about this earlier, I'm positive Wilkes wouldn't have been released in the first place, and we could have prevented two further deaths. But I couldn't say anything while I was still so angry as it was likely to come out wrong, and, to be fair, she was right. There hadn't been another door. Maybe, if it wasn't for the scraping sound, I might not have even noticed it myself. However, I'd have expected them to ask Rebecca if there was another exit, in the first place. Basic policing.

TWENTY-FIVE

I called Will and gave him the update about the drugs. "Can you arrange to have Darren Wilkes brought in for questioning, please? We'll be back as soon as we've informed Rebecca's mother."

Finding the drugs was a major coup for the team working the investigation and meant we had something concrete to go on. I intended to keep schtum about the fire-escape for the time being. Once it was common knowledge, the press would have a field-day, not to mention what Janine would do—she'd have a fit.

Fifteen minutes later, we arrived at our destination. A middle of the row terraced house in Toxteth. The first part of the street had seemed relatively tidy—mostly red painted brick exterior walls and front doorsteps. Even pretty, lace curtains adorned most of the UPVC windows. But then, halfway down the street, things took a serious nosedive—boarded-up windows, metal shutters, graffiti, and litter. Rebecca's mother lived in the middle of that lot.

We climbed from the car, the curtains twitching all around us, and approached number 54. A scruffy youngster was playing on the doorstep with a matchbox car. He wore a dirty white vest and nothing else, his little bare arse in the air for all to see.

"Charming!" I said with a smirk. "Is your mummy home?"

"Mummy's gone. What's your name, mista?"

"I'm Dylan, what's yours?"

"None of your fucking business, you nonce." He ran inside screaming for his nan.

I looked at Layla, in total shock. "Did I just imagine that?"

She shook her head. "Unfortunately, no."

I knocked on the painted black door that had several chips showing the previous colour used to be bottle green. "Hello? Mrs Preston?" I stepped inside the hallway onto old linoleum flooring that had definitely seen better days.

"Who are you?" A woman appeared at the top of the stairs, pulling up her bright pink jogging bottoms. She appeared to be in her late fifties with cropped peroxide blonde hair and the pallor of a heavy smoker.

"DI Dylan Monroe and DS Layla Monahan." We both flashed our ID. "Are you Angela Preston?"

She eyed us warily. "Yes."

"You called the station earlier today to report your daughter missing."

"I reported my *son* missing. Rupert was born a boy, no matter what he calls himself now he'll always be a boy to me."

"I see. I apologise. Do you mind if we come in for a few minutes?"

She rounded the bottom of the stairs and headed towards the back of the house. "Scuse the mess."

I glanced back at Layla and raised my eyebrows. The kitchen, to be fair, apart from a dirty plate in the middle of the small square table, was neat and tidy. Much tidier than I'd expected.

The cheeky little brat was slumped on a beanbag, watching a small portable TV in the corner.

"Keanu, go and put some bloody pants on. You're worse than your dad for stripping off." She swatted at the young boy and chased him from the room. "So, did you find him? He was meant to come to my birthday bash Saturday but didn't bother to show up."

I waited until we'd all taken a seat around the table before I responded. "We've just come from your son's home, Mrs Preston."

"And?" She looked from Layla to me, her eyebrows knitted.

"There's no easy way to say this, I'm afraid."

"No. No. Don't tell me. No." She began flapping her hands in front of her and this soon changed to her slapping herself in the face.

Layla jumped to her feet and grabbed the woman's hands to prevent her hurting herself any more.

The kid appeared in the doorway. "What have you done to me nan?"

I groaned. This was going from bad to worse. Layla was trying to calm the hysterical woman down, but we still hadn't told her what had happened and now the feral-like grandchild was on my case. "She's just received some bad news. Is your daddy about?"

He turned and legged it up the stairs, screaming for who I suspected to be his father.

A huge bald man covered in tattoos and wearing a pair of off-white cotton boxers entered moments later, the brat at his heels. "What's going on?"

"And you are?" I asked, getting to my feet.

"Robin Preston—her son. What's happened?"

I found it astonishing little Rebecca, or Rupert as I'd better get used to calling her around these people, was from the same gene pool as this lot. "Maybe you should take a seat."

"It's Becky, isn't it?" he said.

"I'm afraid so. We found Rupert-Rebecca this morning after your mother reported her missing. We believe she was killed at home on Friday evening."

Mrs Preston began wailing again.

Taking obvious offence at this, the youngster rounded on me and kicked me in the shin.

"Hey. Stop that!"

Robin grabbed the lad by the ear and marched him from the room. It was total chaos.

Once we were back in the car, I called Will again.

"How's it going?"

"Darren Wilkes is sitting quietly in a cell. He doesn't seem bothered by his arrest, but won't cooperate without Nigel Warfield, his solicitor, present."

"So, get him in then."

"I tried. Warfield's currently in Manchester and won't be back in Liverpool for a couple of hours."

"Then we play the waiting game." I ended the call. "Do you fancy some lunch?" I asked Layla.

"Yeah, sounds good to me." She seemed in a slightly better mood than she had been all morning.

"I fancy a burger." I'd been planning to pop in and say hello to Kimberley sometime this week. I hoped she might have her ear to the ground and reveal something about Wilkes that might help bring him to justice.

"That was crazy back there," I said, once we were en route.

"I know. I almost died when that kid booted you. Did it hurt?"

"No. He didn't have any shoes on, thankfully."

My stomach growled and I looked forward to stuffing my face. I was meeting Steve at the gym later and would work the calories off there.

"How's things with Max and the kids?" I asked, just for something to fill in the time with.

"I don't wanna talk about it right now, if you don't mind."

"Got it." Her problematic private life was definitely beginning to take its toll. She was often blunt and came across as officious and, while still presentable, she'd lost the edge she usually had with her appearance. Her face was makeup free and her hair had been scraped back into a tight ponytail. But, if she didn't want to talk about it, that was her choice.

We stepped into the diner, the aroma making my mouth water.

A waitress approached. "Table for two?"

"Yes, please," I replied with a smile.

We were seated quickly and efficiently. "Kimberley, your waitress, will be with you in a few moments," she said before zooming off to another couple who had just entered behind us.

"Thank you," I said, pleased.

"Kimberley..." Layla was putting two and two together. "The one from Dorothy's?"

"Yeah, but don't mention what we do for a living."

"I'm not stupid, Dylan."

Kimberley approached, looking less glamorous than she had on Friday, wearing tight jeans, a branded blue T-shirt with an apron tied around her waist, and a cap on her head. She still wore a full face of makeup, but nothing over the top. "Good afternoon, my name is Kimberley and I'll be your waitress today."

"Hi, Kimberley, it's good to see you again."

She looked at me, trying to place where she might know me from. "Sorry, but have we met?

"Yeah, last Friday at Dorothy's—you told me to pop in next time I was in the area."

"Dorothy's?" She studied my face. "I'm not sure... oh, hang on a minute. Avaline?"

"The very same," I replied, my voice rising a few octaves.

"Bloody hell!" Her face was a picture of surprise. "I'd never have recognised you walking down the street. You're gorgeous as a man too."

"Well, thanks." I didn't know how to respond to the compliment. "This is my good friend Layla and, during the day, I'm Dylan."

She laughed at my crappy attempt at humour. "Hi, Layla, I think I remember seeing you on Friday too. How are you?"

She was observant which was a good sign for me.

"I'm good, and you?"

"Busy as usual, but you know how it goes." She looked to me again. "Wow, Dylan, I can't believe the difference. Most drag queens I could spot a mile off, but not you."

"Really?"

"Yeah, totally. Although you don't seem the usual type."

"I guess I'm not your run-of-the-mill queen. I always had the urge to dress up and perform but was too scared in case my friends found out, which is why I arrived and left in full drag."

"Whatever works for you, doll." She pulled the pad from her apron, poised to take our order. "You looked fantastic. I'll be there on Friday and hope to see you perform, but I'm on prep duty again Saturday so won't be able to stay past 11. Make sure you say hello if you see me."

"Of course I will."

"Okay, what are you having?" She looked to Layla first.

"The classic cheese burger meal and a diet cola," Layla replied.

"Same for me."

"Great, help yourself to the salad bar when you're ready."

"Will do, thanks. So, have you been to Dorothy's since Friday?" Not wanting her to leave just yet.

"I haven't but I was speaking to a friend of mine on my break earlier and remember that guy I was speaking to at the bar?"

"Yeah."

"Well, he's only been arrested for murder this morning."

"You're kidding me?" I couldn't believe the jungle drums had been beating already.

"No," Kimberley replied. "Another girl was found dead earlier–a right mess she was in, apparently."

"Shit!" I said, feeling bad for my deception. "Makes me nervous working there if some loony is after the girls."

"You'll be safe," Kimberley added. "Unless you're T, Darren wouldn't be interested."

"So you think it's him?"

"Like I said to you at the bar, he's an evil bastard."

"But murder though?"

"Who knows? It's just odd that three girls he's been mixed up with have ended up dead. Might be a coincidence but I wouldn't bet my life on it. Still, I feel a little safer with him behind bars. Let's hope they find something on him."

"Yeah," I said. "Just be careful coming and going in the meantime."

"Thanks, doll." She placed a hand on my shoulder.

"Right, is that it? I'm starving and all this talk of dead people is making me feel sick," Layla said rather brusquely, obviously not in the mood for idle chit-chat.

I was pissed off. Layla knew I was here to scout for information and had butted in at the wrong time.

"I'll leave you to it, Dylan." She glowered at Layla, seemingly unimpressed with my moody partner.

"Did you have to be so bloody rude?" I hissed once she'd gone.

"She doesn't know anything and I'm starving."

I wanted to make allowances for Layla even though she'd

really annoyed me. Manners cost nothing, but I wasn't about to cause an atmosphere taking her to task about her behaviour. It wouldn't do me any good. "It's nice being away from work, don't you think?"

"Yeah," she replied, quietly. "The constant noise in the office drives me to distraction. It's hard to think sometimes."

"I know what you mean." She appeared to be mellowing, so I thought I'd chance my luck and find out how things were going in her personal life. "You're having a rough time of it at the moment, so cut yourself some slack."

"I'm not the first or last person going through a divorce, Dylan."

"I know that." I offered a smile. "How are things with Max anyway?" I waited for her to tell me to mind my own business and was surprised when she didn't.

"Shit if I'm honest, but if I'm not enough for him..." Her words trailed off.

I didn't want to play counsellor as nothing I said would make her think differently about why Max had left her. It was clear she blamed herself for the breakup of her marriage, which was understandable, I guess. But, in my experience, it takes two to tango and Max had been the one who turned to another woman instead of trying to fix what he already had.

"Are the boys still upset over his visit the other night?"

She shrugged. "That's anybody's guess. I try to talk to them, you know, get them to open up but they keep a lot inside."

I felt for her. "That must be hard, worrying about them on top of everything else."

"Yeah, it is, although I'm more worried about Jake than the others." She blinked away tears. "It's bad enough he's acting up at home but being disruptive and disrespectful at school isn't doing him any favours. I've been called in for a meeting with the Headmaster." There was a slight hint of anger in her voice. "This is all since Max left so it's clearly affecting him."

"How do the other two seem?"

"Sad and hurt, which is understandable, but they seem to be coping much better than Jake."

"Max has a lot to answer for, doesn't he?"

She nodded and dabbed at her eyes. "I hate him."

I knew they were just words said in the heat of the moment. If she did indeed hate him, she wouldn't be hurting as much as she was right now.

"Do you have any other men in the family you can turn to, that could talk to Jake? Somebody he might open up to, maybe?" I was clutching at straws trying to find a resolution for at least one of her problems. "What about your dad?"

She shook her head. "I don't know where he is most of the time. He left Mum when I was nineteen and I'd already left home by then."

"And he didn't keep in touch with you?"

"Yeah, for a while. But the last I heard he'd gone to France—chasing some woman, no doubt. He's a waste of space to be honest."

"At least he had the decency to stay around until after you'd left home."

"Yeah. Although he was rarely home for the last few years I lived there, anyway. He worked away a lot."

My stomach growled, breaking the flow of conversation.

Her eyes widened with surprise. "What the heck was that? You sound like you've got a wild animal shoved up your shirt."

"Hey, cheeky. I'm starving."

"Come on then," she said, pushing herself away from the table. "Enough of my woes, let's eat."

Forty-five minutes later, stuffed up to the eyeballs on burgers and salad, we headed back to the office to await the arrival of Wilkes' solicitor.

———

At two o'clock that afternoon, Darren Wilkes sat in Interview Room 2 with his solicitor finally in attendance.

Layla accompanied me.

Once the recording had started, I began my questions.

"For the recording, can you please confirm you are Darren James Wilkes of Wapping Quay, Liverpool Three?"

"You know I am," he grunted. "Or I wouldn't be sitting here wasting my fucking time."

"And for the recording, acting as representation for Mr Wilkes is Mr Nigel Warfield of Layton & Warfield Solicitors. Is that correct, sir?"

"That is correct." Warfield nodded, his jowls jiggling.

"Thank you," I said, picking up my file from the desk. "Now, Mr Wilkes, can you confirm you know a Ms Rebecca Preston?"

"Yeah, I know her." He was slouched in his chair and I felt like kicking it out from underneath him—his attitude made me wild and tested my patience.

"And would you please detail the nature of your relationship with her?"

"There isn't a relationship, but we hook up sometimes."

"Would you clarify what you mean by hook up?"

Darren sat up and leaned towards the recorder. "It means we fuck sometimes. Clear enough or do you want me to draw you a picture?"

"Yes, clear enough. Thank you." I turned to look at Layla. Her lips had almost disappeared into a thin line.

"And when was the last time you saw Ms Preston?" I continued.

"Sometime last week," he answered.

"Where?"

"At her flat."

"Do you remember the exact day?" I asked.

"No–my days kind of melt into one."

"So, sometime last week but you can't remember exactly when?"

"I just said so, didn't I?"

"What was the purpose of your visit?"

"I was horny."

"So you and Ms Preston had an intimate arrangement, shall we say? "

"I'm intimate with a lot of people," he snapped, picking up the fizzy drink from the table and guzzling it.

"Are you intimate with many transsexuals?"

Warfield suddenly piped up. "What does that have to do with anything, detective?"

"If you'll allow me to explain–we have it on good authority, you are well known to the transsexual community, and I was merely trying to ascertain—"

Wilkes interrupted me. "I like to fuck trannies. It's not a crime, and they enjoy it, so what's the problem?"

"Any form of consensual sex is legal, Darren. But dealing drugs, namely unprescribed hormone medication isn't."

"I ain't been dealing nothing."

"We have evidence to the contrary."

Warfield jumped in again. "Then stop dancing around with this silly line of questioning and advise my client what you think you have."

"Fine," I said, irritated by the smug git. "Fingerprints were recovered from Ms Preston's property, and on several items inside, namely a bag used by the aforementioned to store drugs that had not been prescribed by her GP."

"Really, that's all you have to go on?" Warfield said with a grin. "My client already told you he had a casual relationship with Ms Preston, and has often visited her home, so the fact you have his fingerprints isn't a surprise. As for this bag, my client could have picked it up out of simple curiosity—it doesn't prove he's a dealer or a murderer, as you well know."

I hadn't yet mentioned Rebecca's death, but as Warfield clearly knew, it was time to change my line of questioning.

"As you may be aware, the body of Ms Preston was discovered in her apartment earlier today."

"I don't know anything," Wilkes snapped. "If she's dead, you ain't pinning it on me. You lot already tried that with Jade and that had nothing to do with me either."

"So, two individuals you were intimate with are found murdered, mutilated." I watched as he flinched at my words. "And it's just a coincidence?"

"Yeah, I guess it is."

"I see," I said, desperate to wipe the superior expression off his face. "Well, I'm sorry to burst your bubble, Darren. But not only are you a prime suspect for Rebecca's murder, but you're back in the frame for the death of Jade Kelly."

He jumped to his feet, the metal chair slamming backwards onto the concrete floor. "Bullshit! I was cleared for that! The CCTV camera proved it."

"Sit down, Mr Wilkes." I grinned, loving the fact I'd finally provoked a reaction from him.

Warfield picked up the chair and Wilkes sat down again.

I continued. "Yes, well, unfortunately, my colleague wasn't a well man and missed the fact there was actually a rear exit from Rebecca's flat. You could have come and gone un-noticed anytime. Rebecca hadn't provided you with an alibi for the entire night. She vouched for you arriving and the fact you were there in the morning, but she didn't know what you got up to during the hours in-between while she was sleeping."

He shook his head, clearly exasperated, and looked at his solicitor for help.

Warfield shrugged and glanced down at the papers in front of him.

"So, by your own admission, you called in to see Rebecca a few days ago. Thursday at 7:34pm to be exact, as you entered via the front door and left at 8:05pm—you were picked up on the CCTV."

"So what? I already admitted seeing her last week, what's that got to do with anything?"

"Well, I'm pretty certain you used that visit to plan your next move."

"What the fuck's that supposed to mean?"

"I believe you released the fire-escape ladder, in order to let yourself in undetected on Friday night."

"This is all purely circumstantial, detective. None of it's going to stick," Warfield said.

"Then I'll have to make sure I find enough evidence to *make* it stick. Won't I?"

I stormed back towards the incident room with Layla trailing behind me.

"Slow down, Dylan," she called.

I carried on walking. "That slimy bastard is right. We need more evidence."

"We don't know what Lauren will find yet so calm down and let's just wait and see."

"People are dying, Layla. We don't have time to wait and see."

"I didn't mean it like that."

"Will," I barked, pushing the double doors open. "Any news on the CCTV?"

"Yeah, just in, boss. The cameras didn't pick anything up."

"How is that even possible?" My blood was now at boiling point. "Can you explain it? Because for the life of me..." I stopped and shook my head, pinching the bridge of my nose.

Will approached. "Maybe our killer knew where the cameras were located and avoided them."

"You're kidding me, right?"

Will shrugged one shoulder.

This was beyond ridiculous. "How does any member of the public know where all the cameras are?"

"Search me," Will replied.

"*I* don't know where most of them are. That's impossible, isn't it?"

"What other explanation could there be?" Will asked, returning to his desk. "Not one camera picked up the Transit van on Friday, but there could be another explanation and don't have a go as it's just my opinion."

"What?" I asked.

"Maybe you didn't see the van after all?"

"I didn't imagine it."

"You'd had a busy day—"

"I saw the fucking van, Will. Trust me on that."

"Okay, okay, it was just a suggestion, boss."

I could feel a headache coming on and sat at my desk pinching the bridge of my nose again.

TWENTY-SIX

Bella's invite for coffee couldn't have come at a better time. I was more stressed than I'd ever been and couldn't speak to Layla without her biting my head off.

She opened the door and I was surprised to see she was back in her jeans.

"Wow! You look great."

"Hiya, gorgeous." She beamed.

I pulled her in for a hug.

"Come in, the kettle's already on."

I followed her through to the kitchen. "What are you cooking? It smells delicious."

"Lasagne, for dinner. You can take some home for later, if you want?"

"Sounds good to me. Is Simon not joining us for coffee?"

"He'll be home soon. He's just taken the baby around the block in the pram."

"How's everything?"

"Baby's been a little unsettled today. Simon thought the motion of the pram might send him off to sleep."

"Aw, I can't wait to give him a cuddle. Can I help with anything?"

"Nope. Sit down and relax."

She handed me a steaming mug of coffee "So, tell me what's going on while we have the house to ourselves."

I sipped at my drink. "This makes a change from the muck they give us at the station."

"Come on. What's going on?"

"The whole case is a nightmare—you've seen the news, I'm guessing?"

"Yeah, I see there's been another murder but they don't give the specifics."

"You don't wanna hear them, trust me."

"That bad?"

"Worse." I placed the mug down onto the table. "I've seen some crime scenes over the years, but this was fucking barbaric—what he did to her sickens me."

"Are you any closer to solving the case?"

"We've got Darren Wilkes in custody right now. We can't hold him forever, but that's more complicated than it sounds."

"How so?"

"Our latest victim gave Wilkes the alibi for Jade Kelly's murder—he was supposedly with her all night, but there's a hole in his alibi."

"A hole?"

"Yeah," I said, feeling like a traitor for what I was about to reveal. "Fred Savage and Layla investigated Jade's murder, and interviewed Rebecca, but both of them failed to notice there was a rear entrance to the place with a fire-escape ladder that rolled down to the alleyway behind her property."

"Shit!"

I nodded. "Wilkes was seen arriving at Rebecca's and leaving the following morning, but he could have snuck out when she was asleep and used the other entrance, and we'd be none the wiser."

"And neither of them picked up on it?"

"Nope."

"Did you mention it to Janine?"

"I haven't said anything yet because I don't want to hang my own partner out to dry."

"You have to tell her, Dylan."

"I know, but Layla doesn't need it right now."

"Are things still bad for her and Max?"

"I assume so, but I don't know for sure. She won't talk about him anymore."

"That's understandable."

"Yeah, I get it, but missing something as important as that is a massive fuck up, and if it turns out Wilkes is our killer and two of our officers screwed up, it's gonna cause a massive stink."

"Yeah, I don't envy you right now. You'll have to speak to Janine."

"Then face the wrath of the rest of the team—that lot will never trust me again, and you know it."

"Tough." Bella pushed her mug away. "People are dying, Dylan. You don't have any other choice right now. Tell Janine because if you don't and she finds out some other way, she'll hand your arse to you on a platter."

"I'll tell her when I get back to the station, but I need to let Layla know first so she can come up with some sort of explanation."

"There isn't an explanation for misconduct, Dylan."

Bella could be a hard-faced, bitch sometimes and, while I knew she was right, Layla was still my partner, albeit temporarily. I didn't want to feed her to the wolves, but I had no choice. "Yeah, I know. I'll sort it." I got to my feet.

"Are you going already?"

"Yeah, I'm sorry, this is playing on my mind, and I need to deal with it."

"Let me plate that food up."

"Sorry for being such a misery, Bells. I'll try to come back tomorrow for a cuddle, if that's okay?"

"Sure, but Simon might not like it."

"Ha bloody ha, you know I meant the baby." It felt good to smile, but once I returned to the station, I knew my mood would darken.

"I'll see you Friday night anyway, remember. Roy is picking me up and bringing me to Dorothy's. I can't wait."

"Oh, joy," I replied, sarcastically. "Just what I need, but I'm glad you reminded me because I need to call him and see if he's still helping me out on Friday. I was a bit of an arse when we lost the Transit van."

"Erm, what am I missing?" She handed me two large tubs full of Lasagne.

"Sorry, I forgot to tell you, but I'll fill you in tomorrow."

"You better."

"Promise," I said, heading for the door. "Thanks for the food and make sure you give Lily and baby Dylan a kiss from me."

"Will do," she said walking me out. "Cheer up. You're doing a sterling job."

"I'm not sure I share your optimism, but thanks."

I leaned in to kiss her cheek. Once I was at the car, I called Roy. He answered after a few rings.

"Well, hello, darling."

"Hiya, Roy. How are you?"

"Rushed off my size nines, but that's nothing new."

"Sorry to hear that, but I'll only take a minute of your time."

"What is it?"

"I was hoping you'd still be up for helping me on Friday?"

"Why wouldn't I be?"

"After making you play car chase the other night, I thought I might have put you off?"

"It played havoc with my nerves, darling, I'm not going to lie, but it was the most excitement I've had on a Friday night for ages. So don't worry, of course I'm still going to help you, especially after seeing the news about that poor young girl."

"Thanks, Roy, I couldn't manage without you."

"No thanks needed. Now, have you decided on what song you're going to do this week?"

"I really haven't."

"And what about what you'll wear?"

"You're gonna hate me but I haven't a clue about that either."

"No matter," he replied. "I have the perfect outfit in mind, but it's very daring."

I wasn't in the mood to argue. If I had to wear it, then I'd wear it. After all, I couldn't be petulant because Roy was doing this as a favour and in his own time.

"So, what colour is the dress?" I couldn't believe I was even asking that.

"It's a lovely shade of lime green, darling, but not exactly a dress."

"Then what is it, dare I ask?"

"It's more of a tight sequinned body stocking, but you'll need some tucking panties. I think I have some lying around that should do the trick."

"Oh, God." My heart sank. "How tight is this body stocking?"

"Skin-tight, but with your figure, you'll look sensational. Add a pair of Cerise Pink knee-high boots and matching wig, you're gonna look out of this world."

Something told me Roy was enjoying using me as his very own *Barbie* doll. "Jesus, isn't that a bit in your face?"

"You're a drag queen, not a Miss World contestant."

Well that told me. "Okay, you're the expert."

In my mind's eye it made for a revolting combination, but I'd grin and bear it. "Do you think it's a bit camp?"

"Totally over the top, but that's what you want. If you're gonna do something, make it count."

"Okay," I replied, dreading Friday more than ever. "I'll think of something to lip sync to. Are you free on Wednesday evening? We can have a run through of the performance and I'll cook you some dinner."

"Sounds good to me. You know Bella's coming on Friday, right?"

"Don't remind me."

"Okay, darling, I must go. If you think of a song, text me and I'll get my thinking cap on in the meantime."

I turned the engine on, the loud music pumping out of the radio making me jump. But I'd just had an idea what song I could lip-sync to and texted Roy straight away.

What do you think about Express Yourself by Madonna?

I really wasn't a Madonna fan at all, but I knew this song well and thought it would get the crowd going.

PERFECT!

That was a relief. I would need to download it when I got home and put some moves together before seeing Roy on Wednesday. I couldn't leave everything to him.

TWENTY-SEVEN

I hesitated before knocking on Janine's door, not in the mood to take an ear bashing for something that was beyond my control. The station was famous for second-hand gossip, and what she needed to know was better coming from me. I couldn't put it off any longer and decided to bite the bullet.

I knocked quietly.

"Come in."

Turning the knob and pushing the door, I peeped my head around. "Got a few minutes?"

"Sure, come on in."

"Thanks."

"Take a seat."

I sat opposite her and took a deep breath.

"Something tells me I'm not going to like this, Dylan."

"You're not, but I'd rather you heard it from me."

"Go on then, spit it out."

"While investigating the Rebecca Preston case, I discovered a huge fuck up pertaining to the Jade Kelly murder."

"And you're about to tell me it was something to do with forensics, right?" That was wishful thinking on her part.

"I wish that was the case."

She clasped her hands together as if in prayer and rested them on her desk, leaning closer. "Go on."

"It seems two officers overlooked another exit at Rebecca's flat."

"What do you mean?"

"There was a fire escape exit—"

"And you're telling me two of our own didn't spot it?"

"Correct. Which means the alibi given by Rebecca for Darren Wilkes won't stand up in court. He could've left her flat and returned without her knowing."

She exhaled loudly, her cheeks looking flushed. "This is the last thing I wanted to hear, Dylan."

"I know."

"Who are the officers in question?"

"Fred Savage and Layla Monahan."

Janine's eyes narrowed into tiny slits. "Fuck."

"Exactly. I wanted to keep you informed, but it doesn't sit right with me dropping my own partner in the shit. However, the ramifications are huge. If Wilkes *is* our man, our error allowed him to roam free and commit another two murders."

"You did the right thing. Savage I can do nothing about now, but Layla has screwed up big time and there will be consequences."

I was worried. Not just for Layla and what she was going through right now, but the overall morale of the team. "I'll handle this any way you need me to."

Janine pinched her bottom lip, something she always did when thinking. "Ask Layla for a written account of what happened on the day in question."

"What good will that do?"

"It leaves a paper trail for one, in case Wilkes *is* our killer."

"Okay, and then what?"

"I'm unwilling to take it down the disciplinary route at this stage, but if it comes up at a later date, the statement from Layla shows we knew and acted accordingly."

"Got it."

"In the meantime, have a quiet word with the team and tell them no more fuck ups will be tolerated."

"I'll sort Layla first then have a briefing."

"Anything else, come straight to me. The powers that be are breathing down my neck on this one, and with no solid leads, we're looking more and more inept as the days go by."

"It's only gonna get worse because I think we'll have to release Wilkes, for now at least. We have nothing concrete to pin on him."

She shook her head. "He's like a cat with nine lives that one. Do what you can. He's the only suspect we have right now."

"I'm on it." I got to my feet.

"Thanks, Dylan."

I nodded then closed the door behind me, dreading this next conversation.

———

I dialled Layla's mobile.

"Hello?" she answered, sounding puzzled.

"Hi, Layla. Do you have a few minutes?"

"Sure," she replied. "Where are you?"

"Interview Room 3."

She paused. "Oh, okay. Give me two minutes and I'll be there."

I ended the call, hoping she would understand the reason for the meeting and realise my actions weren't personal.

Moments later there was a tap on the door. "Come in," I called.

Layla stepped into the room and took a seat opposite me. "What's all this about, Dylan?"

I decided it was easier to get right to the point. "I spoke to Janine earlier and had to tell her about the exit neither you nor Savage noticed."

The colour drained from her cheeks. "Am I gonna lose my job?"

"God, no. Nothing like that, but I had to tell her. You understand that, don't you?"

Tears filled her eyes. "My job is all I have."

"You won't lose your job, Layla," I couldn't guarantee that, but I could see she was hanging on by a thread. "You'll need to provide a written statement about the day in question–Janine's orders."

"I bet she thinks I'm useless." Tears trickled down her cheeks.

"She never said anything of the kind, but thinks a written statement is the best way to go in case Wilkes *is* the killer."

"You know Savage liked to fly solo. He would get me to stay office-based more often than not, so I wasn't about to question him when he did let me tag along. Now, if Darren Wilkes is the killer, I'll refuse to take the blame. He was the senior detective, not me."

"I know that, we all do."

"But what if it turns out it was Wilkes? What then?"

"I don't know. That wouldn't be up to me to decide."

"So I could still lose my job."

"Getting Wilkes off the street is the most important thing right now."

"Maybe for you, but I'm a single mother and have three kids to feed. Max is being a total arse right now and without a job that would be impossible."

"Try not to worry. I'm sure it won't come to that. If you could get me that statement by the end of the day, I'd—"

"Yeah, I'll give you the evidence you need to get me fired." She pushed her chair back and jumped to her feet.

"Layla, it's nothing like that, I promise—"

"Don't bother making excuses, Dylan." She stormed out of the room.

I followed swiftly behind as she barged into the incident room, drawing all eyes towards her.

"Layla, please, not here."

"If I'm gonna lose my job, I'd rather it wasn't all hush hush."

All eyes now turned to me. I could see the confusion as well as the suspicion behind their glares. Layla was one of them, just like I used to be before my promotion. Now, all the hard work I'd put in to win their trust was about to be blown out of the water.

"You're not going to lose your job, but please, let's discuss this in private."

"Fuck you, Dylan." She grabbed her bag from under her desk, then pushed past me, rushing out of the room and along the corridor.

I ran after her. "Layla, please, talk to me."

"Don't follow me," she screamed, disappearing through the doors at the end of the corridor.

I didn't want to upset her any more than I had already and decided to let her go. Hopefully, when she calmed down, we could talk, and she would see I was on her side. I felt horrible about the whole situation.

Back in the deathly quiet incident room, the team simply stared at me. I shouldn't discuss anything private with them, but they needed to know about Savage and Layla's screw up.

Will was the first to speak. "What's going on, boss? Is Layla getting the boot?"

"No, Will, she's not."

"Then why is she in that state?" Joanna asked.

Will spoke up again. "Come on, Dylan, we need to know what's happening."

"I'll tell you what I can." I took a deep breath. "You might already know this, but when Savage and Layla interviewed Rebecca Preston, they messed up and missed a window exit with a fire escape ladder."

"What does that mean for the investigation?" Joanna asked.

"Rebecca gave Wilkes an alibi over Jade's death, saying he was with her all night, but it's not as cut and dried as it appeared because Wilkes could have used the window exit and returned without Rebecca knowing anything about it. CCTV wouldn't have picked him up which means not only did he have the motive but also the opportunity to murder Jade."

"And Layla will have to take the fall because Savage is no longer here?" Joanna shook her head, a sneer on her face.

"No, it's nothing like that at all, Jo."

"Then what is it?" Will asked.

"I don't know why I'm even having to explain this to any of you, but I will anyway."

"Go on then," Tommo said.

"If Wilkes does turn out to be our killer, the fact two of our own screwed up allowed him the freedom to commit two further murders. It's as simple as that. Can you imagine the headlines?"

"And if he isn't the killer?" Joanna asked. "What then?"

"Then nothing. We get on with what we're paid to do." I decided I might as well lay my cards on the table. "But, if he is, you all know what that means. Take Layla out of the equation for just a moment and tell me what you think would happen to *any* officer who was negligent to the point a killer was released back into the community to brutally murder two more people." I looked about the room. "Well?"

"We get it, Dylan." Will didn't look happy. "But she's one of us and—"

I interrupted. "And she's *my* partner, or did you all forget that part?"

Joanna put her head down. "I'm sorry, Dylan."

"I don't want your apologies, but you might try to keep in mind I'm still part of this team, regardless of my position." My blood was at boiling point. "I never have and never will hang any of my colleagues out to dry, even if they *have* fucked up. I'd always do my best to help them, and you lot would do well to remember that."

"We don't think you'd hang any of us out to dry, boss," Will mumbled.

"Layla has a lot going on right now with her personal life, we all know that, but she's still one of us." I needed a strong drink by this point. "I'll fight for her as much as I can, like I would for any of you in here, but both she and Savage fucked up and that's the black and white of it."

"I'll call her after work and see if she needs anything," Joanna said.

"You do that. I'll be speaking to her myself later. Now, if there's nothing else, I need to get on with my job."

TWENTY-EIGHT

"Penny for them," Steve said the next morning as he handed me a steaming mug of coffee.

I shuffled up in the bed to a sitting position. "Oh, thanks. I could get used to this." I grinned.

"So, what's wrong? You were miles away then."

I exhaled with a controlled blow. "It's just this case I'm working on. We think we know who the killer is, but can't catch a break at all. We're gonna have to let the scumbag go today, by the looks of things."

"Do you tail your suspects these days?"

"We didn't just step out of an episode of *The Bill*, you know?" I laughed.

"Shut up. I know that. But sometimes going back to basics is the best way. I could come along with you to the stake-out. Bring my flask of tea and egg mayo butties."

I gagged. "You'd stink like you'd shit yourself in the confines of the car—no thanks."

"Charming. That's all the thanks I get for putting my life on the line in the name of love."

I knew he was joking, but his use of the 'L' word made my stomach flip. "Well, maybe we could make a deal—lose the fart sandwiches and we can re-negotiate."

"Too late. I revoke my offer."

"That was quick!" I chuckled, taking a sip of the coffee. "When did you have a shower anyway?" I said, noticing his wet hair.

"While the coffee was brewing and you were snoring."

"I don't snore!"

"Really? How do you know you don't?"

"I just know."

"You do this real cute snorty thing, like a little pig."

"Fuck off! No I don't."

He nodded, annoyingly. "Yeah, you do."

He got up off the bed and let the towel drop to the carpet, displaying his toned body.

Taking one final sip of coffee, I jumped out of bed and ran for the bathroom—distractions were definitely not allowed until I had solved this case.

Freshly showered and wrapped from the waist down in a towel, I returned to the bedroom.

Steve, now dressed, stood in front of the full-length mirror fiddling with his tie. He was every inch the typical accountant.

"You came prepared." I nodded at his overnight bag.

"Is that a problem?" He eyed my reflection.

"Not at all. In fact you could always leave a few bits here. The spare bedroom has an empty wardrobe and chest of drawers if you wanted to make use of them."

"Really? You don't mind?"

"I wouldn't have offered if I did."

"It *would* make life a little easier if I didn't have to lug a bag with me every day."

Things did seem to be moving pretty fast since we'd decided to turn the relationship up a notch, but it felt like a natural progression—we'd been seeing each other casually for a few months already.

I dressed in grey slacks and a light blue shirt—my usual work attire—then kissed the tip of his nose before darting from the room. "Will I see you tonight?" I called over my shoulder.

"Can do. Shall I bring dinner?"

"Sounds good. Take the spare key from the drawer beside the kitchen door in case you get here before I do." There, I'd done it. Giving him a key was definitely taking things to the next level. I'd never let anyone have a key to my place before, and yet I'd done it so easily with him. This was the way things were meant to be—effortless—cruisy.

I found a muesli bar in the kitchen cupboard, slipped my shoes on, and grabbed my jacket off the hook before heading out the door.

In the car, I called Will. "We're going to have to let Wilkes go, unless there's anything else we can use to keep hold of him?"

"No, boss. Nothing. And his brief is shit hot and is already putting pressure on us."

"Damn. Okay, you better arrange for his release then. Oh and get someone to tail him for a while. You never know, he might just lead us to the van, or something we're missing."

"I'll sort it," Will said. "Leave it with me. Did Layla get hold of you, by the way?"

"No. I tried to call her last night but she wouldn't pick up."

"Well, she just rang here looking for you, she wanted to leave a message but I told her to get hold of you direct, so expect a call."

Just then, my phone vibrated in my ear.

"Gotta go, Will. See you soon." I answered the call then turned on the engine. Layla's voice came over the loud speakers.

"I won't be in today. I'm sick."

"Really? Nothing too bad, I hope."

"Women's problems."

I knew it was a lie, she was still licking her wounds from yesterday, but there was nothing I could do about it. "Can we find some time to talk? I think you got the wrong end of the stick yesterday."

"I don't want to talk about work—I'm on the sick."

"Of course. Hope you're feeling better soon. Call me tomorrow if you're not coming in again." I said, tight-lipped and silently seething. We were now three people down. How the hell was I expected to catch a psychotic killer when I didn't even have a full functioning team at my disposal?

The day was uneventful. In fact, it couldn't have been any more boring. I had a mountain of paperwork to catch up on so I got stuck into that which took the majority of the day and I still hadn't finished. Not only did I have my own work to complete and file but Savage hadn't been at the top of his game in the paperwork department.

I was glad to finally get home, relieved I didn't have to cook because Steve was bringing takeaway. Slouching onto the sofa, I heard the key in the lock, and, for a moment, forgot I'd told Steve to take it.

"I'm in the living room," I called out.

Steve popped his head round the door and smiled. "Good day?"

"Crap to be honest, but seeing you, it just got better."

"You're only saying that because I have bags of food in my hands?"

The aroma from the food soon captured my attention "I'm saying nothing," I replied, teasing.

"Right, you stay there and put your feet up and I'll get the plates and bring everything to you."

"No, it's okay, let's eat at the table."

"Are you sure?"

"Yeah," I said, hauling my arse off the sofa and planting a big kiss on his cheek.

TWENTY-NINE

Still nothing to go on the next day, I completed the last of the paperwork. Afterwards, I began trawling through the case files once again, positive we must be missing something, but it was a fruitless task. I packed up early and headed home to prepare for Roy.

An expert at preparing comfort food, I'd cooked a nice, hearty meal and hoped Roy would enjoy it. I'd told Steve I was busy tonight, not ready for him to see me in all my Avaline glory just yet.

It had been pissing down for half an hour when the doorbell rang. I dried my hands on a tea towel then rushed to answer it.

"About time, darling," he snipped.

"Hello to you, too." I stepped aside allowing him entry.

"Sorry, today has been hellish, but I'm here in one piece and something smells divine."

"Braised steak, mashed potato, carrots and green beans."

"Lovely," he said, weighed down. "Let me put this stuff down somewhere and I can give you a hand."

"Dinner is already cooked and ready to serve." I took hold of the zipped up bag with the hanger attached, and the heavy makeup case, placing them carefully on the sofa.

"Thanks," he replied. "Yes, if we eat first, it gives us time to get on without interruption. Afterwards, I can steam your outfit again and make sure it looks ready for showtime."

"Sounds good to me." I led him into the kitchen. "Do you want a tea or coffee?"

"Strong black coffee please, no sugar."

That was easily sorted. "Take a seat while I make the drink and dish up."

"It's very kind of you to invite me round for a bite to eat. I usually eat alone, unless you count Liza for company."

"Liza?"

"My cat."

"Oh," I said, trying to keep a straight face, making a mental note to send any scraps of meat home with him. "Well, you're welcome here anytime."

"You know, I thought you didn't like me."

"What gave you that idea?" I felt bad because he was a great guy.

"Oh, I dunno, most gay guys like you run a mile when they see an effeminate man."

"I *was* wary, I won't lie, but now I've got to know you, I feel like I've found a friend for life."

"Awww, don't," he said, wafting his hand in front of his face. "I've got a touch of makeup on and you'll have me looking a mess if it runs."

"A touch of makeup–you're kidding aren't you?" I don't know what possessed me but I'd said it before I could stop myself.

"Cheeky bitch," he said with a glint in his eye.

And we both laughed which was why I liked him so much. He was easy to talk to. I enjoyed the time we spent together.

"I mean what I say—you're welcome here anytime you feel like some company."

"Thank you, darling, that means the world to me. Now move your arse—I could eat a horse."

"Yes, sir," I replied sorting the drink.

We laughed over dinner and Roy indulged in second helpings which was good to see, so my cooking can't have been that bad. It was a shame we couldn't partake in a glass of wine or two, but work beckoned.

Moving into the sitting room, he unzipped the outfit on the hanger.

"That *isn't* what you described to me."

"I know, I know, but you're doing the Queen of Pop so I thought we'd go full throttle. I even found a monocle you can use."

"A monocle, what do I need a monocle for?"

"Pass me that phone and I'll show you."

He showed me a video of Madonna performing *Express Yourself* live on stage, wearing a man's suit with a pink conical bra underneath the jacket. She used the monocle as a prop to great effect. Shania, I could just about pull off, but this was ambitious to say the least.

Five minutes later, my heart was in my mouth. "And you really expect me to be able to do that?"

"No chance, but even a few moves with a nod in that direction and you'll be a smash, trust me."

"I'm not sure about this, Roy."

"Nonsense," he replied. "Did you download the song?"

"Yeah." I was trembling with nerves.

"And you know the words?"

"I do."

"Then we're halfway there. Sit there for a moment and watch me, okay."

Still wary of the neighbours, I closed the curtains then plonked myself down on the sofa, and pressed play on the remote as an incarnation of Madonna emerged before my very eyes.

After the song had finished, he took a bow.

I clapped, massively impressed.

"See, it's easy."

"For you, maybe, but I'm not sure I'll look anywhere near as good as you did."

"You'll be fine. A few slut drops here and there, that lot will be asking for autographs."

"Slut drops," I shouted out. "I can't do a slut drop, in or out of heels, Roy."

"Have some faith, please."

Faith was one thing, but delusions were another.

―――――――

"Not bad, darling, but let's go through it a few more times and I think you're there," Roy said.

"I told you I couldn't do a slut drop."

"We can take that out—it's supposed to be sexy, but you looked like you'd thrown your back out."

I burst out laughing, despite the insult. "Thanks. But I'd rather try—I'm not one to be beaten."

"You're welcome. And it's up to you. Now hit the play button and focus, we don't have long to have you looking halfway decent."

THIRTY

I hadn't heard a thing from Layla, so assumed she would be in the office when I arrived.

To my surprise and annoyance, she wasn't there.

"Morning," I said looking towards Joanna and Will. "Is Layla about?"

Will popped his head up from behind his computer screen. "Morning, boss. Not seen her yet. Have you, Jo?"

Joanna shook her head. "I haven't seen her either. Isn't she supposed to be on the sick?"

I didn't want to answer her question. "If you hear from her can you let me know? I was expecting her in today."

"No worries."

I turned to Will. "I'm just gonna head in to see Janine."

"Right-o," he replied.

"Jo, I need to have a quick word after I've seen Janine, don't go anywhere."

She looked at me and I could see her mind ticking over, wondering if she'd done something wrong. "Okay."

I made my way down the corridor and knocked on Janine's door.

"Enter," she bellowed.

I stepped inside. "Morning, Dylan. Come on in."

"Thanks." I took a seat. "I'll apologise beforehand but I need to have a moan."

She rolled her eyes. "Go on."

"First of all, Layla is a no show this morning and she hasn't called me to say she won't be in."

"Have you called her?"

"Not yet."

"Then do it."

"Now?"

"No better time," she snipped. "If Layla isn't going to be in, she knows the procedure."

"Guess so," I said pulling my phone from my pocket and dialled her number. It went straight through to her voicemail. I hated leaving messages, but did so anyway, asking her to contact me urgently.

"Let me know what's happening with her, will you?"

"Will do."

"What else do you want me for?"

"I need more officers urgently–we're grossly understaffed, and with Layla sick, I'm three people down."

"I can't just snap my fingers and magic three new people, Dylan. There are other cases besides yours."

"Well, when the shit hits the fan, don't say I didn't try."

"Is the pressure getting to you? You seem a little snippy today."

"No, the pressure isn't getting to me in that way, but I'm busting my balls here trying to find this lunatic, plus Jade Kelly gets cremated this afternoon, and I don't know how I'm going to face her family."

"It happens to us all, but I'm confident you're doing all you can to solve this, but leave it with me and I'll do my best to get you at least one other person to cover by tomorrow. Will that help?"

"Anything will help."

"Let's hope Layla's back soon."

"I know it's against policy, but I'm going to head around to see her if I don't hear anything in the next few days."

"If Layla doesn't follow absence procedure, the end of her marriage won't be the only thing she has to worry about."

I didn't want to get into a bitchfest about my partner, and so I excused myself.

Coffee called, so I headed straight to the staffroom and grabbed a cup, taking it back to my office, almost forgetting I needed to speak to Joanna.

"Jo," I called. "Can I grab a quick word now?"

"Sure," she replied, plonking herself down on the chair on the other side of the desk.

"It's nothing urgent but as I don't know what's happening with Layla yet, I wondered if you'd mind accompanying me to Jade's funeral this afternoon?"

"Of course, I will."

"Great, we'll take my car."

The tiny crematorium was packed to the rafters with people from all walks of life. They congregated on the front steps and just inside the miniscule foyer, either hugging and comforting one another, or eyeing each other with disdain and indifference—no different to any other funeral I'd attended. All families are complex, no matter how small and tight-knit. I've found there's always a black sheep, a sleazy uncle, and at least two people who haven't spoken in years.

Joanna and I watched from the car initially, not wanting to intrude on anybody's grief but needing to witness any odd behaviour or identify any dodgy looking mourners.

"So what now?" Joanna asked. "I've not been to a victim's funeral before."

"We watch and wait. Once everyone goes inside, we can slip in the back. Hopefully they'll have a sign-in register in the foyer we can photograph and check out any names we don't recognise and their connection to the victims. We'll be able to cross reference that list with those who attend Gina's funeral too."

We waited until everyone vanished through the doors before leaving the warmth of the car and heading inside.

It was standing room only at the back of the chapel. Joanna and I slipped in, relatively unnoticed, and scanned the room.

All I could see was the back of everyone's head, but I couldn't see anyone who resembled Wilkes anywhere. Maybe he wouldn't turn up, but I would be surprised. The narcissistic prick wouldn't be able to help himself.

Halfway through the service, I noticed a movement beside the door and a collective hushed whisper spread around the room, accompanied by several disgruntled people who'd turned to face the door, shooting daggers at someone.

Stepping forwards, I finally caught sight of what had caused the commotion. Darren Wilkes stood just inside the doorway, wearing a full length burgundy coloured overcoat which caught everyone's eye in the sea of black and sombre colours. "Bingo," I muttered to Joanna, nodding my head in his direction.

The sound of running footfalls caught my attention, seeming strange considering the circumstances, and a young man, probably in his early twenties, flew up the aisle towards Wilkes, his huge fists balled, ready for a fight.

Also running now, I headed for Wilkes putting myself in-between both men.

"Get outta my way!" the young man yelled at several other mourners who had seen and pre-empted what he was about to do and blocked his way.

I turned and bundled Wilkes out the door, shoving him harder than I needed to when we got out to the concrete.

He stumbled, but unfortunately managed to stop himself tumbling down the steps. "What the hell are you doing?" he roared at me.

"Saving your bacon, you ungrateful little prick," I hissed.

"That's assault. You assaulted me."

"Believe me, if I assaulted you, you wouldn't be standing there whinging about it. Now, it looks as though you're not welcome here, so do yourself a favour and leave."

"I'm here to pay my respects. Jade *was* my girlfriend when all's said and done."

"If you set foot back in there, don't expect me to save you from getting lynched. Now, if you've got any decency, you won't make this day any harder for Jade's family—just go."

He scratched his head, took a few paces towards the doors again, where Joanna stood observing, threw his hands up, sucked in air over his teeth and stomped off towards the carpark.

The rest of the service went without a hitch.

I was glad to get home and decided to get a practice run in on my performance ready for Friday. Steve was coming for dinner and I wanted to be done by then.

Roy told me to practise in front of a mirror, but I hated seeing myself flouncing about pulling all manner of strange faces. While I admit to enjoying the actual performance on stage with the audience egging me on, the preparation was hell, and the heels weren't helping matters at all. I found a new admiration for female performers and women in general—heels were murder on my feet *and* my back.

I put the shoes away, and any evidence of my upcoming performance just before Steve arrived laden down with takeaway bags. He was a welcome sight. I was starving and tucked into the Indian food with gusto.

I had to laugh at Steve. He was struggling with a simple korma while I shovelled a red hot vindaloo into my mouth.

His face was red and sweat ran down his forehead. "My gob is burning. I don't know how you manage to eat that vindaloo."

"The hotter the better for me," I said in between bites of naan bread I was using to mop up some of the curry sauce.

"Your arse will be on fire in the morning."

Steve could make me laugh so easily. His humour was on par with mine. "Behave yourself or I'll dish it up for breakfast."

He laughed too. "No chance."

I put my fork down on the plate and rubbed my belly. "I'm stuffed up to the eyeballs."

"Not surprising really. I've never seen somebody eat as much as you do and not gain weight."

"If I carry on like this, I'll be as fat as a pig. Unless that's your plan?"

"You've rumbled me–dammit." He smirked.

"Yeah, I know your game—turn me into a chunker so nobody else wants me."

He leaned in to give me a quick peck on the lips. "That's all you're getting until you brush your teeth."

"Cheek!" I pushed myself up, wanting to rinse the dishes and shove them in the dishwasher out of the way. "You'll have to wait until I sort this mess out."

"I'll give you a hand."

"No, it's okay, you stay there. It won't take me long." I stacked the plates and picked them up. "You can decide what we're going to watch."

"Oh, don't leave that decision to me. Any requests?"

"See what movies are on Netflix, but no horror."

"You know what? For a copper, you're a big baby."

"I see enough blood and gore at work thank you very much."

"Yeah, I didn't think about that."

"Maybe that new *Lost in Space* series I've been dying to watch."

"Okay," he replied.

I walked into the kitchen and set about clearing up. My mind wandered to the case and of course, Darren Wilkes wasn't far from my mind.

Closing the dishwasher, I looked around to check nothing had been missed. The place was spotless. Now I could snuggle up to Steve and relax in front of the TV, with a well-deserved glass of wine.

I turned the kitchen light off and walked into the living room.

Steve was pawing through the case file I'd brought home and he obviously hadn't heard me.

"What do you think you're doing?"

He turned to look at me, shocked I'd caught him in the act. "I-I was just curious that's all."

I stormed towards him and snatched the file out of his hands. "You shouldn't be reading that. It's highly confidential." I was fuming.

"I'm sorry, but you've been so wrapped up in this case and, after everything I've seen on the news, I just—"

"My work is my work and nothing to do with you, got it?"

"I didn't mean to upset you."

I slammed the file down on the table. "I think you should just go home."

"Come on, Dylan. I screwed up, but I didn't mean any harm."

"Trust is everything to me, Steve."

"Are you saying you don't trust me now?"

"What would you think if the shoe was on the other foot? If you found me poking into stuff that was none of my concern?" He didn't answer. "Well?"

"Look, I'll go. But I'll call you tomorrow."

At that moment I couldn't care less if I never saw him again. "Suit yourself," I replied, picking up the file and stomping off upstairs.

A few minutes later I heard the front door slam slut.

THIRTY-ONE

I hadn't slept too well, still blazing with Steve for nosing through my files.

But I couldn't afford to dwell on it as today was going to be a long one. I didn't have a clue what time I was on stage at Dorothy's, so it could turn out to be a very late night.

Sliding out of bed, I hurried into the bathroom desperate for a pee. When I'd finished, I took a hot shower.

I was dressed and out of the house by 8am, wanting to beat rush hour traffic. As I pulled into my allotted parking space, my phone rang. It was Steve. I debated answering, but, as I'd mellowed a touch, I decided to get the conversation out of the way.

"Morning," I said, speaking through my handsfree kit.

"I'm glad you answered. I didn't think you would," he replied. "I just wanted to apologise because I was well out of order."

"You had no right to go through my things, Steve,"

"I know, and I wish I could turn back the clock."

"Look..." I said, not wanting a long drawn out conversation

about it. "... my work is very important to me, and as long as you respect that, we won't have a problem."

"So you forgive me?" He used a cutesy voice that made me cringe a little, but I wasn't the type to hold a grudge.

"If you promise not to do it again, yeah."

"I promise."

"Then, let's forget it, shall we?"

We only spoke for a few minutes because I had so much to do. But I promised to call him when I got home from Dorothy's.

I felt better after clearing the air and walked into the station, much chirpier than I'd been an hour ago.

"Morning, boss." Will popped his head up.

"Christ," I said, surprised to see him. "Are you always in first?"

"I like to get a head start before the rabble get here."

"Don't blame you." I plonked my things on my desk. "Hey, I don't suppose you've heard anything from Layla the last few days?"

"I haven't. Has she not called in sick?"

"Between us, no, and if she doesn't play by the rules, it'll become an HR matter."

He raised an eyebrow. "Do you want me to call her, see if she's okay?"

"No, it's okay, but thanks anyway. I was thinking of swinging by her place tomorrow morning to find out what's going on."

"Max is a bell-end and has a lot to answer for–putting her through all this because he couldn't keep it in his pants."

"I couldn't agree more, but my job now is to make sure Layla keeps her job."

He gave me that look. We both knew what unexplained absences would look like on her record. Any chances of promotion would be blown sky high, and it irked me because she was an extremely capable officer. "I hope she appreciates you looking out for her."

"I hope so too, but I can't shield her forever."

"S'pose not, boss."

Once again, the day was uneventful, and with no new leads to go on, I decided to get an early dart and prepare myself for Dorothy's.

When pulling out of the carpark, I wondered if Will had found any CCTV footage from outside the sex shop. He would be on the ball with it, I knew that much, but I made a mental note to ask him Monday morning anyway. My phone rang and moved my train of thought.

I accepted the call. "Hi, Lauren. How are you?"

"Busy as ever," she replied. "Especially when I'm acting as your unpaid PA."

"You've lost me."

"Gina Elliot's body was released to her family yesterday afternoon."

"Then, how come it's only you that seems to tell me these things?" I was pissed off to have been kept out of the loop yet again.

"God knows. Check Savage's inbox—they might be going in there."

"Ah, yes, probably. Thanks for calling me." I would kick somebody's arse on Monday morning and remind them of the importance of relaying such information to *me*, not Savage anymore. "Any idea when the funeral will be held?"

"Sometime next week I would imagine."

"Damn."

"Have I said something wrong?"

"I was only at Jade Kelly's yesterday and wasn't anticipating having to attend another quite so soon."

"Perks of the job," she joked. "But don't hang your funeral suit up too quickly because Rebecca Preston won't be on ice for much longer either."

"Charming," I said, a little grumpy. "But I guess you're right."

"Hey, I'm only the messenger," she replied. "Anyway, gotta go."

"Thanks, Lauren. I owe you dinner and drinks when this is all over with."

"I'll hold you to that."

She ended the call.

I made another mental note to ask Joanna if she would mind accompanying me to Gina's funeral.

I stood in front of Roy, awaiting his critique. "Well, how was I?"

He looked me up and down. Now I knew how X Factor contestants felt facing Simon Cowell. It's a no from me, was the response I'd been expecting.

"You've been practising, darling,"

"Can you tell?"

"Oh, yes," he said with a smile. "You're quite the revelation, do you know that?"

"Eh?" I didn't have a clue what he meant. "In what way?"

"Never in a million years did I think you'd have it in you to pull this off."

"Really?"

"Of course not. The big butch cop morphing into a drag queen—you couldn't write it."

"It's not that hard with a bit of practice."

"Some people are born to entertain and you're one of them."

"I wouldn't go that far, Roy."

"Well, take it as the biggest of compliments because I don't dish them out often. You're going to knock 'em dead tonight."

"I'm glad you'll be there. I feel more confident when you're around."

"I wouldn't miss it, darling."

"Maybe tonight will be my last performance."

"What makes you say that?"

"Wishful thinking is all."

"The case not going well I take it?"

"I shouldn't say this, but he's fucking clever and outsmarting us at every turn."

"People screw up all the time, just wait and see. You'll find something and get him."

"Before he strikes again, I hope."

"Well I know it's easy for me to say, but focus on what you have to do tonight—you got into Dorothy's so you could keep your ear to the ground, and trust me, once the queens in there get to know you, they'll be flapping their gums like their lives depend on it."

"I hope so."

"Mark my words."

"We haven't got anything we can use yet."

"You will, but I'll keep my ears open tonight."

"You're a star, Roy."

"Yeah, yeah, I know, now shut it. Let's go again, and this time, pound your pussy on the floor."

I burst out laughing, bent double. "What the hell does that mean?"

"It means get down and dirty. When you do that slut drop, make sure you drop it as low as you can go."

"Got it," I said, still laughing.

He clicked his fingers. "Come on. Focus."

I assumed my opening pose. He hit play, and I went through the routine one more time, remembering to drop it low.

"How was that?"

"Magic, darling, magic."

Roy dropped me off at the stage door.

"I'll go and pick Bella up now, but don't worry we'll be back by show-time."

"You could always call her and say you've got a flat tyre."

"Not a chance, darling. My life wouldn't be worth living, and besides, I'm looking forward to seeing her."

"Traitor," I replied, shaking my head as I watched him drive away,

I banged on the stage door, feeling like an idiot in the red sequinned dress Roy insisted I wear. I'd wanted to wear my stage outfit, but Roy said if I was going to linger in the bar area pre-show, I should leave my performance outfit as a surprise. He did have a point. I banged again, feeling irritated. A minute later, the same security guy from last week opened up and let me in.

I was less nervous with it being my second performance and, once I'd locked my bags away, I entered the club and headed towards the bar. There was no way I was sitting in the smoky dressing room with a gang of bitchy drag queens giving me the side eye again.

Kimberley spied me and approached—all smiles. It was good to see a somewhat familiar face. She looked sensational in a tiny, silver dress topped off with a denim jacket that was covered in badges.

"I was hoping to see you." I gave her a hug.

"How are you?" she asked. "Looking forward to your show?"

It was hardly a show, but now wasn't the time to debate the issue. "I'm good and yeah, I can't wait to get up there."

"What time are you on tonight?"

"Last up, I'm afraid."

"Oh, no! Again? I won't be able to stay that late."

"Well, if you've gotta work, you've gotta work."

"Yeah, but next weekend I'm off, so I'll be able to see you perform then."

"I'd like that." I didn't know if there would be another performance, but I wasn't about to tell her that.

"Your friend not in tonight to watch?"

I had to think who she meant for a moment then realised she was talking about Layla. "Afraid not. She has kids and is feeling a bit under the weather right now."

"Pardon me for saying, but she seemed a right grumpy cow the other day."

"She's not usually like that, but she's going through a messy divorce at the moment."

"Ah, got it," Kimberley said, a glum expression on her face. "I feel bad now."

"Don't," I said. "She wasn't at her best the other day but you weren't to know that." I still hadn't heard from Layla and wondered how she was. I would definitely call round to her house and see her tomorrow. Not as her boss, but as a friend. Hopefully I'd be able to talk some sense into her, at least with regard to following absence procedure.

"I'll be right back," she said suddenly, seeming a little on edge. "Gotta see a man about a dog."

"Okay, but while you're gone, I'll get you a drink. Same as last week?"

"Yeah, thanks," she replied.

I watched as she walked towards the other end of the club

then I was distracted by the handsome barman I hadn't been introduced to yet.

"What can I get you, gorgeous?" he asked with a wink.

"Rum and cola, and a soda water please."

"My name's Samuel," he said. "And you're Avaline I take it?"

"News travels fast around here."

"You've been the talk of the place all week," he said, tending to the drinks.

"Some people are too easily pleased."

"Blanche thinks you're the second coming—a class act as she describes you."

"Oh, God," I replied, embarrassed.

"You should be honoured." He placed the drinks down and smiled. "Give me a shout if you want anything else."

"Thanks, Samuel."

I wondered where Kimberley had got to, then a commotion drew my attention and, to my surprise, I watched as the club's two burly security guards dragged Darren Wilkes across the dance-floor. He struggled but couldn't shake himself loose from their grip.

"I'll fucking kill you," he yelled as the music cut out.

"Shut it, Darren. You've caused enough trouble tonight," one of the guards said.

"You owe me, you cunt." Darren's face twisted in fury as he turned his head in the direction they'd come from.

I looked about, curious to know who had provoked such a response from him, then Kimberley appeared, her hand holding the side of her face.

"You're not getting another penny out of me," she screamed. "I paid my debt already."

Security dragged him up the stairs kicking and screaming.

"You're dead, Kimberley," was his parting shot before his voice was drowned out by the return of the music.

I raced over, wanting to get her out of harm's way. Wilkes was unpredictable and I worried he would suddenly reappear. "Come over here and let's have a look at your face."

"It's nothing, really."

She moved her hand and I could see the bruise forming under her eye, snaking down her cheek.

"Shit!" I said, wanting to beat the living daylights out of him. "Samuel, can you get me some ice in a tea-towel, please?"

Samuel handed me the ice bucket and a cloth.

I wrapped the ice in the cloth and placed it on her face. "What was all that about?"

"He reckons I owe him money."

"And do you?"

"No."

"He seems pretty adamant you do."

"Darren used to help me out and he insisted I paid him in kind."

"Ugh," I replied.

"He's off his face and horny and because I won't go home with him he's decided to change the terms of our agreement."

"Do you need money?" I was concerned for her. "I can help you out."

"Nah, not at all. I won't tolerate him bullying me. I owe him nothing."

"Does he know where you live?"

"Yeah, but he's all mouth. He'll go home and sleep it off. I'm not worried."

"The bruise forming under your eye tells me another story."

"He's pissed and drugged up to the eyeballs. Trust me, this isn't the first time. He'll have forgotten all about it by tomorrow."

"How are you gonna get home?" I briefly considered blowing my cover and making sure she got there safely.

"Same way I got here, on foot. I don't live too far away."

"Here, drink this."

She slugged it back. "Thanks, I needed that."

"Look, I'm worried he'll be waiting for you. Please get a taxi home."

"You're sweet to worry, but I'll be fine, really."

"Do you want me to get on that stage and forget my routine, 'cos that's what will happen if I have to worry about you?"

She rolled her eyes and grinned. "We wouldn't want that, would we?"

"Exactly," I replied. "I'll speak to security and make sure they see you safely into a taxi. That way, if Darren *is* outside your place when you get there, you can tell the driver to bring you back here then I'll take you home myself. I'm not scared of that idiot."

"My own personal protector."

I grinned. "Let's swap numbers so you can text me when you're home."

THIRTY-TWO

With her face still throbbing, Kimberley left Dorothy's on the arm of a hulking great bouncer who made sure she was safely inside the taxi.

As the taxi pulled up outside her house, she sent a quick text to Dylan, thanking him for caring. It felt nice to have someone giving a damn about her, even if she didn't really know him. He'd been sweet, making sure she didn't leave the club alone.

The security light flashed on as she approached the front door of her quaint two-bedroomed end terrace she rented off her uncle Merv. Pulling the key from her jacket pocket, she opened the door and stepped inside.

A sudden flurry of movement startled her, and Felix, her house cat, made a dart for the door, escaping through the gap in a flash.

"No, Felix, come back!" She chased after him but the naughty cat was too fast and launched himself over the small brick wall and off into the bushes that bordered the piece of woodland beside her property. Totally frustrated, she headed back inside.

Felix had been getting smarter recently. She'd made the decision to keep him as an inside cat because the *Ragdoll* breed was usually laid back and too trusting—unaware of danger, and Kimberley didn't want him run over or eaten by the neighbour's dog. But since he'd snuck out a couple of weeks ago, entering and leaving the house had become like a military operation. She'd just been distracted tonight because of that dickhead, Darren.

She hung her jacket on the hook just inside the door and eased off her shoes. She'd need to wear something a little more suitable if she was going to have to climb trees to rescue a frightened cat. This was where being born a boy came in useful, her tree-climbing skills were second to none.

She headed upstairs to get changed, and, after slipping out of her dress, pulled on a pair of jeans, a T-shirt and her running shoes. She'd need to go and look for him otherwise she wouldn't get a wink of sleep tonight.

Back downstairs, she headed to the living room window, opening the heavy cream-coloured curtain just far enough to peek outside.

There was no sign of him.

She puffed out a breath, frustrated and exhausted. She'd been on breakfast duty all week and found the early morning starts a killer. She could do without this, tonight of all nights—her face and jaw throbbed like a bitch.

Grabbing a pouch of cat food, she emptied it into a saucer and headed back outside. "Come on, puss, puss, puss," she called quietly, hoping not to wake the neighbours.

She walked along the tree-lined street to the clump of bushes. Tapping the fork onto the saucer she expected him to appear. Nothing kept Felix from his food, but it had no affect this time.

Meandering through the bushes to the larger trees at the back, she stopped, listened, and prayed he'd appear so she could get her arse into bed.

Nothing.

She gave up and headed back inside, to make a hot drink, leaving the saucer on the door mat. She clearly wasn't going to get to sleep anytime soon.

After making herself a strong black coffee, she settled on the sofa and reached for her phone.

She trawled through *Facebook*, *liked* a few posts, and checked her messages. Being a bookaholic, she was an active member of several online book clubs—her virtual family. A lot of her best friends were members of these groups, and the sad thing was, she'd never actually met any of them in person.

My cat has done a bunk, she posted to her own page with a gif of a cat running out of the door.

Oh no! Naughty pussy. One sleazy smart-arse said.

Lock her out, that'll learn her, another person suggested.

She's a he, and Noooo! He's my baby, Kimberley responded. ***Cats aren't supposed to be kept inside— that's cruel.***

Kimberley shook her head, "Shoot! They're all on form tonight," she muttered.

The sound of something outside had her on her feet and back at the window. She swished the curtain aside again and scanned the doorstep. The saucer was still there and full of food. "Where are you, Felix, you rascal?"

Closing the curtain, she drained her cup and returned it to

the kitchen. Then, slipping her jacket back on, she headed out the front door once again. "*Chh, chh, chh,*" she called into the night.

Picking up the saucer again, she walked down the side of the house. It was much darker down there suddenly, and she felt wary, wishing she'd brought her phone for the torch app to light the way. "Felix! *Chh, chh, chh.* Come here boy."

Something moved in the bushes startling her. "Felix, come on, puss, puss, it's late," she groaned, and tinkled the fork on the saucer again.

Ten minutes later, frozen to the bone, she headed back to the house, horrified to see the front door swinging open. "Bloody hell, Kimberley, you're asking for trouble tonight!" she whispered.

Stepping inside, more than a little freaked out, she felt wired and every detail seemed to jump out at her in the tiny hallway. The scratch marks on the carpet at the bottom of the stairs that Felix insisted on using as a scratch pad—the three-globe light fitting had two of the bulbs blown—the scuffmarks on the wallpaper caused by her neighbour, Carly's, feet when she'd fallen down drunk after popping over for a bottle of wine one night. All so familiar, yet strangely different somehow. What had changed?

Was she being paranoid?

Had Darren followed her home after all?

She'd been stupid for not locking the door when there was a potential killer after her. Not that she actually thought Darren was capable of murder, but the police clearly did and, after his crazed antics tonight, maybe he was.

Closing the door behind her quietly, she locked it, and picked up the cast-iron doorstop standing beside the wall that was shaped like a quaint cottage. It would certainly give an intruder a terrible headache if she clocked them with it.

She methodically went through each room of the house, looking under beds, in wardrobes, even behind the shower curtain but there was nothing. Feeling pretty silly, she returned to her place on the sofa.

Maybe she should've just given in to Darren. Her new hormone supplier had let her down and she'd approached Darren to score. She'd always identified as a female, even as a youngster, but her parents wouldn't hear of it. As highly respected members of the community, they had been mortified their only son would embarrass them like that—as though that was the only reason. Idiots.

She first met Darren while she was still in school and he introduced her to hormones. Taking them at such a young age had prevented her voice deepening too much and helped to shrink her testicles. She'd been lucky—being so young, she hadn't developed an Adam's apple and the leathery jaw of most men. Her skin was smooth and feminine looking, and her breasts well-developed. She'd never be an underwear model, but she was happy with what she had. She wouldn't need a boob job to accentuate her curves, put it that way. All she'd needed was an endless supply of the drugs and she'd be happy as Larry—or Lucy, as the case may be.

But, a few months ago, Darren began holding out on her, making sexual demands that, at first, she had no choice but to accommodate. So, she asked around and found another supplier online. Darren hadn't been best pleased. However, he'd approached her last week and seemed relatively friendly, and tonight, with her new supplier messing her about, she mentioned, in passing, she might need some goodies from him. He'd demanded sex right away. His usual line up of trannies were thinning out rapidly—all murdered and she told him there was no way she would become his or some other crazed killer's latest victim.

He'd gone berserk, resulting in his fist connecting with her face, and a tirade of filth spewing from his mouth. He liked to be the one in control.

Easing out of her shoes, she rubbed her achy feet. Where the hell was that cat? He'd probably got the scent of a floozy in heat and gone around there trying to woo her with his ultra-groomed hairdo and batting his baby blues. No lady cat would be able to resist, she was sure.

Resigned to sleeping on the sofa, she got to her feet for one more peek outside.

She pulled the curtain aside and froze—a scream caught in her throat.

A man dressed in black stepped out from behind the curtain, a knife raised above his head.

She screamed as the blade slammed into her forehead.

THIRTY-THREE

I felt better seeing Kimberley escorted out by security. They weren't pleased having to play babysitter, but I was prepared to take her home myself if they didn't play ball. Let them explain to Blanche why the closing act had walked out.

Roy and Bella arrived.

She looked amazing, and I was surprised to see only a hint of a baby bump. People wouldn't have a clue she'd not long given birth.

I kept my distance, not wanting to be seen with Bella, but as per usual, she had no problem speaking to strangers. The last I saw, she was engaged in animated conversation with Blanche and a young guy who was hanging off his arm like some sort of trophy husband.

With only twenty minutes until show-time, I waved Roy over to go backstage. He whispered something to Bella then sauntered towards me. Thank God he was back in time because I hadn't worn my performance outfit in full yet and he'd offered to help me into it to make sure I looked the part.

"Are you nervous?" he asked.

"Not at all," I replied, stepping out of the sequinned red number I'd been wearing.

"Just do it like you did earlier and you'll be fine."

"I'll try my best."

Ten minutes later, I was ready and said goodbye to Roy. "I'll wait outside the stage door for you, darling."

"Thanks."

I hung about and watched as another of the drag queens galumphed around the stage to a Lady GaGa number. There was nothing graceful about the performance and I suddenly realised why I was closing the night again—most of the acts lacked a certain finesse.

The song faded as the DJ's voice boomed out of the sound system. "Let's give a big cheer for the fabulous Polly Wanakracker."

A smattering of applause rang out as she took her bow and pirouetted off the stage.

The curtains closed and I rushed to my spot and waited for the music to start.

"And now, let's welcome a class act." The room was silent. "Give it up for the divine Miss Avaline Saddlebags."

I heard the roar from the crowd and adrenaline exploded and coursed through my body.

The opening bars of the music kicked in as the curtains parted, revealing me in full-on Madonna mode. Another roar lifted my spirits, pushing me to give it my all.

Come on girls, do you believe in love?

I used every part of the stage, just like Roy had taught me, and allowed my inner showgirl to burst forth.

Before I knew it, the song was over and the place erupted. Cheers and screams from the crowd almost deafened me, and as I took my final bow, feeling elated, I watched Roy and Blanche hugging each other at the side of the stage, obviously pleased with the performance. Bella was jumping up and down on the spot. She whooped and hollered with the rest of the crowd.

The curtains closed and I made my way back to the dressing room to collect my gear from the locker.

Polly Wanakracker was waiting for me, a cigarette dangling from her bottom lip. "That was shit hot," she said. "I've never seen anything like it in this dump."

"Thanks," I replied. "You were great too."

"Where d'you learn to dance like that—stage school?"

"God, no," I replied. "Just practising at home."

"Come off it, you're a pro. Anyone can see that." Polly looked me up and down. "I mean, look at that outfit. Quality that is." She pawed at the jacket. "Is it Gaultier?"

"Eh?" I had no clue what she was yapping on about.

"That outfit, you know, is it couture, you know, designed by Jean-Paul Gaultier?"

"Christ, no," I said, finally cottoning on. "Nothing like that. I have a friend who makes my stage outfits for me." I was lying through my back teeth, but I didn't have time to go into the specifics.

"Lucky bitch. I wish I had a dressmaker."

"There was nothing wrong with your outfit," I said, trying to make her feel better about herself. "You looked good up there."

"That's kind of you to say, but it's hard when you're carrying a few extra pounds, you know, trying to get something that looks good. Mind you, I save a bleeding fortune on padding–these hips and thighs are all mine."

"Don't knock yourself." She seemed sweet if a little naïve and eager to please. I looked down at the impressive cleavage. I bet that was all hers too. No breast plate required.

"It's not that honey, I just wanna be the best at what I do. It's hard work being this fabulous, but for some it comes easy."

Was she having a dig at me? I wasn't certain. "Not for me

it doesn't, trust me on that. Tonight was the result of hours spent rehearsing, and I don't even get paid for it." I pulled my phone out. Thankfully, Kimberley was home safe and sound. There was a text from Roy too. I didn't read it because I'd guessed what it would say. Gossiping with Polly, I'd forgotten the time and the fact Bella and Roy were waiting outside for me. "Shit, I gotta go, sorry, my lift is waiting, but if you're here next week we can have a drink and a chat at the bar if you want?"

"Sounds good to me, doll."

"Okay, Polly, see you next week." I tottered past her and headed for the stage door. I felt bad because I didn't know if I'd be here next week.

At the car I noticed Bella was in the back and so I climbed in beside her.

"You took your time," she said. "Were you signing autographs for your adoring fans?"

"Ha bloody ha, Bells," I said. "One of the other drag queens collared me."

"You were amazing tonight," Roy piped up. "I just wanted to tell you."

"Thanks, Roy." I was chuffed. "Did I spot you and Blanche hugging?"

"I was flabbergasted, darling. I tell you."

Bella tittered in the back seat. "Oh, dear," she said.

"You're a big softie, Roy," I teased.

"He's right, Dylan, you were bloody fantastic. It's like you've been doing it all your life."

"It's just me up there pretending to sing a song I don't even particularly like."

"Matters not, Avaline, love," Roy said. "You wowed us all, and if that's you performing something you don't like, then find something you love and the drag world will fall at your feet."

It was weird hearing him call me Avaline and not Dylan. "I'm a copper, or did you forget that part?"

"I know, but don't you think DI Saddlebags has a nice ring to it?"

Bella burst out laughing.

"Piss off the pair of you," I said. "Roy, drive, I need to get this bloody wig off, my head's itching like mad."

"Yes, m'lady," he teased. "Right away, m'lady."

After dropping Bella off at her gate, Roy turned the car around and headed directly to my house.

"Do you want to come in?" I asked, remembering the farce of last week. "I could make you a bit of supper?"

"No, it's okay. I'm pretty tired, actually. I'll get going home if you don't mind?"

"Of course not. What about the outfit though?"

"I can grab it off you next week." He fumbled in the glove box and pulled out a bottle of makeup remover. "Here, you'll need this."

"Oh, shit. I meant to buy some of this, thanks mate—you're a star."

"You can keep this one, it's a spare."

"Goodnight then, mate." I tottered out of the car and into the house, kicked the shoes off at the door and groaned—my feet were killing me.

Collapsing on the sofa, I reached for the TV remote and froze. A bump from upstairs had me on high alert.

Getting up, I crept into the hallway and picked one of the shoes back up, and made my way upstairs—my heart thudding in my chest.

At the top of the stairs, I scanned the empty bathroom, then pushed myself along the landing to my partially opened bedroom door—the shoe raised above my head, and my breath held tight.

The door swung inwards with a creak.

Steve lay on the bed, partially covered with a single white sheet, a long-stemmed red rose held firmly between his teeth, a box of Belgian chocolates sat on his bare chest.

I exhaled noisily. "Bloody hell, Steve. You freaked me out."

"What the hell?" He discarded the rose, his face a picture.

"What?" It suddenly dawned on me, I was still in full drag—wig and all. "Oh." I laughed. "Steve, meet Avaline." I curtsied.

THIRTY-FOUR

Steve was up at the crack of dawn, banging and clanging in the kitchen and whistling some god-awful tune.

I groaned covering my head with the pillow which seemed to do the trick until the clomping of Steve's boots on the wooden staircase chased the last vestiges of sleep away.

"Wakey, wakey, sleepy head—I've made you some breakfast."

"Do I have to? It's Saturday for God's sake."

"Tell that to your phone, it's been vibrating for over half an hour."

I jumped up. "Really? Bloody hell, I forgot to turn the ringer back on after my performance last night."

"Here, don't panic." He handed me my phone.

My heart dropped to my stomach as I checked the screen. "Five missed calls, all from Will. Shit!"

"Is that bad?"

"It means something's happened." I returned the call and Will picked up immediately.

"Sorry to disturb you on a Saturday, boss, but you'll wanna hear this."

"Oh, God. What now?"

"We've found another body, I'm afraid."

"Fuck! Same MO?"

"I'd say so."

"What are the details?"

"Konrad Walker. He, or I should say she, was found by a neighbour this morning. 79 Sundown Avenue, Toxteth."

"I'm on my way. Where are you?"

"I'm already there. I didn't hang around when I couldn't get hold of anyone."

"Good. Keep everybody out, I won't be long." I hung up and turned to Steve. "Sorry, but I've got to go."

He glanced down at the fried eggs and bacon congealing on the plate. "Oh, well. I'd best eat it myself. Drink your coffee though."

I grabbed one of the triangles of toast and took a bite, then, after slurping a mouthful of hot coffee, I kissed the tip of his nose and headed to the bathroom.

Being Saturday morning, Sundown Avenue was heaving with a mixture of kids and adults, all trying to get wind of what had happened at the bottom of the street.

I parked as close as I could then walked the rest of the way, stepping over the police cordon.

Will met me at the front door.

"What do we have?" I asked.

"The next-door neighbour, Deborah Mitchell, noticed the victim's cat out this morning, which struck her as odd as he wasn't usually allowed out. She caught him and brought him home. When there was no answer at the door, she knocked on the window and spotted a load of blood spatters on the curtain. She called the station right away. Uniform discovered the body shortly after."

"Has Lauren been informed?" I asked as I climbed into a pair of overalls and bootees Will had left beside the front door.

Will nodded. "Yes, she's on her way."

I stepped inside.

"First door on the right," Will said. "I hope you've not eaten."

"Thanks for the warning." I glanced around the small, tidy hallway and, spotting a jacket covered in small badges, my blood ran like ice water. I gasped and rushed into the lounge. There my fears were realised. Kimberley's dead grey eyes stared up at me. Her forehead had been split in two as though someone had smashed her with an axe. I rushed to the kitchen and, not wanting to contaminate the crime scene, I threw up in a cup.

"Sorry," I said to Will once I returned.

"I take it you knew her?"

"Sadly, yes. Get Darren Wilkes picked up now."

"You think this was his doing?"

"Yeah." I thought of the sweet girl, now lying dead on her floor and felt the threat of tears. "He assaulted her and threatened to kill her last night in Dorothy's."

Lauren arrived shortly after me and got straight to work but I didn't need her to tell me the murder had been committed by the same killer. Because Kimberley was pre-op she hadn't had her penis mutilated, but the opposite was true of her breasts which had been butchered beyond recognition.

"He was trying to remove the implants, but this little lady

didn't have any," Lauren said, inspecting the tattered remains of Kimberley's chest. "This guy is a right sicko."

I turned away, not able to look at poor Kimberley any longer. "He's a sick bastard, alright, but I'll make sure he doesn't do this to anybody else."

Will was waiting for me once I'd finished with Lauren.

"Her parents live in West Kirby—A Jemima and Rex Walker."

Just what I needed right now; a trip through the Liverpool tunnel in Saturday traffic. "You want to head over there with me? I could do with the company."

"Of course. Do you want to drive or shall I?"

"We can drop your car off at the station, if you like, and then I'll drive."

"Sounds good."

I followed him to the station and then together we headed to West Kirby, an upmarket town on the north-west corner of the Wirral peninsula.

Forty minutes later, we pulled into the grounds of an impressive detached house—a far cry from where Kimberley's life had been savagely snuffed out.

A top of the range silver Mercedes and a sleek red Audi were parked on the drive outside the open garage which was big enough to accommodate most people's houses and still have room for a couple of cars. A man in his late twenties, dressed in black sweats, was busily cleaning them. Sounds of Ed Sheeran filled the air between us.

The man's feet almost left the ground when he spotted us standing behind him, and he leaned inside the Audi and turned off the music. "Sorry, guys. I didn't see you there," he said with a broad cockney accent.

I held up my ID. "DI Monroe and DC Buckley. We're looking for Mr and Mrs Walker."

"I think they're both inside, shall I check for you?"

"No, it's okay, I'll find them."

We approached the front door and a woman in her sixties, who was very well presented for a Saturday morning, answered the doorbell.

"Mrs Walker?"

She eyed us suspiciously then shot a dirty look towards the guy in the drive. "Yes. Can I help you?"

We showed our badges.

"DI Monroe and DC Buckley—may we come in please?"

"What's this about?" The woman had a definite haughty attitude, so unlike her daughter.

"I'll tell you, just not on the doorstep, if that's okay?"

"Very well." She allowed us to enter and then led us through to a conservatory at the back of the vast property.

A man, dressed a little more casual than his wife, jumped to his feet, folding the newspaper, startled by the intrusion. "Oh, good morning."

Once the introductions were out of the way, Mr Walker offered us a seat.

"So, cut to the chase. What are you here for?" his wife snapped.

"We're here about your son, Konrad, or Kimberley as she was also known," I said.

"Not in this house, he wasn't," Mr Walker said.

"What the hell has that boy done now? As if he hasn't brought enough shame on this family," his wife sneered.

I felt the hackles rise on my neck and it took all my self-control not to bite. "He's done nothing, actually. Konrad was attacked in his home last night. I'm sorry to inform you, your son's dead."

The next twenty minutes turned out to be the most bizarre of my career to date. Kimberley's parents were more upset about the shame this would bring on their family and career than they were to hear their only child had been brutally murdered.

I couldn't wait to get out of the place before I said something I'd regret. Poor Kimberley deserved a family that would grieve her death—to mourn her absence—not be embarrassed at the way she chose to live her life.

"Hateful bastards," I said to Will once we were back in the car. "Let's go to the station and see if they've picked up Darren Wilkes yet. I'm in the mood to tear him a new arsehole."

THIRTY-FIVE

I waited at the station for a good three hours before deciding enough was enough.

A squad car had attended Wilkes' apartment and gained entrance from the building manager, but he was nowhere to be found. Only upon further questioning did the manager inform them Wilkes hadn't been home all night.

Where the hell was he? I was beyond irritated the slimy little shit had evaded me and issued a warrant for his arrest. He wouldn't get far.

Walking out of the station I decided to pay Layla a visit. Janine was on my case, and, with having no contact from her, I couldn't keep her out of the firing line any longer. Monday morning she would be getting a letter from HR and I wanted to do the decent thing and pre-warn her. That way it wouldn't come as too much of a shock.

Pulling up outside her house, I noted the curtains were drawn and it looked like nobody was home, apart from the fact Layla's car, which also happened to be covered in bird shit, was parked on the driveway. I wondered why she didn't use the garage, but that was the least of her problems right now.

Stepping out, I walked up the path to her front door and knocked.

One of the twins, whose names I couldn't remember pulled the door open and glared at me.

"Is your mum home?"

"We don't want any," he grunted and made to close the door.

"I'm not here to sell you anything. I want a word with your mum. She works with me."

"She's in bed," he snapped.

Friendly little bugger, I thought. "Would you mind waking her up? This is important."

Just then I heard Layla shouting from the top of the stairs. "Who's at the bloody door?"

I poked my head inside. "It's only me, Dylan."

She rushed downstairs and peered around the door. "What are you doing here?"

I noticed how dishevelled she looked. "I hadn't heard from you so thought I'd pop round and see if there was anything I could do to help."

"I'm on the sick, Dylan. You shouldn't be here."

"But you're not on the sick, not officially."

Her tone changed instantly. "What's that supposed to mean?"

"Look, I don't want to shout your business all over the close. Why don't you invite me in for a coffee and we can talk? It really is in your best interest, Layla,"

She wasn't pleased by my presence, but if she valued her job, she would listen to what I had to say.

The door swung open. I was surprised by her fluffy pink pyjamas. "You better come in then but let me run upstairs and put some clothes on."

"Thanks."

"Take a seat in the living room." She turned to her son and ushered him towards the stairs. "You get up there and clean that bedroom."

"I wanna go and live with my dad."

"Tough luck, buddy. He doesn't want to live with you."

I flinched at her harsh words.

The kid ran up the stairs and the house shook when he slammed a door.

Layla came down a few minutes later, wearing faded blue jeans and a baggy top. Her dark hair had been scraped back into a messy ponytail. "What are you really doing here, Dylan?"

"You called in the first day to tell me you were sick, then nothing. What's going on?"

"I'm sorry, I meant to, but I couldn't face talking to anyone."

"You could have emailed me, text, anything, just so I had some sort of explanation to give to Janine."

"I'm gonna lose my job, aren't I?"

"Not if I can help it, but I won't lie to you and say everything is hunky dory."

"I don't wanna get fired."

"Look, I'll do what I can, but you can't go AWOL again. Make sure you message me if you're not up to talking until you get a sick note. I assume you *are* going to go to your GP?"

"Yeah, I have an appointment on Tuesday next week."

"Good, but keep me in the loop, and I'll try to square it with Janine and HR, tell them it was an error and you didn't realise you had to call daily because you can self-cert for a week."

"Thanks, Dylan."

"I'll help you as much as I can, but you have to start helping yourself. This isn't you."

"I don't have the energy to do anything right now."

"Are you still having problems with Max?"

She looked on the verge of tears. "I hate him so much for what's he's done to me and the kids."

"Marriages end all the time, Layla, but you can't allow yourself to fall apart, for your sake and the boys."

"Have you ever felt so mad inside, or felt such hatred for one person?" She pulled anxiously at her top, and my heart went out to her. Her fingernails were bitten down to stumps, and for the first time, I saw my partner on the edge. One more push and she'd topple over.

"I get why you hate him, but if you don't get a grip on yourself, you're gonna end up losing your job, and right now, you need it more than ever."

"My job is all that is keeping me sane."

"Well, that's good then. Focus on that and the kids. Day by day, you'll start to feel better, I promise."

"It'll take more than that. But I'll try."

"I can help you to clean up the place if you want me to? I'll even clean your car and park it in the garage."

"It won't fit."

"How come?"

"My dad's storing his stuff in there until he gets back from France."

"Okay, but your car's covered in bird shit. Do you want me to clean it for you?"

"No. It's fine, really. I'll pull myself together and take it to the carwash in town."

"Are you sure? I don't mind."

"You've done enough."

I didn't know if that was a good or bad thing. "I'm only a phone call away."

"I know, and thank you for being a friend, I do appreciate it, now if you don't mind, I'm gonna get this house into some semblance of order and tidy myself up with it."

I got to my feet. "Please see your doctor on Tuesday and get the sick note in as soon as possible. I'll speak to Janine first thing Monday morning, but you still need to text me daily till you get the sick note from your doctor." I made my way to the door and left, not bothering to discuss the latest murder with her. She was off sick and discussing the case wouldn't be professional as I was there as a friend, not her boss.

THIRTY-SIX

Sunday started no better than Saturday had.

Darren Wilkes still hadn't been located, which only served to prove his guilt in my eyes. But his car had been found parked in the street at the back of Kimberley's house. Why had he left it there?

I wanted to catch the bastard and throw the book at him but trudging around his usual haunts on Saturday had proved fruitless. Nobody had seen him,

Making enquiries in Dorothy's was out of the question for me, so I sent Joanna instead.

"He hasn't been seen since he was thrown out for attacking Kimberley. The manager gave me the CCTV footage, though. And all the staff are on high alert. If he shows up there, we'll know about it, believe me."

"Good thinking, Jo. Let me know if the footage picks up the assault."

I hung up, feeling totally frustrated. What that monster had done to Kimberley sickened me, and one thing was clear; the attacks were becoming more brutal and savage. We needed to find Wilkes, and fast.

"I'm back," Steve shouted when he returned from the shop. He'd offered to get the local newspaper for me.

I rushed downstairs, desperate to see what had been reported.

"Thanks," I said, kissing his cheek.

"You're not gonna like it."

Grabbing the paper from him, I looked at the front page.

"Shit," I said, rushing back upstairs for my phone.

"Told ya," Steve called out.

"I need my phone. Janine is gonna go fucking apeshit when she sees this."

Janine answered after a few rings. "Please tell me you're calling this early on a Sunday to give me good news."

"I wish I was. Have you seen today's paper?"

"Not yet, why?" Her tone had changed.

"Darren Wilkes has been named as a suspect in the murders."

"Where have they got that from?"

"I have no idea, but I'm just gonna get dressed and head into the office."

"I'll meet you there, and Dylan...?"

"Yes?"

"If the press are camped outside, say nothing. You and I need to work on a carefully worded statement."

"No problem. See you in about an hour."

I felt like the worst boyfriend in the world abandoning Steve again, but he understood it was the nature of my job.

After resolving to make it up to him with a dirty weekend away once this case was over with, I kissed him quickly, then rushed out to my car.

As I drove to the station, my mind replayed the last conversation I had with Kimberley on a loop. I liked her and she hadn't deserved to die that way. Now, this case had become personal, making me more resolute to catch the animal and put him away for life.

As I feared, the press were congregated outside the station, waiting in the staff car park, like vultures circling for every scrap they could find.

I pulled into my parking space and pushed the car door open.

Cameras flashed. A red-haired female approached, shoving a microphone in my face. "DI Monroe, what can you tell us about the latest victim?"

My heart sank when I thought of Kimberley lying in a morgue with her head caved in. I pushed the camera away. "No comment," I grunted, not in the mood to deal with them.

A man I recognised from the local TV news stepped in front of me. "DI Monroe, is it true you have Darren Wilkes listed as a person of interest?"

"No comment," I said once again, side stepping him.

"Come on detective, there must be something you can tell us?" the red-head said, fishing for the tiniest crumb of information.

"There will be a statement made in due course, but until then, no further comment."

I pulled the station doors open and stepped inside, breathing a sigh of relief.

"Get that lot out of the car park, now," I barked at the desk Sergeant, irritated he'd allowed them to trespass in the first place. "Janine will bust your balls if she drives into that circus."

"Sorry, I've been snowed under here, but I'll get rid of them."

"You do that and before she gets here—she's on her way in now."

His face paled. "I'm on it. Sorry, sir." He looked to his left then shouted to a colleague. "Oi, Jane, give me a hand getting shot of this lot will ya? Janine's on her way in."

I grabbed a coffee from the canteen and made my way to the incident room half expecting Will's head to pop up from behind his monitor and offer a good morning.

The place was deathly quiet.

I leaned on Joanna's desk and looked at the images stuck to the walls—innocent victims, butchered in the prime of their lives because they just wanted to be themselves. It sickened me and I knew the killings would continue, unless I found a way to put a stop to him.

Lauren popped into my mind. I made a note to call her first thing tomorrow. I had to know if Kimberley suffered, and deep down, I prayed, whatever he had done to her was quick and she hadn't realised what was coming.

Janine pushed the doors open, startling me.

"What a fucking mess—those gobshites have taken over the car park."

"I hoped they'd be gone by the time you got here."

"They better be by the time we leave or Sergeant Dildo at the front desk will be getting his marching orders."

I snorted out a laugh. "So, what are we going to say in this statement?"

"Well, they already know Wilkes is a person of interest, but what they don't know is, he's done a runner. We might as well be honest with them, because the shit is going to hit the fan sooner or later and I don't want to look a fool when it does. If they know what we know, to a certain extent, it will look better when the powers that be come charging in."

"Is it that bad?"

"You tell me—we've got a serial killer out there, and whether it turns out to be Wilkes or not, people want him caught. I've already been fielding calls from my boss today and he never calls on a Sunday unless he wants to tear me a new one."

"But we're doing all we can."

"It's not enough though. You're working undercover as a bloody drag queen for God's sake and still nothing."

"We need to find Wilkes."

"You definitely think it's him?"

I shrugged my shoulders. "It appears that way." The truth was, I had my doubts. While I'd been sitting there, staring at the incident board, it suddenly struck me. Wilkes being the killer seemed too easy, somehow. Although every single murder pointed at it being him, my gut told me we were wrong. He was the common denominator, the only one we could find—a drug dealer with a fetish for trannies. It was motive enough, but would it be sufficient to secure a conviction? I didn't think so, and there hadn't been a scrap of DNA found on the victims up to now. Lucky? I doubted it, more like somebody who knew what he was doing.

Janine's eyebrows furrowed. "You don't think so?"

"It certainly appears it's him. But don't you think it's just a little too convenient? Contrived even?"

"What aren't you saying, Dylan?"

"The killer's smart. Nobody's seen him coming or going at any of the crime scenes. He's left nothing for us to go on—no clues of any kind, or DNA evidence."

"Means nothing. He could be a clever little bastard who knows what he's doing. Christ, any fool could commit a crime and get away with it these days. There are enough TV shows that tell them how to do it."

"I guess so, but something is niggling me." I walked to my desk and unlocked it, grabbing the case file for Jade Kelly. I flicked through the autopsy notes. "Hmmm."

"What are you looking for?"

I picked up Gina Elliot's and read her autopsy findings, then moved onto Rebecca Preston's. "Lauren notes on each of the autopsies that they were all victims of blunt force trauma to various parts of the body which shows our killer is extremely strong and overpowers his victims quite easily and with little fuss."

"What are you thinking?"

"That Wilkes isn't that tall and yeah, I know he works out, but the first three victims were about five-nine, five-ten, in height, and Wilkes is only five-eight."

"So?"

"I may be totally wrong here but I think our killer is some-body much bigger in size, who is able to overpower his victims much quicker than Wilkes could."

"Sounds like you're reaching to me..."

"I've always had good instincts and right now they're screaming we're focusing on the wrong man."

"Then why has Wilkes gone missing? If he's innocent, why run?"

"Because he knows how bad things will look for him. He'll have seen the news and would assume he'd be our prime suspect."

"I'm not convinced, Dylan. Sometimes two and two do make four, you know? And don't forget Wilkes car was found aban-doned close to the latest victim's house."

"I know, I know. I might be way off the mark and if I am, you can shove me on traffic duties, but something isn't adding up, something we're missing that's right in front of us and we're not seeing it."

"So, are we telling the press Wilkes is just a person of interest and not a fully fledged suspect?"

"I think we tell them he's wanted for questioning and leave

them to speculate further. The only other thing we can tell them is there was another murder and we believe it to be the same killer."

"They'll want more, you know that."

"Tough, they're not getting any more."

"Come on then, you can do the talking, but tell them only what we agreed. Okay?"

We made our way outside to the front of the station where the press were now camped.

As soon as the doors opened, they flocked towards us, firing questions.

"Ladies, gentlemen," I yelled above the din. "I have a very short statement to make, so if you'd be so kind as to zip it, I'll make a start. But before I do, there won't be any questions answered from myself or anybody else at the station."

There was absolute silence as I began to speak.

I could see how disappointed they were, but they knew as much as we were willing to share.

Afterwards, we about turned and re-entered the station leaving the reporters behind us. Hopefully, they'd soon get tired and go home, or back to their offices to twist everything I'd said into some semblance of a story.

I left Janine at the station soon after and battled through the reporters still wanting their pound of flesh.

On the drive home, I called Steve to see if he fancied lunch in town.

"Yeah, sounds good to me," he said.

"I could do with a couple of drinks, if only to take the edge off my nerves," I admitted.

"Okay, I'll see you when you get back. We can get a taxi so I can have a few drinks too but remember I'm in the office tomorrow."

"See you soon." I ended the call, my mind wandering back to the case files I'd looked through earlier. Something about this whole case niggled at me, but I couldn't put my finger on what it was.

THIRTY-SEVEN

Monday morning came around much too fast for my liking. After glugging back a glass of water to combat the dry-mouth-horrors brought on by yesterday's impromptu drinking session, I raced from the house, eager to get to the station to find out if there had been any news on Wilkes. In the back of my mind, I knew they'd call me if there was, but it didn't stop me from hoping.

I pulled up the collar of my jacket and quickly walked around the back of the crowd of reporters camped out on the front steps. I managed to get inside before anyone spotted me.

"That was a bit of nifty footwork," Ian, the desk sergeant, said.

"I know, but I'm not in the mood for that lot. I haven't had my quota of coffee yet."

I heard him chuckling as I let myself in through the security door.

Will was already at his desk as usual and the rest of the team filtered in over the next half hour. All except Layla. I hadn't heard from her since I left her house on Saturday, and I hoped my warnings had sunk in but it soon became evident she wasn't going to call.

"Can I have your attention please, guys?" I called out to the room.

A sudden hush followed.

"Okay. As you're all no doubt aware, we had another murder on Friday night. Konrad Walker, AKA Kimberley Walker, was attacked in her own home." I glanced around them all, and each of them nodded their head.

"I'd actually spent time with her on Friday in Dorothy's and was present when she was attacked by Wilkes. He was last seen being escorted from the premises and I saw to it that Kimberley was put into a taxi for her own safety. Wilkes' car was discovered parked up close to Kimberley's house. Why did he leave it behind? Did something happen to him? Maybe Kimberley fought back and injured him somehow? Or he could've dropped his keys somewhere and had no choice but to leave it behind. All but one of the four victims were known to have been intimate with Wilkes at some time or other, so it's imperative we locate his whereabouts ASAP."

"I'm currently in the middle of trawling through the CCTV footage from Friday night-Saturday morning, boss," Will said.

"Surely you'll find something," I said, scratching my head.

"You'd think so, wouldn't you? I'll scale the search to include a wider area—you never know, something may show."

"Thanks, Will. Are any of you working on other leads?"

Joanna cleared her throat. "I've got an appointment to meet Kimberley's boss at the diner, then I'll have a chat with her workmates."

I nodded, glancing around the others.

Tommo shuffled in his seat. "I'm currently going back over all the crime scene images, boss. See if there's anything that jumps out that we may have missed."

"Good idea. I'm planning on updating the incident board today for the same reason. As of yet, the killer hasn't left any DNA or fingerprints at any of the scenes and there's no reason to believe this latest scene is any different. There's no hair, footprints, tyre impressions—nothing. I don't know how he's doing it, to be honest. However, if Wilkes is our killer, any fingerprints and DNA could be argued in court because he's been in three out of four victim's houses multiple times. So we'll need something conclusive we can pin on him."

"He's a slippery fucker, boss," Pete said.

"You're not wrong. But the fact he publically attacked Kimberley and now he's gone AWOL works in our favour. We just need to find him—and fast. I know uniform canvassed the area yesterday, but maybe a couple of you can do it again. Take a photo of Wilkes this time and see if anyone can recognise him."

"I'll do it, boss, once I've finished here," Will said.

"I was informed this morning that Janine has arranged for some cover in the absence of Layla and a Genevieve Tanner will be joining us shortly. Will, can you settle her in please?"

"Of course. She can even come door knocking with me."

"Good idea. Make sure all statements are properly documented, no matter how insignificant you might deem them to be."

"Of course," Will said, appearing a little miffed.

"Sorry, I don't mean to patronise you but Wilkes has a lot of money at his disposal and can afford the best solicitor so we need everything signed and sealed if we're going to make any charges stick."

"I know. Don't worry, boss." He nodded.

"Jo, can you look into Jemima and Rex Walker—Kimberley's parents. Something about them seemed off on Saturday. I couldn't put my finger on what, but do a bit of digging for me, please?"

"No problem," Joanna said.

"Right. Getting back to Kimberley. It appears from the blood spatter on the back of the curtain that the killer was hiding behind it. He'd gained access through the back door, a small window had been smashed and the key had been left in the lock. Drugs found at the scene were similar to the ones Wilkes deals in, yet the packaging was different. Kimberley did tell me she'd ceased contact with him, so maybe she'd found another supplier. Heather, can you access Kimberley's phone and emails, maybe we can glean something from them?"

"On it, boss."

"Also, we need to nail down the timeline. She left the club in a taxi at around eleven. Can you contact the taxi company and confirm if she went straight home? Did she stop anywhere along the way? Did she pick anyone else up? Did they make small talk? Get everything, no matter how unimportant it might seem."

Heather nodded, scribbling in her pad.

"Why was the cat outside? The neighbour said it was an indoor cat and Kimberley would never let him out. Did the killer let him out? We have the glass from the window being analysed—hopefully when we pick up Wilkes we will find one or two fragments of glass to connect him to the scene. The murder weapon, one of Kimberley's own knives, had been wielded with such force that... well, need I say any more, the pictures tell their own story." I held up a gruesome image showing the gaping wound in Kimberley's skull.

A collective groan spread around the room.

"Wilkes is a dead man if we don't get to him soon. Thanks to the press naming him as a suspect, the trans community will lynch him if they find him before we do so the pressure is on. Good luck team. Let's get this cleared up this week."

There was still no sign of Wilkes by the time I left for home. I was feeling pretty dejected and frustrated with it all by now and was surprised Janine hadn't been on my case again.

THIRTY-EIGHT

I spent Tuesday morning in the station, once again, poring through the case files, positive there was something I was missing. So far, a breakthrough eluded me.

I looked at my watch–it was gone eleven am.

"Jo, anything on the Walkers yet?"

She looked up from whatever she was reading. "Both are squeaky clean up to now. Mr Walker is listed as managing director of a structural engineering firm on Companies House, while his wife is the company secretary—married for nearly thirty years, with one child. They're pretty normal folk from what I can see up to now."

"Keep looking," I said. "You never know what could turn up." I didn't know what I was hoping to find, and a part of me knew I was clutching at straws.

"I'm on it."

I turned to Will. "Any contact with Layla?"

"Nothing, boss."

"Shit," I whispered. To my dismay, Monday had passed me

by in a blur of activity and I'd meant to call her, but totally forgot. Another day she hadn't followed procedure, so now, on top of everything else, I had her to worry about.

"Do you want me to call her?" Joanna offered.

"No, it's okay, I'll pop round there later." I knew it would be late when I got there because I'd agreed to meet Steve for dinner at Liverpool One. I considered calling in advance but decided against it. She'd just ignore my call anyway. Turning up unannounced would be better. I couldn't shield her anymore and tonight I'd tell her exactly where she stood.

"Let me know if you change your mind."

I nodded and looked up as Pete entered the room. "Any sign of Wilkes yet, buddy?"

"Nothing, boss. He's just vanished into thin air."

"Have you spoken with Nigel Warfield?"

He looked at me with a blank expression. "Erm..."

"His solicitor," I reminded him.

"Oh, no, sorry. Not yet."

"Take a drive down to his office with Heather and see if he's heard from him. For all we know, he could be hiding Wilkes, especially if he's paid enough."

Pete grabbed the coat from the back of his chair. "Do you really think he'd do that?"

"He's a sneaky bastard, so yeah, I think he would."

"I'll call you if I find out anything urgent."

"Thanks, Pete."

I felt I was losing a grip on the case. Something had to give, and soon.

"Anyone fancy a coffee?"

"I wouldn't mind one," Joanna said.

"Nothing for me," Will said. "I'm trying to give it up."

"Okay, won't be long."

I pulled my phone out, hoping Layla had called and I'd missed it, but nothing. There was a text from Bella, which made me feel slightly more cheery. I'd grab the coffee for Joanna, then take an early lunch, and head around to see Bella and the baby. She was probably lonely now Simon had returned to barracks.

Bella stepped aside, allowing me in. "You're a sight for sore eyes."

"It's only been a few days," I replied, my tone reflecting my mood.

"Ooh, what's the matter with you?"

I walked towards the kitchen. "Make me a coffee and I'll tell you."

"It must be bad."

I sat at the table. "I only came around for a moan and to have a cuddle with the baby."

"Well moan away, but little Dylan is fast asleep, thank God, and I'd like him to stay that way."

"He's always asleep."

"Trust me, he isn't." She grinned. "I made a lovely lemon sponge earlier, want a slice?"

"Yeah, I do, but I won't."

"Come on, it'll cheer you up."

"Cake isn't going to change my mood, Bells, but if you're so insistent, shove a few slices in a tub and I'll pig out tonight once I get home."

"No problem." She carried on making the coffee then sat opposite me.

I picked up the steaming mug. "Just what I needed."

"Come on then, face ache, spit it out. What's going on?"

"This bloody case. We've got nothing to go on, and the bodies are piling up. It won't be long before I'm booted off it and they'll bring in a competent detective."

"Piffle! That won't happen. You know you're an ace detective and so do they. It's just unfortunate your first case as DI is a doozy and there's no evidence to sink your teeth into. That's not your fault."

"I'm not so sure, but as well as this case wrecking my head, Layla is doing her level best to get the sack."

"What do you mean?"

"She's off sick and hasn't been calling in."

"Have you spoken to her?"

"Yeah, I called round to her place at the weekend. She looked terrible but promised she'd sort herself out and call me daily until she handed her sick note in."

"So, it's long term then?"

"Looks like it, but we have a replacement for her–Genevieve Tanner."

"Oh, I know her. A right frosty-faced cow she is."

I laughed. "Give the girl a chance."

"I know, I know. Just saying is all."

"You're such a bitch, but I miss you. I can't wait until you get back from maternity leave."

"Me neither."

––––––––––––

"Sorry," I gasped, as I rushed over to Steve already seated at the table. "Rush hour traffic was a nightmare."

"Don't worry about it. I ordered just like you said."

"Good, I'm starving."

"Haven't you eaten anything today?"

"I called round to see Bells for lunch but decided not to have the cake she tried to tempt me with."

"You're mad, I would have had it."

"I need to watch what I eat. You won't want me if I turn into a lard arse."

"That's true," he said with a straight face.

"Cheek!" I laughed.

Just then, the waiter arrived. The food smelled delicious, but the starter, vegetable spring rolls, was gone too soon. I practically inhaled them. I was thankful for the large main course that arrived soon after. I spooned boiled rice onto my plate then mixed it in with the curry sauce, using the Naan bread to mop it up.

We made total pigs of ourselves, but it was good to spend some quality time together. Steve really was one of the sweetest guys I'd ever met, and I could see a future for us and looked forward to our dirty weekend away. I hadn't mentioned it yet due to the case but would surprise him once it was booked. I'd decided I would take him to Sitges in Spain. I'd been there once before, many years ago, and I'd always wanted to go back. It would be the perfect place for us to be alone.

After dinner, I dropped Steve off at my house and told him I wouldn't be long.

Against my better judgement, I had tried to call Layla, but as I suspected, she ignored me.

It was dark by the time I drove into her close, and rain had started to fall. My windscreen wipers squeaked against the glass.

Pulling up just before I reached Layla's place, I noticed all the house lights on. At least she hadn't gone to bed. I cut the car's engine and was just about to get out but stopped as I noticed a woman, with shoulder-length blonde hair, lower herself into a red Audi TT convertible that was parked across the road.

I saw Layla on the doorstep. I'd never seen her look so angry and wondered if this was the other woman, the one that had destroyed her marriage? "Piss off and don't come back, or you'll be hearing from my solicitor, do you understand me?"

She slammed the door and the hallway light went out.

I caught a quick glimpse of the driver as the Audi slowly passed by. Then, I climbed out of my car and walked up the path to Layla's house. I knew it was a bad time, but I was here now, and we had urgent matters to discuss. What harm could my visiting her do? I knocked.

She peeked from behind the living room curtain, then I heard her shout up the stairs, warning the kids to stay in their bedrooms. Moments later, she almost pulled the door off its hinges. "How long have you been there?" she snapped.

"Only just arrived," I lied, not wanting to embarrass her by admitting I'd seen the woman leave. "Why?"

"You'd better come in."

I stepped inside. "Thanks, I'm sorry to call unannounced but..."

"Do you want a drink?"

"No, I'm good. It's just a quick visit to ask why you haven't been in touch like you promised."

"I didn't think it was worth it."

"Why not?"

"I got a letter from HR yesterday and they want to see me anyway."

"So you just thought you'd make things worse for yourself?"

"Look, Dylan, if you've come around here just to have a go, don't bother–"

"I haven't. I just don't want whatever is going on in your private life to affect your job, and, let's face it, you're already at that stage."

"I'm gonna lose my job anyway, so I might as well get used to it."

"Have you been to see your doctor yet?"

"No, I should have gone today, but I couldn't face going out."

"Can't you get them to do a house call?"

She laughed. "When did you last see a GP? They don't do house calls."

"Even if you explained..."

"It doesn't happen, Dylan."

"Then you have to go to them, I can come with you. Where's your surgery?"

"Greenfield Road—just around the corner."

"Then I'll come and pick you up tomorrow. I'll take you myself then bring you home."

"Why are you doing this, Dylan?"

"Because you're my friend, and I care."

Tears filled her eyes. "I've lost everything."

"No, you haven't. You can turn this around."

"Do you really think so?"

"I know so." My eyes were drawn to a family portrait of her, Max and the kids, hanging on the wall above the fireplace.

They were a good-looking family. I couldn't begin to imagine why he would do what he had to the people he was meant to love more than anything in the world. "I'm sorry this has happened to you, Layla. I know it doesn't seem like it now but, one day, you'll be happy again."

She dissolved into floods of tears and my heart broke for her. I wanted to give her a hug, show her I was there for her, but she didn't want to be touched and kept me at arm's length.

Silently, I cursed Max for treating her so horribly and hoped the time would come when he would be forced to sit and think about his actions and the havoc they had wreaked on Layla's life.

She eventually stopped crying and rubbed at her eyes. "I will go to the doctor's tomorrow, but you don't need to take me. I'll be fine."

"Are you sure?"

"Yes. Thanks though. I do appreciate it, Dylan. And I promise I'll sort my shit out."

Knowing how mentally fragile she was, I wouldn't get my hopes up.

THIRTY-NINE

Exhausted, I climbed into bed beside Steve, who was already out for the count and snoring gently.

Even though I shouldn't, I felt a little guilty again. Something I promised myself I wouldn't do.

Steve didn't complain or give any indication he was pissed off with me. The guilt was born from a combination of a heavy workload and a history of needy and jealous exes.

When I'd told him I had to stay up and read through the case file, he didn't seem to mind. He just kissed the top of my head and toddled off upstairs to bed. I hadn't intended to stay up so late, but something was niggling at me and I couldn't put my finger on what.

Snuggling in to him, I felt contented and secure. A nice feeling I wasn't used to.

As I drifted off, images of the dead girls filled my mind—no doubt brought on by my choice of bedtime reading. I still couldn't shake the huge sense of loss I felt for Kimberley, a girl I didn't really know but, as Avaline, I'd developed a connection with her and liked her—a lot.

Her death made me doubt my ability as a detective. It didn't bode well for me if I couldn't protect someone under my very nose like that. While I was parading about the stage making a complete fool of myself, poor Kimberley was having her head staved in. This knowledge made me shudder.

Then there was Layla. If I wasn't mistaken, she was heading for some sort of breakdown—screaming from the doorstep like some fishwife. And who the hell was that woman anyway? She'd certainly seemed familiar. It wasn't her mum, of that I was certain—her mum was short, petite even. She was the complete opposite of Layla who was tall, almost six foot and statuesque. In fact, kickboxing clearly kept her in fine physical shape. I wouldn't like a kick around the ear-hole from her, put it that way.

I yawned, more than ready for sleep to take me for a while.

Steve changed his position and snaked an arm around my middle, holding me tight.

I smiled in the darkness and felt myself slip away.

It was out of my reach. I needed to get to it but it was just too far. Shifting my position, I lifted my head, opened one eye and peeked at the clock. 5:49am. I groaned and buried my head underneath the duvet. I'd only had a couple of hours' sleep, if that. What the hell had woken me?

I'd been dreaming but what about? I felt I should remember but the more I tried to focus on it the further away the memory seemed to be.

Something suddenly occurred to me. Was I being stupid? It certainly seemed far-fetched. I was still half-asleep after all.

Sliding from the bed, I tiptoed downstairs. After locating my phone, I trawled through reams of photographs until I found what I was looking for. The face of the woman I'd seen at Layla's gazed back at me.

"Oh, my God!" I gasped. After hurriedly getting dressed, I scribbled a quick note for Steve, and left the house.

By the time I got to the station I'd convinced myself I was totally wrong and put my wild imagination down to over-stimulating my brain before bed. That would teach me.

I stared at the incident board—unsure of what the hell I expected to find, but willing myself to see something, anything. We'd still had no joy with the traveller who'd bought the van, even though Will had contacted all the surrounding stations for assistance. If the van was still in the area, it would've been found by now, surely.

It still niggled me about the sex shop and the fact I kept forgetting to ask Will if he'd got any further with it. All that was written beside it on the board was the name of the manager.

I sat at my desk and googled Damien Robinson, just for something to do. When the page loaded, I gasped, my thoughts in a spin. "What the actual fuck?" I said aloud, in total shock.

It turned out Robinson's business partner was none other than Monahan Holdings. Further delving named Maxwell Monahan as the managing director.

I felt sick to my stomach. I'd hoped and prayed I was barking up the wrong tree, but I clearly wasn't. I knew in my heart of hearts I was right. But what was I going to do about it?

I went into one of the side rooms and began writing on the white board fixed to the wall.

. . .

I drew a brainstorming graph—a circle with several lines going off it.

In the centre I wrote MAX.

I shook my head again. How could this even be possible?

From the lines I wrote;

-Inside knowledge—access to the file?

    -Connection to the transgender community.

    -Access to the prosthetics.

Layla could've left the file lying around at home and Max could've read it just like Steve had. But there were still a few things I couldn't link to Max

-van??

    -connection to each of the victims?

    -Who had access to the back staircase at Rebecca's?

    -CCTV–knowledge of camera placement.

My chest tightened. I could barely breathe. Goosebumps covered my entire body. Was I deluded? I'd need firm evidence before I could mention this to the rest of the team or they'd think I'd lost my marbles, and who knows, I may well have done.

Rubbing out Max's name from the centre of the circle I hesitated, then wrote, LAYLA.

FORTY

By the time Will arrived, I'd compiled a list and got my head around what I was going to do.

I quickly erased the name from the middle of the circle—not ready to share my thoughts with anyone just yet. I needed to do one final thing first. There would be no point letting the cat out of the bag without something concrete to back up my wild and far-fetched theory.

"Bloody hell, boss," Will said. "You startled me then. You're in early."

"I've been here hours already."

"Why? Has something happened?"

"Not really. But I am working on a theory."

"Can you share?"

"Soon, just not yet. Wish me luck." I gathered all my stuff together from the spare desk and crammed it into my satchel.

Twenty minutes later, I parked my car a little further up the street from Layla's house. Then, I sat and watched in my rear-view mirror.

I didn't have to wait long. Slumping down in my seat, I saw Layla and the three boys pile into her car and drive from the street.

Once she'd gone, I turned on the car engine and drove onto her driveway.

Eyeing the house, I was certain nobody was home, but I needed to appear genuine, just in case. I approached the front door and knocked. After waiting a sufficient amount of time, I headed down the side of the house alongside the garage. I stopped and pressed my face up close to the window. It was so dark inside, I couldn't make anything out. I needed to get inside.

Around the back of the house, I knocked on the door before trying the handle. No luck. Then I froze. A car had pulled up outside the front of the house.

"Fuck! That was quick," I muttered rushing back down the side of the house. I took a deep breath and fixed a smile to my face before stepping out front.

"Oh, hello, Dylan isn't it?"

I exhaled as Layla's mum suddenly appeared in front of me. "Oh, hi, Pixie. I was looking for Layla."

"She's taken the boys to school. She shouldn't be too long. Do you want to come in and wait? I wouldn't mind a word with you in private, actually."

"Of course." I was willing to agree to anything if it meant I'd have a few minutes to get into that bloody garage.

She opened the door and ushered me in. "I was just wondering how I could get hold of you, and here you are—seems someone must be looking down on me."

"Intriguing." I smiled as I followed her to the kitchen, quickly scanning the doors off the hallway to work out which of them led to the garage. I deduced the door at the very end had to be it, as the others were all open.

"I'm worried about my daughter, Dylan. I can call you Dylan, can't I?" Pixie continued, dragging my attention back to her.

"Of course you can. What are you worrying about? Is it this business with Max?"

"She told you?" Her eyes almost shot from her head.

"Yeah. We don't *just* talk about work, you know. I'd like to think we're friends as well as colleagues."

"I'm astounded she would tell you something like this though. But she's not coping. She told me she made a mistake at work and that she's in big trouble."

"I can't really discuss it, but there's nothing that can't be fixed."

She began filling the kettle. "Oh that's a relief. Layla refuses to discuss it. Between you and me, I don't think she could take much more. Tea or coffee?"

"I'd love a coffee," I said. "But do you mind if I use the loo?"

"Of course, do you know where it is?"

I nodded and left the room, heading straight for the garage door. I was relieved when it opened.

It took a second or two for my eyes to adjust. The garage was full of boxes, and two huge objects, both covered with a tarpaulin, stood side by side in each of the parking bays.

"Did you get lost?" Pixie said, suddenly behind me.

"I did, I could've sworn it was this room.

"No, the one next door."

I headed into the bathroom, my heartbeat going ten to the dozen. If I was right—Layla was definitely our killer. I just needed to check what was underneath those bloody tarpaulins.

Pixie was hovering in the hallway by the time I'd finished in the bathroom. "Coffee's ready," she called.

There was no chance of me getting back inside the garage. I'd need to think of another way to find out what was in there. I returned to the kitchen and sat at the dining table.

She handed me a mug of coffee and it smelled divine. "Thanks. This is the first one I've had today. I'd usually be onto my fifth cup by now."

"Layla drinks far too much coffee as well. It must be something to do with the job."

"Yeah. No doubt. We rarely get time for lunch so we live on the stuff." I smiled. "I was surprised by everything in the garage. What are those two big things covered over?"

She rolled her eyes. "My ex's belongings. It was only meant to be here for a short while until he got himself sorted, but he took off to France and Layla hasn't seen him in ages."

"Really? What are they?"

"A caravan and a vehicle of some kind. Don't know, really. I've told her I'd scrap them if I was her. They're not worth anything."

My heart was racing. "A caravan? Seems strange to leave a caravan with somebody."

"It's his mum's. He had it when we first got together and it's just a pile of crap now. But it's all he has to his name. I suppose I shouldn't have expected anymore, marrying a traveller."

Her words sealed Layla's fate. Layla's dad was the traveller who bought the van. The last loose end was finally tied.

"What time did you say Layla would be back?"

"I thought she'd be here by now. Maybe she's gone to see Max again—they've been arguing a lot lately."

I thought I'd bite the bullet and ask her outright. "So, what do you think about him being a transsexual?"

"I think it's disgusting. I mean, I have no problem with transsexuals in general, if that's what a person feels then fine. But why wasn't he honest with everyone prior to him getting married and having three kids? It makes me sick."

It took all of my self-control to be able to remain calm. I got to my feet and put the cup in the sink. "I can't wait any longer. I'll come back later to see Layla."

"Don't tell her I spoke to you—she'll go mad at me for interfering."

"Maybe it's best she doesn't know I stopped by then?"

"Good idea. I'll see you out."

FORTY-ONE

I rushed back into the office, wondering how I was going to explain my findings, and make everyone see I was telling the truth.

I burst in through the doors, all eyes turned to me. "We need to get a team round to Layla's right now."

"What's going on, boss?" Will asked.

"I think Layla is our killer." I was aware how crazy I sounded and even though, in my heart, I knew I was right, saying it out loud was another matter.

"Are you winding us up?" Joanna asked, her face a picture of confusion.

"No, I'm not." The room descended into chaos as we all talked over one another.

"What the hell is going on in here?" Janine roared as she came crashing into the room.

"Dylan thinks Layla's the killer," Pete added.

"Our Layla? A killer?" She turned to me. "Have you lost your mind?"

"I know it seems that way, but we need to get around there, like now."

"Hold your horses, Dylan," Janine ordered. "Are you seriously accusing a long-serving member of your team of murder? Have you taken leave of your senses?"

"I know how crazy it sounds, but listen to me, please, or we could all be making the biggest mistake of our careers."

I had the attention of the whole room.

"Talk and make it fast," Janine ordered.

"I popped round to visit Layla last night to see if there was anything I could do for her, and, as I pulled up, I witnessed Layla basically throwing a woman out of her front door."

"So what?" Janine commented. "It could have been this other woman of Max's."

"That's what I thought, initially, as she rushed past my car. I didn't get that good a look at her, but something about her must have caused a trigger because I woke up dead early this morning and realised who she was."

"Yeah, yeah," Janine said, having lost interest. "This is all very well and good, but why would it make you think Layla is the killer?"

"Because the person rushing out of Layla's house was her ex-husband, Max."

"Hang on a minute..." Janine looked confused. "... you just said it was a woman leaving Layla's house. Make up your mind, Dylan."

The rest of the team tittered at what they clearly thought was a badly executed joke.

I was pissed off they weren't taking me seriously. "I know what I said, but Max *was* the woman leaving the house, and he's transgender." I looked around the room. The whole team stared at me open mouthed.

"Is it April Fool's Day, or something?" Janine asked, sarcastically. "Very funny."

"I know you think I've lost the plot but please give me the benefit of the doubt here, and if I'm wrong, I'll resign. But we have to get around there, now."

"No, Dylan." Her eyes narrowed. "You're not leaving here spouting this madness about one of our highly respected officers."

"Layla is our killer, Janine, I know it."

"Give me some proof and we'll talk," she said. "For all you know, Max could have been going to a fancy-dress party. *If* it was Max you saw."

The team laughed.

I wish it was as easy as that because I wouldn't be responsible for taking down my own partner. "Please, I know I'm right about this."

Janine exhaled. "Then let's suppose for a moment I believe what you're telling me–what evidence do you have?"

"For starters, Layla's Mum, Pixie, confirmed that Max is transgender."

I noted the expression on Janine's face. "You're serious, aren't you?"

"I wouldn't joke about something like this, but there's more. Max is managing director of Monahan Holdings and they own the sex shop where the prosthetics were procured."

"Oh, my God," Will said. "But didn't Layla volunteer–"

"To go round there and speak to the manager." I finished his sentence. "Yeah, she did, but according to her, there was no CCTV or anything that could lead us to a suspect."

"Dylan, you have to be certain everything you are saying is correct because the fallout will be..." Janine shook her head.

"I know it's definitely her. There's a vehicle parked in her garage and I'm certain it's the Transit van. Pixie confirmed it belonged to her ex-husband and he's a traveller."

"Heather, Pete stay here and see what you can find out. Get in touch with Max's GP and confirm he's trans. Will, you're with me and Dylan." She was halfway across the room while my mind was still whirling. "Come on, you lot, move it, now."

"Pete, get uniform round to Layla's stat, but make sure you tell them she's possibly armed."

I jumped in behind the wheel. Janine sat beside me, and Will in the back.

"I can't believe this," Will said.

"Me neither, I'd give anything to be wrong." I sighed.

"Layla told me herself; Max had another woman," Will added. "It doesn't make sense."

"Max *is* the other woman, simple as."

"But why didn't she just tell us what was going on? There's no shame in it. We would have supported her no matter what."

"I'm no psychologist," Janine said as I shot out of the car park. "But imagine how you'd feel if your marriage was a sham and you found out your husband was going to have his dick cut off."

I cringed at Janine's analysis, knowing there was so much more to what the transgender community went through before surgery was even discussed.

Traffic was building and we were slowing to a halt.

"Shit," I said, banging the steering wheel.

"We don't have time for this, Dylan, get the blues and twos going and shift this lot out the way."

I did as she ordered and minutes later we were speeding down the dual carriageway.

"Why don't you try to call Layla?" Will asked.

"I'll do it," Janine volunteered.

"No offence, but if *you* call her, she'll know something's up. I'll do it." I hit redial.

We were only a few minutes from her house now, but I was desperate to talk to her, knowing what was coming. If she heard the sirens, would she suspect her time was up?

She didn't answer.

The tyres screeched as I rounded the corner.

"Jesus, Dylan," Janine shrieked. "This isn't an episode of Cagney and Lacey, you know." She was holding onto the dashboard.

I turned into Layla's estate. "She's still not here. Her car's not here."

"It might be in the garage," Will added.

"I already told you, the Transit is in there."

I pulled the car to a stop.

"Let me go first. Will, you go and make sure nobody is trying to get out the back."

He disappeared down the side of the house.

I banged on the door.

Janine stayed behind me.

"Hang on, I'm coming." It was Pixie. She pulled the door open and looked surprised to see me standing there. "Oh, hello again. Sorry, but Layla isn't back yet."

"Have you heard from her?"

"No," she said, looking at Janine. "Is everything okay, Dylan?"

"We need to find Layla as soon as possible. Do you know where she is?"

"She took the kids to school. I told you that earlier. Now, what's going on?"

Janine stepped forward. "My name is Janine Kerrigan and I'm Layla's boss. Can we step inside for a moment, Pixie? I don't want the whole street hearing this."

"Well, yeah, I suppose, but I need to call my daughter and make sure she's okay."

Pixie turned and we followed her inside.

Will was now at the French doors.

"Who the hell is he?" Pixie's voice had raised a few octaves.

"He also works for me. Do you mind if I let him in? We need to conduct a search of the property."

"Hang on a minute. You didn't say anything about that. This is my daughter's house and she won't be pleased with people rifling through her things."

I decided to be honest. "Listen, Pixie. I'm not going to bullshit you, but I believe Layla is responsible for the recent murders, you know, the ones on the news."

"The trannie murders?" Her eyes widened with shock.

I didn't have time to debate with her. "Yes, the trannie murders."

"Don't be so bloody stupid. She's a cop—and a damn good one too."

"You confirmed earlier your ex-husband's van is in the garage, and, if I'm right, it's the same one we spotted on CCTV after a couple of the murders.

She fell back onto the sofa. "I don't believe you."

"I don't want to believe it either, but your daughter is killing innocent women."

Janine stepped forward. "Do we have your permission to search the entire property?"

Pixie nodded, the wind clearly knocked out of her sails.

Just then, I heard a van pull up outside and assumed it was armed response.

"Will, let the guys in please. Then the door at the end of the hallway is the garage—check under the tarpaulins."

"Got it, boss." He looked pale. The shock at what his friend and colleague had done had clearly hit him hard. "I'll get uniform to search upstairs and see if they find anything worthwhile."

I turned back to Pixie. "Can you please try to call Layla to find out where she is? But don't tell her we're here. I don't want her harming anybody else, or herself."

"She'll see our cars if she arrives home, then make a run for it," Janine reminded me.

Pixie grabbed her phone from the coffee table and put it to her ear. "It's ringing."

"Not a word." I held my finger up to my lips.

To my surprise, Layla answered.

"Hiya, love, I was just wondering what time you'd be back?" I could hear Layla's voice, but not what she was saying. "No, not at all. I was just wondering where you are, is all." More words I couldn't make out. "Oh, you don't want to do that love. You know it'll only end in another row. Just come straight home and I'll make you a nice cuppa." Pixie listened, her face stricken with fear. "Okay, well if you're sure, I'll see you when you get back, Yeah, of course. Bye, love. Take care." She hung up and turned to us. "She's going to Max's."

"I need Max's address, now."

"All I know is he's moved into a rental somewhere near Woolton, but the address is on the fridge. Hang on a minute." Pixie rushed to the kitchen and returned with a post-it note. "122 Primrose Gardens. But she won't hurt him, not my Layla. She wouldn't."

"I hope you're right, believe me, I do. But I'm gonna need you to promise me you won't breathe a word of this to Layla. If she gets wind we're onto her, there's no telling what she'll do."

"Boss," Will shouted from the back of the house.

"Coming."

A uniformed officer entered the living room. "Stay with Pixie please."

Janine and I walked into the garage. The tarpaulin had been pulled off the Transit van. There was no doubt it was the same vehicle.

"What have you found, Will?" Janine asked.

"Look here," he replied.

The back doors of the van were wide open.

We stepped closer.

"My God," I said as Will held up voice distortion equipment. "She had it all planned."

"That's not all," Will added. "There're clothes in here, all black, covered in what looks like blood."

"Layla, what have you done?" Janine shook her head, looking weary. "This is going to cause a stink when the papers find out."

"Fuck the papers," I snapped. "She's one of us, and we have to make sure she doesn't hurt anybody else."

"Dylan, she's a cold-blooded killer."

"She's still one of us. You know as well as I do, this isn't her—she's lost it."

"This little lot says otherwise, boss," Will said. "Looks like she knew exactly what she was doing and was one step ahead of us all the way—clever bitch."

I was on the verge of tears. She was still my partner and I was going to be the one responsible for locking her up.

"Dylan, come on, we don't have time for this," Janine said, bringing me back to the moment. "We have to get over to Max's before it's too late."

"I'll stay here, boss. In case she comes back," Will said.

Janine was on her phone. "Get a team round to 122 Primrose Gardens, Woolton, now, but don't go in until I get there."

Minutes later, Janine and I were back in the car and heading towards Max's.

"I pray we're not too late." Surely she wouldn't hurt the father of her children. I had to hold onto that because the alternative was too grim to contemplate.

"The Professional Standards Department will eat us alive,"

Janine said. "We'll all be hauled in for not spotting one of our own is capable of murder."

"They can kiss my arse," I replied. "How were we to know? She never gave us any reason to believe she was acting out of the ordinary. She was going through a divorce and was down about it–which is understandable." I pressed the phone icon on my hands-free kit and hit the redial button. Layla's voicemail clicked in. "Layla, it's Dylan. Call me urgently, please. I'm on my mobile."

FORTY-TWO

After dropping the kids off at school, Layla pulled up in a layby and cried.

Everything had spun out of control. The things she'd done to those men were terrible, she knew that now. Having this time at home to ponder on her actions had made her realise that.

She knew it was only a matter of time before the team discovered she was the killer. Especially now she wasn't there to tamper with their findings. There was also Darren Wilkes' body to consider. It wouldn't stay hidden forever, and she'd killed him with no protective clothing on.

She'd bumped into him as she left Kimberley's house and chased him over the waste ground next door, and through to the mini woodland beyond. After overpowering the scumbag, she'd smashed his skull with a rock, and, unlike the other murders, it had felt so good. It had been at that moment reality dawned on her—Darren had deserved to die, the others hadn't.

She'd had no choice but to leave his body where it was. Because there was an ANPR on the Transit van she'd decided to leave it in the garage at home but parked her car far enough away for it not to trigger any suspicion. She knew, without a doubt, that as soon as Darren's body was found the game would be up for her.

The thought of being taken away from her kids tore her apart. She wasn't a bad person, not really. She'd just made some bad choices. Doesn't everybody at some point in their lives? She hadn't been in her right mind.

The person she should have taken her hurt out on was Max. He was the one who had deserved every ounce of her venom, she could see that now, too. After his visit yesterday, when he told her he intended to fight her for shared custody, Layla knew what she had to do. There was no way she would allow that fucking freak to bring up her boys. No way!

Wiping her eyes, she checked her reflection in the rear-view mirror. She looked like a bag of shite, but maybe that would work in her favour. The doctor would have to take her seriously and grant her a sick-note. There was no point going back to work. Apart from the fact she wasn't fit to tie her own shoelaces most days, she couldn't continue being part of the team investigating the crimes *she'd* committed. Day after day, she'd been forced to listen to them slagging off the killer, but they didn't know the motives and hadn't gone through what she had—the humiliation, the self-doubt, having to watch her kids fall apart.

She'd done okay at first and had been lucky she was able to intercept when Will tracked down the prosthetics to Max's shop. But that had been her only mistake until Darren, and thankfully she'd managed to get out of it by saying the shop had no CCTV or records. That hadn't been a lie as she'd stolen the box of dicks when visiting there one evening for a meeting—she was a shareholder in all of Max's companies. What had she been thinking? Had she planned to rid the area of all transsexuals? What would that have solved? Her problem would still exist. Max, or Maxine as he now wanted to be called, would still exist.

She drove to the doctor's surgery, making the appointment by the skin of her teeth. But the receptionist told her they were running behind. She'd been lucky to get a cancellation in the first place when she'd rung first thing this morning, so she couldn't complain. She took a seat and waited.

Her phone rang several times. Bloody Dylan! Why wouldn't he leave her alone? She told him she'd go to the doctors and she'd kept her word. He was acting like her father not her boss, and she already had one waste of space father, thank you very much. She didn't need another.

"Layla Monahan," the receptionist called.

Startled from her thoughts, Layla sprang to her feet. She was living on her nerves and wasn't too far gone to know this couldn't continue. She needed help—and fast.

The doctor, a pompous looking old fart she'd never seen before, didn't even look up from his computer screen when she entered, which irritated her. "Take a seat, please." After a short while, he took off his glasses and turned to her—a bored expression on his face. "What can I do for you?"

She wanted to smash his teeth in. How dare he treat her like this?" She glared at him, not saying a word.

"Miss..." he checked the screen, "... Monahan?" Suddenly his expression changed to concern, or was he just uncomfortable at her odd behaviour? No doubt people didn't confront him very often. Doctors made a habit of intimidating their patients. She'd seen it before, countless times. But she wasn't going to stand for it.

"I came here for help—of course I did—doesn't everyone?"

"Ye-yes." He nodded, sitting up a little taller in his chair. "How can I help you?"

"I don't like you. I don't like your attitude. Let me give you a few home truths, shall I?"

He nodded. "If you like." He fiddled with his tie self-consciously.

"When a person has crashed, hit rock bottom, and needs help, the last thing she wants to do is admit it—to lay her feelings bare for all to see. Doing this is hard even when presented with a gentle, caring face to confide in, but being faced with a pig-headed, uninterested prick like you, I'd rather stick pins in my eyes than tell you a thing. I suggest you work on your attitude, doctor." She stood up with such force the chair toppled backwards crashing into the bookcase behind her.

"Take note of my name. When you next hear it, remember, you could've made all the difference." As she stomped from the room, she heard him chasing behind her.

"Ms Monahan, come back. I apologise if I made you feel like that. It was never my intention."

"Shut it! I'm not interested." By then they were out in reception and everyone had turned to look at them. "Good luck to the next person booked in to see this fucker."

She stormed from the building. No Medication. No sick-note. No better off at all.

Still fuming, she got into her car and slammed her hands on the steering wheel. Why was everything so bloody difficult? Max's confession had started her problems and now, bit by bit, her entire life was cascading downhill fast like an avalanche, and she couldn't see a way out of it.

Max seemed totally oblivious to the mayhem he'd caused. Wrapped up in his own world, he didn't care about the effect his actions were having on his family.

After starting the engine, she did a three-point turn and

headed across the city to Max's new house. She would show him. Let's see how he dealt with *her* confessions for a change.

Her phone rang again. It was her mother. She contemplated ignoring it but what if something was wrong with one of the kids? She accepted the call. "I'm driving, Mum, what's up?"

"Hiya, love, I was just wondering what time you'd be back?"

"Don't know. I've got stuff to do. Why, is something wrong?

"No, not at all. I was just wondering where you are, is all."

"I'm going to see Max. We have things to discuss."

"Oh, you don't wanna do that love. You know it'll only end in another row. Just come straight home and I'll make you a nice cuppa."

"No row, Mum. I promise you. This time I intend to sort out this shit once and for all."

"Okay, well if you're sure, I'll see you when you get back."

"Can you pick up the boys for me if I'm not there in time?"

"Yeah, of course. Bye, love. Take care."

Max's car wasn't parked in the driveway of the fully furnished house he rented.

Layla parked down the street and then doubled back on foot. After searching for a few minutes, she found the spare key under a rock in one of the plant pots beside the front door.

No matter how many times she'd warned him about security, she knew he'd never change. The beeping of the alarm sounded as she opened the door and punched in a sequence of numbers, hoping he'd chosen the same number they'd always used. The beeping stopped.

Once inside, Layla scanned the ground floor, searching for signs of Max having a partner. If he had, would they be male or female? She had no idea. It was pointless looking for evidence of another woman, there were lacy knickers drying on the radiator and silk scarves hanging on the coat rack, but that didn't mean he had another woman, did it? Then, on the other hand, any male items could be his too. She had no clue how it all worked.

Upstairs, in the master bedroom, she found her answer. The unmade bed had only been slept in on one side. That made her feel a little better. She sat on the bed and reached for the crumpled pillow, dragging it to her, and hugging it to her chest. She buried her head into it and inhaled his scent.

She felt as though her broken heart had been ripped from her chest and smashed to smithereens. How could he do this to her? Had their entire marriage been a sham?

Pulling the phone from her jeans' pocket, she dialled Max's number.

"Layla," Max said—or was it Maxine? His voice had a certain softness to it when he was in character. But she just wanted to talk to her husband.

"I'm at your house. We need to talk."

"I'm pretty tied up right n—"

"We need to talk NOW, Max."

"Okay, the key is—"

"I know where the fucking key is. I'm sitting on your bed. Hurry up."

"I'll be there as soon as I can."

"You've got five minutes before I start swinging your golf club around the display cabinets you love so much." She glanced at the three glass cabinets filled with Star Wars figurines—his pride and joy. It didn't surprise her that he had them in his bedroom. He loved them more than he'd ever loved her and the kids. Of that, she was certain.

"You wouldn't," Max boomed, the soft voice forgotten.

"Try me."

"I'm on my way."

Less than five minutes later, she heard a car pull up and high heels click-clacking across the driveway and into the house.

"Layla? Where are you?"

"In your bedroom."

He thundered up the stairs, sounding like an all-in wrestler—not a bit lady-like. As he burst into the room, he scanned the cabinets for any sign of damage.

"Don't fret. I haven't touched them—yet."

She thought he might pass out in relief. "That's not funny, Layla. I almost killed myself to get here."

"I wasn't trying to be funny, Maxwell. I was deadly serious. Now can you get that ridiculous outfit off? I want to talk to my husband."

"I've told you, I'm Maxine now. The doctor said I have to live my life as a woman or they won't consider putting me forward for surgery. Max has gone, so whatever you've got to say, spit it out."

"I have no intention discussing anything with you while you're dressed like that. Have some fucking respect for me and the life we once shared."

He shook his head and sighed heavily. "I don't want to discuss anything with you, Layla. I just want to see my children, like we agreed in mediation."

"You left them, remember," she screamed.

"There was no way I could've stayed, you know that. It was too hard dealing with your hurt on top of everything else I was going through."

"All along it's been about you, Max! You made all the decisions. Neither me, nor the kids, who you say you love so much, had any say in the matter."

"It's not a lifestyle choice, Layla." He sounded frustrated. "Even you're not naïve enough to believe that."

"Just look at the state of you, Maxwell." Layla pointed at him. "All dressed up like a pantomime dame."

"My. Name. Is. Maxine," he said through gritted teeth.

"No. It's. Not." She hissed. "You'll always be Maxwell to me and Dad to our children, no matter how much you want to play dress up."

"I've always *been* Maxine."

"You can pretend to be who you like in your own time, but not in front of the kids. They already have one mother, they don't need another."

He rolled his eyes. "Did you read the book I gave you?"

"No, I didn't read your fucking perverted book, and have no intention of doing so either. Now, I'm warning you, Maxwell. Don't push me, because the mood I'm in, I'll smash every last one of those pathetic figurines and your face with it."

"Okay, okay. But let's go downstairs first."

"I'm not going anywhere. Now, get out of that stupid fucking outfit, wipe that shit off your face, and act like a man. I need some normality before I'm able to discuss the future of my children."

"No! This is me. Get used to it." He put his hands on his hips and eyed her defiantly. "We're getting divorced. I'll no longer be your husband so you can forget it. Nothing you can say will make any difference. I've made up my mind. I'm going for full custody."

She got to her feet and walked towards him. "Seems ironic that the imminent removal of your balls has allowed you to grow a pair, doesn't it?"

He was about to open his mouth to respond when Layla sucker punched him in the stomach. He groaned and bent double.

She expertly positioned him with a series of light foot taps before going in with a front kick to the chest.

He flew backwards, and smashed into the first cabinet, sending shards of glass and his beloved figurines scattering around the room.

She watched him scrambling about on his hands and knees, skirt up around his waist, while frantically trying to retrieve each precious item. He was so far gone he hadn't even noticed the large triangular piece of glass protruding from his temple or the jagged flap of skin on his forearm that was squirting blood all over his pretty peach-coloured blouse.

FORTY-THREE

I banged the steering wheel then pressed my hand against the horn. Adrenaline coursed through my body.

"Move, dickhead," I yelled, as a delivery van pulled to a sudden halt, ignoring the siren.

Janine held onto the dashboard again, as I manoeuvred around the van.

"Dylan, slow down for Christ's sake or we'll end up in an accident."

"We don't have time. For all we know, Max could be lying dead and what then?"

"We don't know Layla's intending to harm him."

"What else would she be going around there for?"

"She might need to discuss the kids, or the house, anything. Just slow down, please."

I didn't listen to her and zoomed out of town, towards Woolton. "Why didn't I see it?" I was furious with myself. Some detective I was that I didn't notice my own partner massacring innocent people right under my nose. "Fuck," I said, out loud.

"None of us saw what was happening, Dylan. She covered

her tracks well. You can't blame yourself."

"Those poor girls. I could have stopped her." I was wallowing, I knew it, but I'd carry the guilt with me forever. Kimberley's face flashed into my mind and I felt sick. Why had Layla chosen her? Was it because I'd introduced them? It had to be.

"Enough, Dylan, just focus on the road."

"I need to call her again."

Janine picked up my phone.

"Press redial then turn the speakerphone on." It started to ring, and I willed her to answer. "Come on, Layla, answer the friggin' phone."

Voicemail clicked in again.

"Let's just focus on getting there in one piece, okay?" Janine said looking as anxious as I felt.

Layla pulled her vibrating phone from her pocket and shook her head—*Dylan again. What is that man's problem?*

She turned back to Max who was still frantically grasping for the figurines and collecting them in a pocket he'd made from his skirt. He seemed unaware of the glass shredding his fingers.

The scorn she felt for him soon turned to anger once again and she stepped forwards and kicked the underside of his skirt, sending the stupid toys flying for the second time.

"No!" he cried. "What's wrong with you?"

"You!" she screamed into his face. "You're what's wrong with me. Don't you get it?" She twisted and kicked him again—the arch of her foot connected with his nose and a satisfying crack reached her ears.

He cried out and began sobbing like a baby.

"Shut up!" she screamed. The state of him appalled her. He was a pathetic excuse for a man. Why hadn't she noticed it before? "I don't believe I took everything you did to me out on all those innocent people. You're to blame for every one of them, Max. You and you alone."

He froze with his hand pressed to his face and stared at her, wide eyed, clearly petrified. "What are you talking about? You're fucking crazy—you know that?" His fingers touched on the shard of glass protruding from his head and, with an anguished cry, he yanked it out.

"I'll show you fucking crazy."

Dragging him to his feet, she attempted to remove his clothing, but he spun around and made a run for the door.

She was behind him in an instant and drop-kicked him in the centre of his back.

He landed with a thud and skidded along the polished wooden floorboards of the landing, stopping just before the top of the stairs.

In an instant, she was beside him and grabbed at the skirt, tearing the fabric with ease.

"Stop, it. Please, Layla. I'm begging you." His words sounded distorted because his face was smooshed up against the floor.

"You had your chance to put this right, but you chose not to."

"Put what right? I've never done anything to hurt you intentionally. I just needed to be true to myself."

With the skirt lying in tatters beside them, she noticed the French knickers. They were harder to accept than the skirt had been. She remembered all the times he'd bought this style of underwear for her. Had he been buying it for himself all along? In a rage, she tore them from him too—his flaccid penis springing free. Then she lifted his right leg, and flung him, toppling arse over tit, down the stairs.

Her phone rang again from where she'd left it on the bed. As she returned to the bedroom, some movement in her peripheral vision caught her attention outside.

FORTY-FOUR

Layla's heart sank when she saw three, armed response vehicles and several armed officers dotted along the road. She jumped back from the window as Dylan's car drove past.

"Fuck-fuck-fuck!" She'd known she didn't have long, but she hadn't expected it to be this quick. Running back to the stairs, she groaned to see Max had managed to wedge himself halfway down them. The idiot couldn't even fall down the stairs right. Furious, she ran down behind him and kicked him the rest of the way.

As he landed on the hall tiles, she realised he was surprisingly quiet. "You'd better not be dead, you fucker. Not yet, anyway."

A thick smear of blood streaked down the stairs and now began pooling underneath him. It was coming from his arm.

"Wake up, Max." She slapped his face.

No response.

"Wake up, you fucking freak." She needed him awake for this next bit. "We don't have much time." She dragged him by the leg into the kitchen. Conscious of the blood, she didn't want to stain the living room carpet.

He groaned, coming to. "Layla, stop this before it goes too far."

"You still don't get it do you? It's *already* gone too far. Those fuckers outside are here to arrest me. But not until I've finished with you, they won't."

"Arrest you?" His voice was barely more than a whisper. He was such a wimp. Once again she wondered why she hadn't seen it before now.

She rummaged in the drawer next to the sink and chose a filleting knife from the selection.

"Why do they want to arrest you, Layla? What have you done?"

"Never mind that for a minute." She dropped to her knees beside him and smiled. "Why did you put me and the boys through this, Max?"

"You know why," he breathed, closing his eyes. The blood pouring from his arm hadn't let up and rivulets of it ran between the tiles creating a grid of bright red square canals leading away from him.

"Tell me again, I need to understand why you decided to do this."

"I didn't *decide*, Layla. I'm Maxine—have *always* been Maxine. I've just decided to be true to myself, that's all."

"That's all?" He didn't get what he'd put them through. That statement proved it.

He nodded, closing his eyes again.

"So what do you want from all of this?"

"You already know. Let's not do this."

"What do you want?" she said through gritted teeth, gripping the handle of the knife tightly.

"To live my life as a woman. I just want to be accepted, is that so difficult for you to comprehend?"

"Not anymore." With precision and speed, she pulled the

knife from behind her back and lopped off his penis. Amidst his blood-curdling cries, she threw the bloody slug-like thing and it splattered on to his chest.

FORTY-FIVE

"Just call her one more time," I urged Janine.

"She isn't going to answer, Dylan."

"Try, please." I was desperate now. I killed the sirens as I approached Primrose Gardens. Turning left, I sped up the road and eyed the large detached houses with perfectly maintained front gardens. "I don't want to alarm her," I said, explaining my silent approach.

"It doesn't matter now, Dylan. Armed Response is already there, look." She pointed to the commotion at the end of the road. Three police vans were parked at different angles, shielding the front of the property.

Max's house was the last on the row, and it had already been cordoned off, a perimeter created to keep members of the public safe. His neighbours had begun to congregate outside their own homes, craning their necks and gossiping. They were clearly itching to know what had interrupted their day.

I slammed on my brakes behind one of the police vehicles, jumped out of the car, and rushed over. "Have you gone in yet?"

"No," one of the officers stepped forward and replied. "We were ordered to wait for Kerrigan."

Janine appeared on cue. "What do you have for me, Phil?" She was obviously familiar with this officer.

"A dark-haired woman has been spotted inside the property, but that's all we know so far. No sight of anyone else yet, but we did hear someone screaming and glass smashing when we first arrived."

"That'll be Layla," I added.

"Is she really one of ours?"

Janine nodded. "I'm afraid so. Inside the property is DS Layla Monahan. This is her partner, DI Dylan Monroe."

I nodded to him.

"DS Philip Lyons." He held his hand out. "I wish we were meeting under different circumstances."

"Yeah," was all I could think of to say. The niceties could wait until later.

"So, you think she's responsible for the recent trannie murders?"

"We think so," Janine answered. "The evidence is stacked against her, and now this... she's our killer I have no doubt in my mind."

"Damn," Phil replied. "Let's keep who she really is to ourselves for the minute if you don't mind."

"I don't want her harmed, do you hear me?" Janine interrupted.

"We'll do our best, Ma'am, but until we know what we're dealing with, I won't guarantee anything."

"I'm going up to the house," I said.

"No, you're not." Phil grabbed hold of my arm. "I'm running this operation, not you."

"She's *my* partner."

"And she's killed how many people already?"

"Dylan, enough." Janine was trying to diffuse the tension between us. "Stand down until you're told otherwise and that's an order."

"I might be able to get through to her." The stakes had never been higher for me. "Please, let me try to call her again, she might answer this time."

"Go for it," Lyons said. "But try to convince her to come out of her own free will."

Just then, I heard a scream coming from inside the house.

I hit redial again. Voicemail. "Layla, please call me back. Nobody is going to hurt you. We just want to talk to you, I promise."

I ended the call just as there was another ear-splitting scream.

"We have to get in there, Janine, before it's too late."

"Wait," she replied. "Leave Phil and his team to do their job."

I acted impulsively and rushed towards the house.

"Monroe, get your arse back here, right now," Lyons called out.

"I can't, I'm the only one who can stop her."

Another scream came from the house.

"Dylan," Janine called. "Be careful, for Christ's sake." She obviously knew I wouldn't be dissuaded.

As I reached the front door, Lyons yelled across at his team. They dropped to their knees, guns cocked and ready. "Cover him, but nobody fires until I give the order."

I banged on the front door. "Layla, let me in." My heart was hammering inside my chest

A few seconds later, I heard her from inside. "Go away, Dylan."

"Come on, we can talk about this before it goes any further."

"GO AWAY," she roared.

"I just want to talk. Open the door."

I could see her shadow behind the glass. "So they can shoot me? Forget it."

"Is Max okay? Just tell me that, please."

"Get out of here, Dylan. It's too late."

"I care about you, Layla."

She laughed. "You only care about yourself."

"That's not true," I needed her to believe I was on her side. "Open the door and let me in. Just me."

I turned to look at Janine and Lyons. Both shook their heads.

"They'll shoot me if I open the door."

"No, they won't. I swear."

"Tell them to back away and I'll let you in."

I turned again and gestured for them to move back.

"Stand down," Lyons ordered. His face was flushed with anger.

I'd broken protocol and knew I was going to get my arse well and truly kicked for this. "Let me in," I said. "They won't hurt you."

I heard her fiddling with the lock. "Promise me."

"I promise."

"I'm sorry, Dylan. It's all such a mess."

"Let me in, and we can talk."

More rattling came from the lock, then the door opened just wide enough for me to slip through the gap.

As soon as I was in, she locked it again.

This wasn't the Layla I knew. Her face was drawn and her eyes were wild with dark circles beneath. It was clear she was dangerously close to the edge.

"Get in there," she said, rushing me through the door. It was then I noticed the blood-covered knife in her other hand.

I jumped away from her. "Layla, put the knife down."

"Get in there, I said." She pointed down the hallway with the knife.

I gasped. A thick trail of blood went from the stairs to the back of the house. "Oh, no! What have you done?" I rushed into the kitchen. Max was lying on the floor covered in blood. "What the hell have you done?" I dropped to my knees, checking for a pulse.

"Leave him," she sneered. "He deserves everything that's coming to him."

He was out cold, but I could detect a faint pulse. He was bleeding profusely from a deep gash on his arm and his head, but it was the genital mutilation that concerned me the most. I needed to get him out of there and fast or he wasn't going to make it.

"I said, leave him!"

I turned on her. "He's the father of your kids. You can't let him die."

"Father," she bellowed, brandishing the knife. "Don't make me laugh."

"Layla, listen to me. Max needs an ambulance, or he's going to die. Do you understand?"

"Of course I fucking understand. That's the point. I *want* him to die. I can't allow him to get my kids." The Welsh lilt in her voice was even more pronounced than normal.

"Think about it, Layla. The judge will treat you more favourably if you show remorse and get him the help he needs before it's too late."

"You can forget it. If he's dead, he won't get the kids. I can live with that."

"Who will look after them, Layla? Your mum won't want them. She's got her own life to live—you said that yourself. You'll be inside. Do you really want your precious boys to be put into care?"

She hesitated. Was I getting somewhere?

"Let me call an ambulance. If you're still not ready to hand yourself over, you can hold me hostage—just let him go. Okay?"

She nodded. "They're not coming in though. Help me get him out the back door."

Minutes later, we'd dropped Max onto the concrete beside the doorstep. His dismembered penis fell to the ground. Then Layla locked the kitchen door again.

I pulled my phone from my pocket. "I'm calling for the ambulance, don't panic." I held my phone up in front of me until she nodded. Then I called Janine. "We need the paramedics here now. Max is in a bad way and he's outside the back door. No funny business and no-one else will get hurt." I hung up, not listening to Janine's chatter, and slowly placed the phone face up on the table. Layla had received the same training as me and I knew what she would be looking for—had I hung up the phone, was I tricking her in some way? I needed to be careful. I'd seen this kind of manic behaviour before and, although she was relatively calm right now, it didn't mean she would stay like that for long.

She paced the floor, going between the kitchen and the living room, peering from the windows. "What have I done? What have I done?"

"It's okay, Layla. The paramedics are on their way."

She spun around, the knife raised, her eyes glinting viciously. "I don't mean that, you interfering prick! I meant why did I let you convince me to get help?"

I raised my hands, taking a step backwards. "Hey, hey. Put the knife down, Layla."

"No. I need to get him back inside. Now! Before anyone comes."

"It's too late. Look." I nodded at the window and the paramedics entering the property who were flanked by two armed officers.

"No!" She ran towards the back door.

I lunged forwards, grabbing her by the waist, preventing her from getting to Max.

She shoved me off and screamed. Then she half-turned, the knife raised, her eyes wild. She was too far gone to register what she was about to do.

I lifted my arms, covering my face. White hot pain tore through my forearm and I fell backwards.

Layla landed on top of me, a snarl on her face, and raised the knife again.

The gunshot seemed to come from nowhere and Layla was blasted backwards, the knife dropping to the tiles. A pool of blood spread from underneath her, mixing with Max's blood.

Looking around frantically, I spotted the armed officer at the kitchen window, his gun still drawn and aimed at Layla.

EPILOGUE

"Aw, look at him. He's so pale."

Bella's voice infiltrated my dream and I forced myself awake.

The sight of her standing beside my hospital bed with Roy caused an unexpected surge of emotion I'd managed to suppress since being admitted. I had to blink back the tears.

"There you are, darling," Roy said, tenderly, patting my hand. I struggled to swallow the huge lump in my throat. "How are you feeling?"

That was a good question. How was I feeling? "Numb," I whispered.

"That will be the shock, no doubt," Bella said.

I nodded. Steve had been fussing around me since I awoke from surgery—Layla had sliced my arm wide open from elbow to wrist, nicking the main artery—and he'd only just left because I needed sleep, promising to be back before long.

"We would've brought you some flowers, but apparently they're not allowed anymore." Bella plonked a plastic bag onto the side table and proceeded to pull out a pile of magazines and several bars of chocolate.

"I don't need flowers. I'm just happy to see you both." I tried to sit up, but gave up on that idea. I ached like a bitch all over.

"Ouch! Take it easy, hotshot," Bella said, placing a hand on my chest. "Are you okay? Shall I call a nurse?"

I shook my head. "No. It's okay, I'm just sore, that's all. Have you heard how Layla is? Nobody's telling me anything, and Steve refused to ask. He's furious."

"Where is Steve?"

"He's gone to pick up a few things for me. But come on. Tell me. How's Layla?"

"Not as dead as I'd like, unfortunately." She scowled.

I closed my eyes briefly, relieved to hear Layla was still alive. She hadn't looked good when they carried her off on a stretcher. "Where is she? Do you know?"

"Janine told me she survived the surgery."

I turned to Bella again. "And Max?"

"In a bad way. They weren't able to re-attach his penis, apparently. Hopefully they'll be able to bump him up the list for gender reassignment surgery—the poor bastard wanted it gone but not like this."

"Let's hope."

"They need to lock that evil bitch up for the rest of her days."

"Don't be like that, Bells. She's clearly not well."

"Not well? She's a psycho bitch who would've killed you by all accounts. Why are you defending her?"

"Because someone's got to."

"I always knew there was something not quite right about her, but I didn't know she could do something like this. I'd rip her throat out if they left me alone with her for just one minute."

I groaned. Although I was used to Bella's no-nonsense attitude, I wasn't in the mood to argue with her right now.

Roy winked at me and changed the subject. "I called Blanche and told her you can't make it on Friday," he said. "She was gutted, but I promised her you'd be back on board by next week with a bit of luck."

"No, I bloody well won't!"

"Come off it, darling! You're the best act they've had in that place for years."

"He's right, Dylan," Bella piped up. "I haven't stopped talking about your performance all week. I told Penelope and she's desperate to come to see you next time."

"There won't *be* a next time. The case is closed and I'm hanging up my heels for good."

"I thought you'd enjoyed it?" Roy pouted. Had I upset him?

"I did enjoy it, I guess. But it's just not for me."

"Bullshit!" Bella said. "You were bloody amazing, Dylan. And I know you were in your element."

"It was a means to an end. Nothing more, nothing less." As I said the words, I remembered the euphoria I'd felt after each performance. The truth was I would miss the buzz of performing to a crowd. "And besides, I'd never be taken seriously as a detective if I was a drag queen come Friday night."

"Do it one more time," Bella said. "Just for me, simply for the thrill of it, and if you honestly don't enjoy yourself, you won't hear another word about it."

"Good idea." Roy clapped his hands. "I'd be heartbroken if all my hard work was for nothing."

"But what about this?" I said, pointing to my bandaged arm.

"I have plenty of outfits with sleeves to be getting on with," Roy said.

Bella nodded. "There you go. No excuses. Is it a deal?"

I groaned. "One night only?"

They both nodded.

"And then you'll leave me alone?"

More nodding. Why didn't I believe them? Although, now I'd

made the decision, a bubble of excitement began fizzling in my stomach.

Maybe I hadn't quite finished with Avaline just yet...

The End

Di Dylan Monroe Investigates: 2 - I am LunaTIC

ABOUT THE AUTHORS

Netta Newbound lives in The Lake District with her husband, Paul, and their adorable grandson, David.

Marcus Brown lives in North Wales with his partner, Jon, their cat Tobias & three adorable dogs, Susie, Sally and Sammy.

For more information or just to touch base with Netta & Marcus you will find them on:

Facebook
Twitter
Instagram

ACKNOWLEDGMENTS

We'd like thank the following...

Our respective families for their never-ending support.

Gloria Nuckols for all that you do.

Marika for her editing skills.

Carol, Donna & Susan for all their hard work on Social Media.

Mel Comley and the wonderful ARC Team.

All of the beta readers

With Love... Netta & Marcus xx

ALSO BY NETTA NEWBOUND

Rage: A Gripping Psychological Thriller

The Watcher: A terrifying psychological thriller

ALSO BY MARCUS BROWN

The Crockworthy Sisters - Parts 1-3

The Nightwalker Mysteries Series: The Complete Series

NETTA NEWBOUND & MARCUS BROWN

DI DYLAN MONROE INVESTIGATES: TWO

I am LunaTIC

FEAR ME

Dylan Monroe Investigates - Book 2

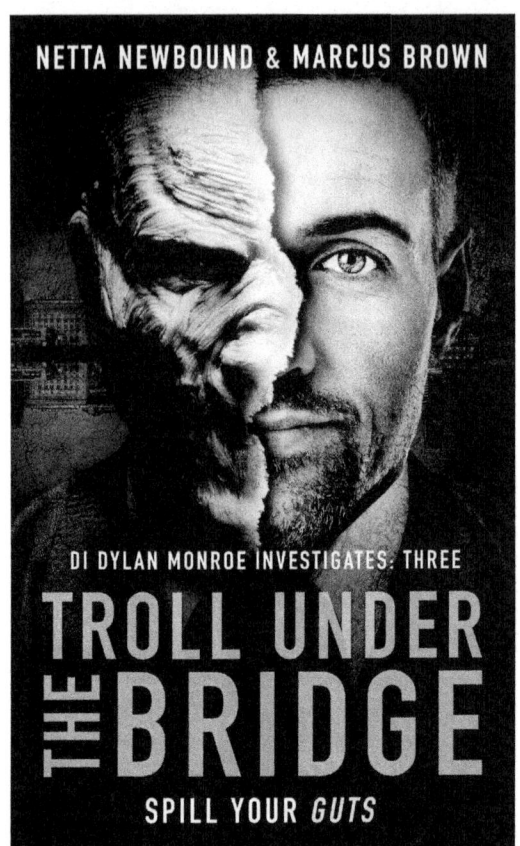

Dylan Monroe Investigates - Book 3

NETTA NEWBOUND
&
MARCUS BROWN

LORI VALLOW

DOOMSDAY CULT MOM: ONE - THE MISSING CHILDREN

True Crime -Lori Vallow

NETTA NEWBOUND
&
MARCUS BROWN

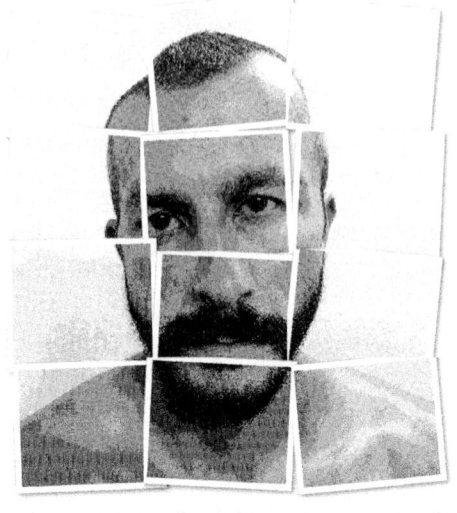

IN COLD BLOOD

DISCOVERING CHRIS WATTS - PART ONE - THE FACTS

True Crime - In Cold Blood

Printed in Great Britain
by Amazon